MY LIFE STARRING MUM

Also by Chloë Rayban from Bloomsbury

Drama Queen

MY LIFE STARRING MUM

Chloë Rayban

BLOOMSBURY
CHILDREN'S
BOOKS

First published in Great Britain in 2006 by Bloomsbury Publishing Plc
36 Soho Square, London, W1D 3QY

A CIP catalogue record of this book is available from the British Library

ISBN 0 7475 7703 X
ISBN 9780747577034

All papers used by Bloomsbury Publishing are natural, recyclable products made
from wood grown in well-managed forests. The manufacturing processes conform
to the environmental regulations of the country of origin.

Typeset by RefineCatch Limited, Bungay, Suffolk
Printed in Great Britain by Clays Ltd, St Ives Plc

1 3 5 7 9 10 8 6 4 2

www.bloomsbury.com/mylife

For Laura Cecil
without whose unreserved enthusiasm
this book would never have been written

Wednesday 22nd January
The Convent of the Sisters of the Resurrection
– otherwise known as School

It was right in the middle of the signing of the Declaration of American Independence that my life changed suddenly, dramatically and for ever.

Maureen Nicholson came bursting into history just as Thomas Jefferson had his pen poised – saying that I had to go up to Reverend Mother's office right away. Leaving the future of the US of A teetering in the balance, I made my way, with a sinking heart, past the plaster statue of the Virgin Mary and the kitchen's burnt cabbage smell. What was it this time? Had someone split on who'd been key mover in the liberation of the biology lab frogs?

Reverend Mother had her 'pained saint' expression on.

'Sit down, Holly, dear.'

I sat.

'Now, listen. I've had a call from your mother –'

'My mother!'

'Well, not, in actual fact, your mother. But that secretary lady who always deals with everything.'

'Mum's PA.'

'The thing is. I don't want to alarm you. But there's been one of those nasty threats again.'

I sighed. I'd become resigned to curfews, all my sports away matches cancelled, being de-listed from form outings. I'd been gated so many times I'd started to forget what weather felt like. I'd better explain. It's all because of Mum. You see, my mum is Kandhi! OK, so now you're doing that big wide-eye thing. And you're going to come out with stuff like: 'No way!' or 'You're kidding!' or 'I don't believe you!', as if anyone in their right mind would claim to be Kandhi's daughter if they could possibly avoid it. A fact which I've managed to keep quiet at my current school since right here I'm called Holly B. Winterman (short for Hollywood Bliss Winterman): Winterman being Dad's name, Hollywood being where I was conceived, and Bliss? Well, that's just typically Mum. I mean, I used to tell people who my mum was at my last school before she got so famous. But even back then they'd started to treat me like my whole body radiated fame like those kids in the hot oat cereal ads. I even got asked for my autograph – *my* autograph – as if her fame had kind of rubbed off on me or got passed down through the genes or something. Pukey.

'It's just that this time,' Reverend Mother continued, 'your mother and, to a certain extent, the school too, are taking the threat seriously.'

'Oh,' I said, unable to think of anything more incredibly deep and meaningful to say.

'Look, I'm really sorry about this, Holly. And we'll miss you.'

'Miss me?' I kind of squeaked.

She nodded. 'I'm afraid the school simply cannot provide the level of security that your mother feels necessary.'

'Oh,' I said again.

Reverend Mother got up and came over to me and patted my hand. 'Your mother is sending a car with full security to pick you up.'

'A car? Security? When?'

Reverend Mother glanced at her watch. 'It should be here within the hour. It'll be lovely for you to see your mother again, won't it? How long is it now?'

'Umm, ages . . . I forget . . . She's been on tour.' My mind was racing. I hardly knew what I was saying.

'Holly, dear. You must realise that this is for the best.'

'But what's going to happen about school and all my work and books and –'

'Don't worry about a thing. It will all be packed and sent on after you.'

'But . . . Where am I going? When am I coming back?'

Reverend Mother dropped her gaze. 'We'll have to review the situation when the time comes. It's really up to your mother. She seems to prefer to have you with her, which is understandable in the circumstances. I'm sure she's got it all worked out.'

'But she can't just take me out of school. There must be laws against it or something. What if I don't want to go?'

9

'Now, listen, Holly. If we have to clamp down on security, everyone's freedom will be restricted. It's simply not fair on the other girls.' Rev Mum's facial expression had changed from 'pained saint' to 'dutiful Head'. 'My dear child, you must see that.'

So there it was. I was given thirty whole minutes to grab some essentials, and leave.

Later: in the limo en route to . . .?

The limo is swishing along and these security outriders on bikes are swishing alongside. I can't believe I was so cruelly rejected by the school. And in my hour of need. I don't think they can even consider themselves Christian any more. Aren't Christians meant to stand by those who are persecuted? Selflessly. Of course, I have to realise that I don't really belong in the school. In fact, I wouldn't have been a pupil at the Sisters of the Resurrection at all if Mum hadn't 'got religion'. It was straight after she came out of rehab. She ordered me back from the States where I was living with Dad and said that she was really and truly going to be a 'mother' to me from now on in. She hung crucifixes everywhere and burned candles all day and ordered loads of books from Amazon with titles like *The True Path* and *Redemption*. Then she signed a brand new recording contract with DBS. And the crucifixes all came down and the books were binned and I was packed off to this convent boarding school. Which I kind of got used to. Even liked. I mean, it was what I called 'home', before I was so heartlessly chucked out.

2.00 p.m., The Royal Trocadero Hotel, Piccadilly, London

So this is where we were heading. Is it plush or what? The doorman's got white gloves on and loads of gold spaghetti on his shoulders. And there's this red carpet leading right down from the hotel doorway across the pavement and into the gutter.

I climbed out of the limo in my school coat and beret feeling so-oo out of place in my current surroundings, but was kind of whooshed in anyway.

Inside, I was greeted by a man in a black suit. Soon as he set eyes on me he did this 'you might well be royalty' half-curtsy-bow-thing and welcomed me to the hotel like he owned it. (I found out later he was only the manager.) I wasn't quite sure if I was meant to shake him by the hand or what. But he turned tail and led me to the elevator. He escorted me up three floors and opened a door to a suite with a flourish.

'I hope you'll enjoy your stay. Just ring down for anything you need.'

The door closed behind him with a kind of muted 'thunk' like a safe door.

2.30 p.m., Suite 6002, The Royal Trocadero Hotel

So here I am, a prisoner in this kind of ultra-luxurious prison cell. Honestly, I swear, the carpets are so thick you squish down into them like walking on sand or something. And you wouldn't know you were in a city because of the double glazing, which means all you can hear is a kind of slow hiss of the air-temperature control. And the door's so thick you wouldn't know if there was anyone else in the hotel. So if you screamed or something no one in a million years would hear. Like if I was attacked I'd have to crawl to that cord in the bathroom which says 'In an Emergency' and pull it. (That's if I was too maimed to get to the phone and ring Reception.)

Not that I'm taking this threat thing seriously. I've kind of got used to threats. Like you do, when your mum is like the tenth richest woman in the world. Mum – if I'm up to date that is – comes somewhere below those billionaire Wal-Mart ladies but before Madonna and the Queen of England. So if I did get kidnapped she'd be able to pay up and get me back, even if they asked for enough to fund a medium-sized war or something. And she wouldn't miss the money 'cos she could just make loads more. Knowing Mum, it would probably come under the heading of 'Publicity' anyway, and she could get like 'tax relief' on it. Which has just given me the horrid little sneaking suspicion that this whole thing might have been dreamt up by her publicists. Because her last solo album only won one Grammy and she apparently totally freaked. Or at least that's what Dad told me. But maybe he was just the teensiest bit jealous. Like, he's not the mega-star he would have been, had he stuck with Mum.

Actually, he hasn't won any Grammys at all. Which he puts down to the fact that the stuff he writes is too 'pure'. But I'm inclined to think it's 'cos he doesn't write that much any more. Since he got that massive settlement when he and

12

Mum divorced, he maybe doesn't have the motivation. After the divorce Mum moved back to the UK and I stayed in New York with Dad. Mum was born in Britain while Dad is American – which makes me half and half, or neither one nor the other, depending on how I feel at the time. Anyway, when I lived with Dad he had this totally cool loft apartment in SoHo where there were loads of other people hanging out a bit like *Friends*, except I got the distinct feeling that some of them were rather more than 'friends'. Oddly enough I never saw any of them doing any work. They seemed to be on a perpetual holiday. Then Mum got this idea in her head about Dad being irresponsible and hauled me over to England and sent me to boarding school. Which Dad totally freaked over. So you see, my parents really don't see eye-to-eye. Sigh.

But Dad and I still keep in touch. Admittedly Dad only communicates by sending me postcards. But I know he cares loads for me deep down.

With nothing more pressing to do I checked out the bathroom and delved into the supply of free stuff in the little basket on the marble vanity top. There was Arpège scented soap and shampoo and conditioner and all these little glossy boxes with the Royal Trocadero crest in gold on them with cotton buds and cotton balls and emery boards and body rub.

I'd just about exhausted the possibilities of total body maintenance when my phone rang. I lifted the receiver:

'Hi, Holly. Is that you?' It was Vix – Mum's PA. 'Kandhi's ready to see you now. You can come up. It's the ninth floor – the Penthouse Suite.'

I swallowed. I always get this kind of jittery feeling when I'm going to see Mum. Like she's going to judge me somehow. And I'm not going to come up to the mark.

I climbed into the elevator to find there was a bellboy with a really cute uniform inside. It was just the two of us so I thought I should say something. I mean, he didn't look that much older than me.

'Hi!' I said. 'Can we head up to the ninth?'

He kind of grunted in reply and looked dead in front of him while he pressed the elevator button. Maybe talking wasn't in his contract.

On the ninth floor, I emerged from the elevator into a corridor wide enough to drive the school bus down. Outside the Penthouse Suite there were loads of big glossy flower shop bouquets piled up as if someone had died or something.

The door was opened by Vix, who held a finger to her lips.

'Hi, Holly,' she whispered. 'We're a bit pushed on time but she can give you ten.'

Beyond her I could see Mum. Or was it Mum? A figure was pinned to a swivel chair swathed in white like the victim of some accident. On all sides of her, people were swarming around. Daffyd, Mum's personal hairstylist, was blow-drying her hair, which was curiously and unaccountably blonde. A manicurist was at work on her nails and June, Mum's make-up artiste, was standing poised ready to move in. And uh-uh, she'd had her lips collagen'd again. She had the phone on speaker and was involved in a loud and public conversation.

'Yeah, I know it's not your fault, but someone must've let

on, or they wouldn't've have known she was there, would they?' Without drawing breath she continued, 'Hollywood Bliss, babe! Come and give your mama a kiss.'

'Hi, Mum.'

I leaned over and received a collagen-y kiss on each cheek.

'(Hold on, Mike . . .) My God, you've grown! What have you got on? . . . (What? So even if they quadrupled security it wouldn't make it safe, would it?)'

'My school uniform?'

'(Look, Mike, I'll have to put you on hold . . .) Now, babes, I've been so worried about you. What with this threat and everything . . .'

'But Mu-um, you can't just take me out of school. I mean, I've got like exams and stuff. I've got a whole load of coursework, which if I don't get in –'

'Look, Hollywood babe, we'll talk about this later. I've got to be on location within . . .?'

'Sixteen and a half minutes,' cued in Vix.

'Right, we've got a lot to fix. Vix, ring through for a complete range of Kandhi Store to be sent over for Hollywood right now. Eights and tens – she looks so in-between. And get her something to wear on her feet. Size . . .?'

'Nine.'

Mum's brow creased. 'Trust you to have your dad's feet.'

'But I can't wear Kandhi Store. That's for kids,' I protested.

'You're not thirteen yet. You are a kid.'

'I am thirteen and two months and eleven days, for your information.'

'Oh, babe, did I miss your birthday?'

'No,' cut in Vix. 'You didn't.'

'You sent a Harrods voucher for £250 and a signed photograph of yourself,' I said.

(For your information, the signed photograph raised more than the Harrods voucher when I put it up for auction on eBay.)

'Whatever. So . . . you can just wear Kandhi Store for the cameras. Vix will get you something else to slouch around in if you must.'

'What cameras?'

Mum looked vague. 'Well, you are my baby, my one and only daughter . . . (You still there, Mike?)'

The hairdryer ceased and June moved in with the make-up trolley. She started massaging in white base-coat. Mum seemed to have forgotten I was there.

'Hang on a minute,' I said. My voice sounded unaccountably loud now the dryer had cut out. June paused, sponge poised. Mum stared up, her eyes looking big and black and scary in her white base-coated face.

'Do you think we could find some time to actually talk?' I asked.

'Talk? About what?' demanded Mum.

'About, like – why I'm here? How long am I staying? Basically, what's going to happen to me?'

Mum and Vix exchanged glances.

Vix ran a pen down her clipboard. 'I think we might be able to fit something in tomorrow around sixteen-ten. Twenty minutes or so, as long as you don't run over.'

'Lovely,' said Mum. 'We can have family tea together. All cosy and English . . . (So, Mike . . . let's talk contracts tomorrow, OK?)'

It seemed I had been dismissed.

Vix got up and began to bustle me out of the suite, meantime firing off directions at top speed about what I was or wasn't allowed to do in the foreseeable future.

5.00 p.m.

Back in my suite it looks like the fairies have been in during my absence. My personal possessions, i.e. comb, toothbrush and ponytail band, have been perfectly aligned on the vanity top. My coat has been hung up and my cardigan folded neatly, both looking shamingly drab in the context of the Royal Trocadero decor.

My bed, only used so far by my teddy, has been stripped and remade. A totally new set of twelve pristine white fluffy towels, a bath mat and a new fluffy bathrobe have magically replaced the ones I marginally shifted during body maintenance. I think guiltily of the hole in the ozone layer which must have gained at least two inches in diameter in the last hour, which will eventually cause the inundation of most of Holland and quite possibly some of Belgium too. And of the rising tide of greyish-white detergent foam which is currently heading on its way down the Thames towards Gravesend (a name which suitably suggests impending doom).

There is a brand new basket of free stuff complete with everything from cotton balls to conditioner. Each glossy monogrammed package no doubt filled by exploited and possibly under-age hands in some distant underdeveloped country.

Sorry about all this. It's Mum that brings it on. Whenever we meet up, I'm engulfed in this huge tidal wave of guilt. Not that I can think of anything to do about it. I mean, Mum's doing her bit. She performs absolutely free of charge at these vast aid events and if the albums she sells top the charts as a direct result, it's hardly her fault, is it?

I was distracted from this train of thought by my mobile. It was a text message:

> **have you been beamed up by aliens?**
> **you just totally dematerialised.**
> **had to torture sister marie-agnes to get the truth.**
> **took six pins before she admitted your mum sent for you.**
> **text me back**
> **Bx**

It was from Becky. She's my ultimate best friend. Like, so close, we practically have synchronised dreams. She's the only girl in the school who actually knows who my mum is. And she's totally unfazed by it. All the girls on our dorm floor have posters with Mum's face plastered over their walls except Becky. She's got this massive poster of Vanessa Mae instead, 'cos Becky's really into classical stuff. In fact, she spends half her life in the music practice rooms with her

violin. Which according to everyone else at school technically pigeonholes her as a nerd. But Becky doesn't care
one bit. Because the way she sees it, her music is far more
important to her than her position on the Sisters of the
Resurrection popularity curve. When I admitted to her
who Mum was, she simply shrugged and said, 'So?' We were
soulmates from that moment on.

I knew I shouldn't tell her exactly where I was in case
my message got hacked into or something. So I texted
back:

> S.O.S from the planet andromeda
> you got it. I was borne off silently in sleek black alien
> vehicle.
> now prisoner in plush pod. non-stop buffy replays on
> cable and
> force-fed mocha chocolate chip haagen-dazs.
> eat ya heart out all at SotR
> love you lots
> keep texting
> HBWx

At that point my door buzzer buzzed and two bellboys came
in wheeling a couple of mobile clothes racks on wheels.
These were followed by a girl with a bleached blonde crew
cut and pierced lower lip who introduced herself as Sam – the
Kandhi Store marketing manager.

'So you're Kandhi's daughter,' she purred. 'Boy, are we
going to have fun dressing you up.'

I gazed at the racks of dazzling Lycra dance wear. I don't think so!

'Yes, I'd say you were definitely an eight,' she continued, looking assessingly at my least spectacular measurement.

I won't go into what followed. It was just too humiliating. Lycra is made to stretch – right? But it has to have something to stretch round (round being the operative word). But Sam wouldn't take no for an answer. She had me looking 'stellar', as she put it, dressed in Khandi Store from neck to thigh, and left me with a whole closetful as well.

Once she'd gone I took to pacing my suite like a caged animal. I'd been told by Vix to stay locked inside and well away from the windows because of this 'nasty threat' thing. Mum was dining out and apparently it would be 'far too dangerous' for me to accompany her. God, doesn't she overreact!

Talking of dinner, my stomach now remembered that I'd missed school lunch ages ago. We generally have supper at around six thirty at SotR and hunger pangs were going off like alarm bells. But I had the feeling that the Royal Trocadero couldn't possibly sink to serving food at such an uncool hour. So I attacked the bowl of complimentary fruit. I ate one mango, one pawpaw, two mandarins, the entire bunch of grapes, two bananas and a lychee. Then I felt slightly odd.

That's when my phone rang.

'Room service calling, Miss Winterman. I don't believe we've received your dinner order yet?'

'Oh, right.' I didn't dare admit I'd eaten practically their whole bowl of fruit.

'You'll find the menu in your Executive Suite folder. Just give us a call when you've made your choice.'

The leather-bound folder had all these glitzy pictures of the dining room, which I wasn't permitted to visit, of course, being as I currently was a maximum security luxury prisoner. I'd checked the security several times. Each time I poked my head out the door the security guy at the end of the corridor kind of leapt to his feet and remembered he was meant to be looking fierce, so I ducked back in again.

I ran through the pages of really lush food like 'Beef Wellington dans son jus de Porto' and 'Escalope de Canard à la Chinois' and 'Sweet and Sour Sea-bass Dans Son Coulis of Mediterranean Vegetables', and felt a strange subterranean rumbling inside. The fruit from various incompatible countries, seasons and continents seemed to have set up global warfare inside my tummy.

In fact, all I really fancied was some toast and Marmite and maybe some cocoa, but I couldn't find any sign of those in the menu choices.

So I rang back and said I'd be OK till breakfast.

Much later that night

I woke up bitterly regretting my dinner decision. Fruit simply doesn't stay with you, as Gi-Gi my great-gran always says. I was so ravenous that I took a pen to the breakfast menu and ticked every single item. Then I went back to sleep.

Thursday 23rd January, 9.00 a.m.
Suite 6002, The Royal Trocadero

I was woken by the buzzer on my door. I climbed into the big fluffy white bathrobe and went to open it. Two waiters swept past me, each wheeling a trolley covered in a pink tablecloth with a vase of fresh flowers and loads of dishes covered in big silver salvers. When they'd gone I took a peek under the salvers.

Oops! Well, maybe I'd gone just the teeniest bit overboard on my order. For breakfast I had freshly-squeezed-orange-juice-tropical-fruit-salad-organic-muesli-peach yoghurt-scrambled-eggs-and-crispy-bacon-sausage-and-tomato-wholemeal-toast-and-butter-waffles-and-maple-syrup-raisin-toast-and-marmalade-mini-Danish-pastries-croissants-and-honey-a-pain-au-chocolat-and-a-double-cappuccino. And there was still loads left. (Which Gi-Gi would've said was a 'wicked waste'.)

After that I went and sat in a hot bath feeling like a bouncy castle. Half an hour or so later I climbed out and reluctantly got back into yesterday's Kandhi Store clothes in order to please Mum. OK, so I now had curves – but in all the wrong places.

3.00 p.m.

I'd watched daytime cable for hours till I got sick of channel zapping. In fact, there was so little on that I decided to ignore the dire warnings about 'the nasty threat thing' and, taking my life into my hands, I went to look out of the window. If there were automatic weapons trained on my suite this was their chance. But as you can see from the fact that my narrative continues – I survived.

But hang on. There was something happening in the street outside. Looked like there was going to be a demonstration or something. The police had put up all these barriers and people kept turning up and craning over them. There was quite a big crowd already. Mostly girls about my age.

I stood on tiptoe to get a better look. That's when a load of them started screaming. I couldn't actually hear them screaming, of course, because of the double glazing and the noise of the air con. But I could see they were.

As the pitch of the screams went up a few decibels, so that they faintly reached me, the door of a limo was opened with a flourish and an unmistakable figure climbed out. Dark glasses, that blonde hair, and – surely not. Wasn't that a fur she was wearing?

It was Mum.

4.10 p.m., the Penthouse Suite (cosy English family tea)

The minute I enter the suite I know something is up. Mum is sitting on this kind of curvy couch thing looking as if creme fraiche wouldn't melt in her mouth. On the table there's this triple-decker cake stand and lacy serviettes and a silver tea service.

But that's not what draws my attention. What I home in on is the guy with the big professional camera and the woman sitting opposite Mum who has a little portable recording machine propped up beside her cup of tea.

'Come and sit by your mama, babe, on the love seat.'

Mum's had a total image change since she climbed out of the limo. June has somehow managed to make Mum, in a kind of weird chameleon way, look as if she could in actual fact be my mother. She, like me, is wearing a Kandhi Store outfit, but the adult version – 'Kandhi Klub Klassics' – which basically means it's the same stuff but made in silk and cashmere. She's played down her make-up and her hair has oddly enough changed to a shade not unlike my own. Could this be a wig? Or was the blonde a wig? Did wigs come in 'mouse'? Or maybe it was her natural colour? Unlikely. Even her roots must've forgotten what that was.

'Mum? What's going on?'

'My, don't you look wonderful!' I don't. I look like a stick of 'Kandhi'. All straight up and multicoloured. I look as though if you cut me in half you'd find my name running through from head to toe.

'But, Mum. I thought it was just going to be you and me.'

'It is just you and me, babe. That's the whole point.'

I stare meaningfully at the woman with the recorder. Mum reacts by giving me a reassuring smile.

'This is Jocelyn. She writes for *Wave* magazine. You must have seen her column: "Family Ties"?'

I had, of course. It's kind of addictive, mums and daughters or dads and sons with cheesy smiles giving you all these 'insights' into what their 'real lives' are like. And like how they have so-oo much in common. Jocelyn is going to have her work cut out on this one.

'I just want you to be really natural. Behave as if I'm not here,' says Jocelyn, leaning forward earnestly.

'Do you think you could move a little closer in, Hollywood,' chips in the guy with the camera. 'You two girls cheek to cheek, maybe?'

Mum puts her arm around me and lurches me towards her. I cannot recall being this close to Mum, ever. Although I must have been once, I guess.

'Lovely. You two look so alike.'

Rubbish. Mum's kind of petite and curvy and I'm like all legs and arms – not to mention feet.

'Now, what are we going to talk about?' asks Mum.

I feel as if the recording machine has grown ears. I can actually sense it listening in judgmentally. I can't think of a single thing to say.

'So. How long is it since you two have been together?' prompts Jocelyn.

We answer in unison.

'A month,' says Mum./ 'Nine months,' I say.

'But I imagine you're always in touch?'

'On the phone all the time,' says Mum, giving me a hard stare./ 'I email Mum from time to time,' I reply truthfully.

'How about holidays?'

'Yes, South of France. My Greek island. Shopping sprees in Paris.' Mum waves an all-embracing hand./ 'I always spend my holidays with Dad,' I say flatly.

'I see,' says Jocelyn. Mum is flashing me icy glances. I feel equally annoyed. How can she be so blatantly untruthful?

Jocelyn is starting to feel the bad vibes. Abruptly she switches her attention from Mum and turns on me.

'Now, Hollywood. Let's just concentrate on you for a moment. Now you're together after . . . errm . . . a while. There must be something you've been dying to ask your mother, face to face?'

It's now or never. This is the chance I've been waiting for. How many girls my age get the opportunity to air their grievances in front of a bone fide member of the press?

'There is, as a matter of fact. Mum, tell the truth. Was that real fur I saw you wearing just now?'

Mum swallows. 'Factory farmed. Humanely killed.'

'But they're still animals! How would you like to be raised in a cage?'

A low-key hissed domestic breaks out at that point. It has been brewing for some time. Years, actually. Jocelyn kind of looks on like a spectator at the Davis Cup, her head going from side to side as we score points off each other.

As our row reaches its crescendo she switches off the recording machine and holds a hand up for silence.

'I can see you two have a lot to catch up on,' she says. 'Maybe we could reschedule the interview for some more appropriate time?'

Vix appears magically at that point. I think, in fact, she must've been hiding in the bathroom ready to prompt Mum if she forgot some key fact about our relationship. Like which of her husbands my dad was, or my name or something.

'I'll give you a ring when I've got Kandhi's diary in front of me,' says Vix, opening the suite door and gesturing violently to me behind Mum's back.

I manage to slip out ahead of Jocelyn and make my escape.

6.00 p.m., Suite 6002

I sit on the edge of my bed with my teddy. He is looking at me disapprovingly. I know I shouldn't fight with Mum. I know, in particular, that I shouldn't fight with Mum in front of journalists. I am going over the ins and outs of the argument in my mind, trying to decide if it was me or Mum who was in the wrong. I mean, I know she shouldn't wear fur, seeing as who she is and how she influences like millions of people. But maybe this is something that I should have brought up in private. Teddy doesn't look as if he's on my side so I put him in the closet and close the door.

Vix rings down at that point.

'How's Mum? Is she furious?'

'Well. Let's put it this way. I'd make myself scarce until tomorrow morning if I were you. She's got a dinner date anyway. That should cheer her up.'

'Oh?'

But she doesn't elaborate. I can hear Mum's voice demanding something in the background, so Vix rings off.

8.00 p.m.

Absolutely nothing has happened. I ordered a steak and chips and ice cream from room service and ate them in front of the TV. They've just been and taken away the meal trolley.

I watched a suspense movie that I'd missed the beginning of and never did get my head around the plot. When I checked down the corridor I found nothing had changed except the security guard. This one was taller. Sigh.

I thought of what they'd be doing right now at SotR. Which was most likely homework and I even missed that. So you can see I was in a bad way. In the end I forgave teddy and took him out of the closet and went to sleep with him.

Friday 24th January, 9.30 a.m.
Suite 6002, The Royal Trocadero

Still nothing happening in my maximum security luxury cell. When I checked down the corridor I found they had changed the security guard again. Yesterday morning's was back. We're starting to strike up a relationship. When I poke my head out of my door he now smiles and nods.

But hey, this is cool! Along with my breakfast comes my post. It's a card from Dad. It's got a picture of King Kong climbing the Empire State Building on the front. And the girl clutched in King Kong's paw looks just like Mum. Dad's added a speech bubble so she's saying: 'Put me down, you beast. Don't you know who I am?'

On the back it says:

Hi Holly-Poppy (Sad but true – Dad's pet name for me)
Hear you're shacking up with your mum.
Just a few tips:

28

a) She doesn't like criticism.

b) She likes to have her own way.

c) She's always right.

Bear these in mind and you're in for an easy ride.

B-C-N-U

Dadx

Dear Dad. I wondered who'd told him I was with Mum. Gi-Gi probably. She's really fond of him.

I've got to tell you about Gi-Gi, my great-gran. Two generations may separate us but I'm closer to Gi-Gi than anyone. She's the one who steps in when my parents forget they have a kid. Which they tend to do quite often – like half-terms or Christmas or Easter – but Gi-Gi is always there. She's the warmest, cuddliest, roly-poly great-gran anyone has ever had. She's Russian, you see, which may account for it, because Gi-Gi says that Russian people are the most loving in the whole world – especially to their families. I don't know what happened to that Russian blood in Mum and my gran Anna. Maybe it skipped two generations. Anyway, hopeless task as it may be, she's all for keeping the family together. She still writes Dad proper letters with pen and paper to keep him in touch.

Speaking of keeping in touch – I've tried texting Becky but it's mobile curfew at SotR, they must all be in class. Sigh.

Eventually in desperation (I mean, I've practically taken to scratching lines to mark the days in the Royal Trocadero wallpaper) I rang through to Vix.

'How's things? Is it safe to come up?'

29

'Fine. She's, errm . . . gone out,' she said.

Odd, I thought. Early for Mum. But maybe she had a video shoot.

'What am I meant to do? I asked.

'What would you generally be doing?'

'Double biology, it's Friday.'

'Oh.' I could hear the boredom in Vix's voice. Clearly, the last thing she wanted was a thirteen-year-old to look after.

'Look,' I said. 'If I take one of Mum's heavies with me, and go in disguise or something, I could spend that Harrods voucher.'

'Well . . .' said Vix.

'Otherwise, you'll just have to come down and play Monopoly with me. Or Scrabble . . .' I threatened.

This had some effect.

'What kind of disguise?'

'My school uniform. Why not?'

'Hmm. Well, maybe. But you'll have to take Sid and Abdul. And you mustn't be more than an hour.'

'OK! Thanks, Vix!'

'I'll probably get fired for this.'

'Only if I get kidnapped.'

'Just don't. OK?'

I flung on my uniform and was totally ready by the time Sid and Abdul rang on my buzzer. They took me down in the elevator to the basement and escorted me along a grotty corridor past the kitchens and out through a door that said 'Press bar to open'.

Outside, Mum's limo was waiting in a back street.

It only took five minutes to get to Harrods.

The limo door was opened by one of the Harrods door-men in his sludge-green uniform. He kind of saluted, which didn't do much for the incognito bit. But in actual fact I did-n't have much faith in being inconspicuous anyway. I mean, a thirteen-year-old girl in school uniform flanked by two seven-foot bodyguards?

Soon as we were inside Harrods I led the guys straight to the confectionery department and stocked up with two kilos of blueberry jelly beans. (Ten quid! Ouch. But this was a wise investment, as you'll see later.) Then we went up to Harrods' young fashions department.

Dazzling racks of Kandhi Store practically filled the sales area. Ignoring these, I headed for the display of jeans. I searched in vain for my leg length while Sid and Abdul stood with their hands crossed in front of them, doing that 360-degree-head-turn-and-eye-swivel thing they teach you at Security School. Shoppers were starting to pause and try to figure out who I was. An assistant who had been alerted by our painfully obvious attempt not to be noticed, homed in.

'Can I help you?' she asked all agog, clearly making mental guesses as to who I might be. (That Onassis girl? Too young. One of Fergie's girls? Too skinny. Madonna's daughter? Too old.)

It turned out that the only place I could possibly find jeans to fit was the men's department, which was handy because I actually got some peace to try them on while Sid and Abdul did some sneaky and totally off-the-record trying-on of a load of Hugo Boss stuff.

I actually bought Sid a totally extortionate black sleeveless polo neck as a bribe not to tell Mum about 'our little outing', seeing as he wasn't interested in jelly beans like Abdul. (He's kind of addicted, but only to the blueberry ones.)

I also bought myself three boys' T-shirts, plain white, plain grey and plain blue, and then I saw a pair of incredibly cool Converse trainers which meant I was left with £57.24 on the voucher and twenty-two minutes exactly until our hour was up.

So I escorted Sid and Abdul up to my favourite part of Harrods – the pets department.

That's where I saw this adorable minute grey angora rabbit. It was in a cage all alone with no other bunnies to snuggle up to. And its nose was kind of wiffling. I mean, it hardly looked old enough to be weaned. And it was only twenty-two pounds. Which apparently is a bargain for a long-haired lop-eared rabbit.

So then I just had enough left for a smart green pet-carrying holdall with ventilation holes. A litter tray. A pack of rabbit mix (junior). And a bag of kitty litter. (But they said it was OK for rabbits too.) And a book called *How to House Train Your Rabbit* 'cos, as you know, I don't hold with keeping animals in cages.

And then we had to rush to be out and back in the limo in time with the whole lot packed in green Harrods bags. Except for the rabbit, which was in the holdall on my lap. Which luckily didn't look like a pet-carrying holdall at all. Because I had a sneaking feeling that the Royal Trocadero might have a negative pet policy – apart from maybe guide dogs.

In the limo I gave Abdul the first kilo of jelly beans (I reckoned it needed a fairly generous bribe to keep quiet about the rabbit). And Sid had his polo neck. So that should be OK.

11.10 a.m. (Back in my suite)

'Thumper' doesn't seem to want to stay in the closet. Although I made it really cosy with a nest of cotton balls in the little basket from the bathroom. Plus his litter tray. He actually prefers to stay inside my brand new T-shirt. So I'm lying on the bed reading aloud to him from *How to House Train Your Rabbit*. You can never start too young, it says – there, you see.

That's when there's a buzz on my doorbell.

'Oops!' I peek through the spy-hole. Oh my God, it's Mum!

With lightning speed Thumper is in the closet and I'm back at the door.

Mum comes in breezily.

'Hollywood Bliss, baby. Isn't this lovely? Don't you just love the Trocadero? It's my all-time favourite hotel. Isn't it just so-oo homey?'

She seems to have totally 'wiped' our fight of yesterday.

'Ummm.'

'Oh, I see Vix got you some jeans. Well, I s'pose you don't want to stay dressed up all day. I remember when I was your age. I was such a tomboy, always up trees.'

My eyes widen. According to Gi-Gi, Mum's encounters with nature were pretty thin on the ground.

There is the faintest scrabbling sound from the closet. It seems Thumper has unfortunately taken this moment to put house-training theory into practice.

'Funny smell in here. Kind of wholesome,' says Mum, sniffing the air thoughtfully.

'It's the flowers,' I say, leading her away from the closet across to the complimentary bouquet. 'I think it's sandalwood.'

'Heaven,' says Mum. 'Now, listen. I know, babes, that I've been a simply terrible mother to you . . .'

'Oh, no.' (A fool would have agreed with her and caused a full-on domestic).

'No, listen. I'm going to make it all up. I've got plans. From now on where I go you go . . .'

'Oh?'

'Umm. So how would you like Paris – this weekend?'

'Paris?' I say weakly. I mean, I'd like Paris. I've always wanted to go to Paris. But it's hardly fair on Thumper, is it? He's barely got used to not being in Harrods. Another change in environment could have serious psychological consequences.

'Well, I'm really happy here –'

'So sweet of you. You don't want to cramp my style. But you won't. It's all fixed. You've got an hour to pack.'

'But what about my school stuff, and weren't we meant to be getting me a tutor and –'

'All in good time. Babe – you know what I think?' Mum

34

kind of grabs me and holds me at arm's length and stares hard into my eyes. 'I don't think you've had enough fun in your life, and Mama's going to put that right.'

'Oh . . . really?'

12.45 p.m. (en route for the VIP Suite London Heathrow)

We're all here. Mum and Vix, Daffyd and June, Sid and Abdul, and me (and Thumper, obediently staying nice and quiet in his carrying holdall).

I mean, I was a bit worried about taking him with us, but I could hardly leave him at the mercy of the Trocadero's chambermaids (and their vacuum cleaners – he's small enough to go right up the nozzle) for a whole weekend. And as I recall, whenever I've travelled with Mum we've gone first class and we've been above queueing up to go through those X-ray thingies like ordinary travellers. In fact, we've kind of been whisked through to the VIP lounge (like now) and then escorted on to the plane.

1.00 p.m. (queuing at one of those X-ray thingies!)

I am totally hyperventilating. It must be the increased security since all those terrorist attacks or something. Or maybe last time I travelled with Mum was only on an internal flight. But anyway, all the bags are so obviously having to go through one of those X-ray machines. Oh, how I wish I had secreted Thumper under my T-shirt or hidden him under a hat maybe. They'd never have been able to tell if he wasn't some extra rounded bit of me. But as it is I can see us both moving up the line. And now they've taken my backpack and my mobile phone . . . and . . .

'Can I just carry this one through? It's got like re-ally breakable, fragile stuff in it. No?' It has to go in the box like belts and loose change and keys and things.

I watch in silent horror as this ghostly image of the holdall appears on the security screen with this tiny, perfect, trembling rabbit skeleton inside.

Oh my God. All these hooters and blinking lights are going and these guys with semi-automatic weapons have appeared out of nowhere and we're surrounded.

'Is this your bag, Miss?'

'Umm . . .'

'Would you mind opening it for us?'

Thumper looks totally traumatised when I unzip the zipper. I mean, you hear about rabbits freezing on the spot, but he's gone totally, totally rigid. If he grows up with a behavioural problem I will sue.

It gets worse. Apparently, I am not just carrying an unauthorised item on-board a plane – like he was a bomb or a knife or something (or a hijacking threat – like he could chew his way through the pilot's neck maybe?). No, I'm also flaunting quarantine laws, animal export regulations, animal cruelty guidelines and all the health and safety rulings of the Ministry of Agriculture, Fisheries and Food. And Thumper only dropped one v. small rabbit poop on the conveyor belt, which I would have thought was like totally forgivable in the circumstances.

And worse still. He is being confiscated. Some evil animal

handler in a white uniform has appeared and he's picked Thumper up by his ears.

So, you can understand why I totally lost it at that point.

In fact, the handler and I had a full-on row in which he insisted that he personally wasn't taking any risks because for all he knew Thumper might be a rabid rabbit.

'A rabid rabbit! No way!' I point out that this rabbit is (or was) travelling from the UK to the continent and not vice versa and that to my knowledge there is no rabies in the UK.

This silenced the handler. But it doesn't stop him confiscating Thumper.

Nor does the fact that I'm currently totally bawling my eyes out. Because I have a horrible suspicion about what happens to confiscated animals.

Saturday 25th January, 6.00 p.m.
La Vendôme Intercontinental, Paris

Mum is a STAR. I know I'm often totally negative about her, but there are times when I'm truly awed by her finer qualities. I still don't know how much money she had to hand over to the RSPCA to come and rescue Thumper. But they can most probably build a whole new animal hospital with it. With a CAT scan and everything (which I guess will do other animals too). But she oh-so stood her ground, refusing to budge until Thumper had been collected by one of their representatives to be taken into a shelter for safekeeping. And the whole of Air France Flight AF 21 had to wait too because our luggage had already been loaded in the hold, so the plane wasn't allowed to take off without us. But Mum saw to it that all the people on board got a complimentary bottle of champagne to make up for the delay, which is so truly romantic when you're on your way to Paris. So in a way, the whole episode has done some good all round. I'm just trying to work out how I can get Thumper back as soon as we return to London . . .

6.30 p.m.

Vix has popped down to say can I be on standby, ready and dressed for dinner at 21h10 (which is the way they write it in France).

'I am dressed,' I point out.

It appears the restaurant we're going to has a no-jeans door policy. I'm meant to be dressed in Kandhi Store.

'Small problem. I didn't pack the Kandhi Store stuff.'

'But you had two whole suitcases!'

My suitcases are standing there beside us in the room, still unpacked and still filled with litter tray, kitty litter, rabbit mix (junior), basket with cotton balls, teddy and a complete rabbit assault course (for essential body development) cleverly contrived from various items loaned from the Royal Trocadero.

Vix lost it at this point and stormed off to consult Mum.

It was Mum who rang down. 'You all right, babes?'

She still had on her 'concerned and understanding' voice. She was being so nice about Thumper. I was starting to feel uneasy. Was she up to something?

'Don't worry, we can just pop out and buy you something hot. I'll meet you in the lobby.'

'But Mum, it's nearly seven. The shops'll all be shut.'

Not a problem. Apparently, Mum only shops when the shops are shut.

So I wait in the lobby until Mum arrives dressed down to look incognito. Mini mac, Dolce and Gabbana stiletto-heeled boots and, in spite of the fact that it's pitch dark and pouring with rain outside – dark glasses.

The minute she steps out of the hotel it's like lightning striking from all sides. Behind a human chain of La Vendôme's uniformed doorkeepers, the photographers have formed a solid wall of human flesh. Each of them is trying desperately to attract Mum's attention.

Mum flashes her dazzling 'publicity smile' while holding up a shielding hand of protest. This always amazes me. How does she do it? I mean, the minute someone trains a camera on me, I instantly lose the ability to coordinate lips, teeth and eyes.

Almost before we know it, Sid and Abdul have frog-marched us down the line and into a limo and the doors have thunked shut. We slide into the night. Only to come to an abrupt halt about thirty-five seconds later. The rue St Honoré, where all the coolest designers hang out, is apparently just round the corner. We've stopped outside a double-fronted boutique that's all glossy and glitzy but has a row of models made out of what looks like straw, giving them the odd effect of a load of fashion victim scarecrows. I note the initials etched into the glass. A.M. Armando Mezzo – Mum's fave designer. The boutique has a discreet 'Fermé' sign up yet, sure enough, there are lights on inside and the doors are sliding open for us.

Armando himself comes out to greet us. He's flanked by three female assistants all looking as if they've just stepped off the catwalk. Once we're all safely in, he and Mum do a load of air-kissing and standing back and admiring each other. Eventually they notice I'm there too.

'And who's thees?' says Armando, giving a pretty good imitation of an Italian accent. (He is in actual fact from the East End of London.) There follows the usual long amazement-session about how tall I am and how could Mum possibly have a daughter so old. The three assistants do a synchronised purr of agreement. Mum brushes it all aside and they get down to the business of what I'm to wear. All eyes focus on me. I wish I didn't feel so totally lame. I can't imagine Armando Mezzo having clothes anyone like me would be allowed to wear.

I cast a nervous glance towards the scarecrows. There'll be no scruffy delving through racks here. The scarecrows are wearing the only clothes in the shop – a minimal body covering assortment of baby pink and blue gingham-checked hot pants and bras trimmed with broderie anglaise. They have matching strappy stilettos and handbags shaped like watering cans. It seems this is Armando's new spring/summer collection.

'And eet's for tonight?' says Armando, looking alarmed.

'You've got it. We're dining at eight thirty sharp,' says Mum, refusing to be fazed.

I can't think why she's making such a big deal about this dinner. I mean, it's just her and me.

'But it's gonna have to be last season's,' protests Armando.

'Look, Armando. No sweat. Anything'll do. So long as it's not jeans.'

Armando and the assistants go into a little huddle. There is a flash of long glossy legs as the three women disappear into the back.

Armando chivvies us along to some squishy sofas. We are offered drinks but Mum declines anything but water – still spa water, no ice.

The assistants are back in seconds. They're now wearing white gloves and each is carrying a huge glossy black box. These are opened in turn. Out of folds of crunchy purple tissue come a strapless white mini evening gown – yumm. 'Too sophisticated,' says Mum. A black leather bustier and tight thigh-length pants – wow! But 'Far too old for Hollywood.' And finally a short sleeveless dress in brilliant coral pink with a jacket to match.

'Perfect,' says Mum.

'Mu-um!'

'Yes?'

'I'm going to look like a flamingo in that.'

'Rubbish. It's fine. We'll take it.'

'But you don't even know if it'll fit!'

'By seven forty-five eet will feet,' says Armando, and he plumps his hand down on a bell.

A minute wrinkly lady all in black with a tape measure round her neck and a pin-cushion attached to her wrist materialises out of nowhere. Before I know it, I've had every single bit of me measured (including my feet) and we're back in the limo.

19h45, my suite at La Vendôme Intercontinental

Not one but five incredibly black, incredibly shiny boxes in various sizes arrived, and inside was everything for the evening, including shoes. Kitten-heel pink pointy shoes – but in the softest leather imaginable. Clutch bag to match. Tights – palest pink too. And the yucky coral pink dress and jacket.

However, I have to put things in perspective. Mum has been a star about Thumper and we are having dinner together. (In PARIS!) And I am ravenous. So I guess it's the least a daughter can do.

20h00

I look totally like a flamingo. I don't even have to stand on one leg to complete the impression. The all-round mirrors in my bathroom confirm the fact. I even look like a flamingo from the back. The dress is v. short and kind of goes in at the hem, from which my legs emerge, looking endless, plus kind of knobby at the knee, which if you've ever bothered to notice is exactly how flamingo legs are. I am so NOT happy in this outfit I am ringing down and telling Mum to cancel and we'll eat in. I'm sure she'll understand.

20h30, La Chasse d'Or

Mum so-oo did NOT understand. I tried to sneak across the restaurant with my mac on but Mum allowed the waiter to take it off me. The restaurant is like all mirrors. So I'm not just one flamingo but a whole flock of them. Everyone else in the restaurant seems to have been tipped off and is wearing black, which makes a flock of stray flamingoes stand out even more.

Mum and I are shown to a table right across the room and I can feel myself blushing from head to toe as all eyes turn on us.

'You look hot, babe. Why don't you take your jacket off?' whispers Mum as soon as we're seated, noting my colour.

'I'm fine,' I say. My arms are about the only bit of me that is reasonably covered. I am certainly not taking my jacket off.

But what with the heat and all the attention I can positively feel my face flaming. I make an excuse to Mum and dash to the loo and plaster powder on my nose to tone down the shine. Then I tug the dress down as far as I can and take a deep breath. This may be the most mortifying night of my life, but I know what Reverend Mother would say: 'This experience, Holly dear, is character forming. You'll look back and be glad you did it.' (Although Rev. M. would be more likely to be talking about doing a Bible reading at the carol service, not walking through a restaurant half-dressed with the whole of Paris gawping at you.)

Anyway, just as I am making my way back to the table I catch sight of . . . You are NOT going to believe this . . . And he's looking just as drop-dead gorgeous as he did in *Loyal Subject* . . . Yes! Oliver Bream. O-L-I-V-E-R B-R-E-A-M! He's by the doors having this discussion with the door guy about the valet parking service and he's doing that kind of frown and smile thing he does – like so all-English irresistibly charming. And I immediately think of Becky and how she would SO-OO like his autograph and then I remember how I am currently a flamingo and totally cannot approach anyone the way I'm dressed, let alone Oliver Bream. So I rush back to our table, which is now kind of easier 'cos the full glare of the attention is now off me and focusing in on the doorway.

I slide into the chair opposite Mum.

'Guess what! You'll never believe who I've just seen!'

'Who?' prompts Mum.

'Oliver Bream!'

This has SO little effect on Mum. I mean, I guess she's used to being with all these celebs and everything. But still – Oliver Bream – and above all right now because everyone knows he's up for Best Actor Award in the Oscars for his role in *Loyal Subject*. I went goosebumps all over actually seeing him in the flesh.

Mum takes a sip of her water and gazes over my shoulder. She's smiling at someone and so I turn and there he is. Oliver Bream's coming in our direction and I think like he's going to sit at the next table and maybe I can just sneak an autograph for Becky after all. But he doesn't go to the next table.

He comes straight to ours and leans down and gives Mum a kiss on the cheek and says, 'May I?' And sits down between us!

'Well, fancy you being here. In Paris!' says Mum.

'Small world,' says Oliver, then he turns to me. 'Hi,' he says. 'You must be Hollywood Bliss.'

And I say really stupidly. 'Hi, you must be Oliver Bream.'

I can feel my whole face fire up to precisely the same colour as my outfit. Even my nose, in spite of all the powder

I've put on in the loo. How could I have said anything so DUMB?

But he seems to think this is really funny and so does Mum. And they both sit there laughing like people do when you're a really young kid and you say something totally STUPID. Like for instance, you ask for cold sore instead of coleslaw. And everyone thinks that's so cute and you hate it.

And then, looking at the two of them, I realise how dumb I actually am. I realise that this was never meant to be a quiet dinner for two, just for Mum and me. Because there are more than two places laid at the table (in actual fact there are four). So they must've planned this all along. And now I'm fuming. I'm really angry. I'm sending silent evil hate-vibes at Mum. Because whatever she says about wanting to do stuff with just the two of us, it's never the case. No, we're always doing stuff that she wants to do. Stuff that's always totally selfish and self-obsessed. And although Oliver Bream keeps on prompting me to say things and he even does his frown and smile charm thing, it doesn't work on me – oh no. I've like totally clammed up, which is handy because I can't think of a single thing to say.

I just sit there staring at this fourth empty place and wondering who's going to turn up next. Jacques Chirac or Michael Jackson or Prince William maybe?

'Shug should be along soon,' says Oliver.

'Shug? He's here in Paris too?' says Mum.

Shug? Who's Shug? Am I meant to know who Shug is? Sounds like a totally stupid name to me.

'Yeah, but we can't count on when he'll turn up. You know Shug.'

Mum knows Shug. I guess the whole world knows Shug 'cept for me.

'Perhaps we should order, then,' suggests Mum.

'You're right. No point in waiting,' agrees Oliver, taking up his copy of the Chasse d'Or menu. 'So what shall we have?'

The Chasse d'Or menus are so large you could live in them. Or use them as a roof at any rate. I bury my face in mine and try to compose myself. With an effort I manage to put my anti-Mum feelings aside as I concentrate on finding something vaguely edible. This restaurant is so classy the menu's got things no one in their right mind would normally eat unless maybe forced to 'cos they'd crash-landed somewhere and had to, to survive. (I know 'cos they have an English translation under the posh French names.) Snails and frog's legs are the least of it. They also have sea urchins, squid in ink sauce, lightly broiled sheep's brains, one-day-old faun and hare cooked in its own blood. This last makes me think of Thumper and wonder miserably whether he's all alone someplace in some cold miserable RSPCA cage surrounded by feral and maybe violent animals.

I can see Mum is having problems with the menu too on account of her current diet. It's a really simple diet. She can eat anything she likes as long as it's raw – which is no big deal if you're having like sushi (she picks out all the rice). It looks like her only choices on the Chasse d'Or menu are caviar and salad. I search for something that doesn't involve blood, insides or baby animals and settle on lobster. I'd had a crab salad at Gi-Gi's eightieth birthday lunch which I'd liked – lobster couldn't be that different.

Oliver has ordered champagne which is opened at the table with a lot of fuss. He makes a big show of sipping it and swilling it round his mouth and then tells the waiter to take it back and get another that's more chilled. After that the head waiter comes straight for me and leans over with a sort of little half bow. To my horror he asks me something in French, indicating that I should go with him.

I wonder if I've done something horribly wrong, like spread my roll with the fish knife maybe, and I'm getting thrown out. But Oliver nods condescendingly.

'Run along, Hollywood. He wants you to choose your lobster.'

'Oh, right.' I get to my feet and follow the waiter to some big glass window thingy set in the far wall.

You are not going to believe this. The Chasse d'Or lobsters are not all pink and and arranged on a plate with little frills of mayonnaise round them like the crab salad was. No, they're in an aquarium and they're alive and they're waving their feelers pitifully at me as if to say, 'Not me, please, not me. I'm too young to die.'

The head waiter gestures towards them with pride and says something which I can only interpret as, 'Look, there's a nice big fat one at the back.'

The 'nice big fat one' seems to have realised that we have homed in on him and is trying desperately to scrabble a hole in the sand and bury himself.

I look the head waiter full in the eyes and come out with (in my very best French): 'Non merci, je ne suis pas un murderer.'

Turning on my heel, I walk with dignity back to our table.

'I'll have the same as Mum,' I mumble.

Mum exchanges glances with Oliver.

'Hollywood is kind of into animals at present. It's just a phase.'

'It is not a phase, Mum.'

'Well, let's not discuss it now. Look, I think that's our caviar.'

Sure enough, four waiters are gliding a trolley covered in a white cloth towards our table. Poised on it is a huge ice sculpture of a mermaid bearing an open ice seashell full of seaweed artfully arranged around a heap of something black and shiny.

'Nice packaging!' says Mum, and delves in with her knife.

Oliver speads a slice of toast and piles some black stuff on for me.

'Try it,' he says. 'It's beluga.'

I have a tentative nibble. It's not bad, actually. Kind of like Marmite on toast but a bit more blobby.

I'm on my third slice when I nearly choke as I hear a voice say, 'Hi, Dad.'

My eyes widen. I didn't know Oliver Bream had a son. He's certainly kept very quiet about it. And I can see why. 'Cos 'Shug' is bigger and older than me. About fifteen in my estimation, which means Oliver must be . . . !!!

This is v.v. bad news for Becky.

And I stare at Shug, wondering how he got in. Not that he's wearing jeans or anything. No, he's wearing a pair of the world's biggest and baggiest combat shorts that are kind of cliff-hanging off his Calvin Kleins. And a ripped T-shirt that says F-OFF. And his hair is all kind of spiked up with gel.

'Hi, Kandhi. How you goin'?'

'And this is Hollywood, Shug,' says Oliver.

Shug takes one look at me, sitting here in my goody-goody pink dress and jacket, and he snorts and sits down without saying a word.

'Caviar?' asks Oliver.

Shug eyes the mermaid up and down. 'Nah, I'm not eating that black shit. Look where it's bin.' He stares rudely at where the mermaid would have had a lap if she hadn't had a tail. Then he beckons to the head waiter and says, 'Can you guys fix me a burger and fries?'

I reckon that head waiter deserved an Academy Award for expressionlessness – he wandered off without saying a word.

'Shug's setting up a band,' says Oliver in a bright conversational tone.

Shug looks as if he's about to put his trainers up on the table and then thinks better of it. He rocks his chair on to its back legs instead.

All eyes turn on me. It's my turn to say something.

'Oh? I say through toast. 'What kind of music?'

'For sure it's nothing like your mum's shit,' says Shug dismissively.

I see a brief look of hurt flash across Mum's eyes. Amazingly for someone so famous, she still can't take criticism.

Some instinct deep down inside me leaps to her defence. I redirect my silent hate-vibes towards Shug.

Oliver doesn't seem to have noticed. He's chatting on, still being really pally with Shug, when any other dad would have frogmarched him outside and told him to take a cab home. I sit silently munching my salad, observing them in action. Quite a double act. You could see the family resemblance. They have precisely the same size egos.

Over the next hour or so our table provided a kind of impromptu floor show for all the tables within earshot, as the two of them competed for the title of 'World Record Difficult Diner'. Oliver sent his side order of spinach back three times till they got it steamed to precisely the nth second and Shug sent out first for ketchup and then for Pepsi 'cos the Chasse d'Or only served Coke.

Even Mum had gone quiet. She kept avoiding Shug's gaze. I could tell she'd had a run-in with him before. How long had she known Oliver, I wondered?

I confronted her with it in the limo going back to the hotel.

'So, you might have warned me.'

'Warned you? Of what?'

'That you were . . . "going out" with Oliver Bream.'

'But I'm not "going out" with Oliver as you so quaintly put it. He just happened to drop by.'

'Drop by! No way. You'd planned it all along.'

'What makes you think that?'

'For a start there were four places at our table.'

'What is this, an inquisition?'

50

'Mum, can't you ever just say something straight? Are you, or aren't you, going out with Oliver Bream?'

Mum pouted and stared at her reflection in the window. An unreadable smile played across her lips. 'Maybe I haven't decided yet.'

'Well, when you decide, do you think you could let me know? These things kind of affect me too, you know.'

Mum looked at me innocently. 'Affect you, babe? How?'

'Mum, give me a break. If you go out with Oliver he's going to be, like, around the place all the time. Or were you just going to keep him in the closet and bring him out when he matches your outfit?'

'There's no need to be sarky, Hollywood.'

'No, but see it my way. If he's around all the time, so will that Urrrrrgh! of a son of his.'

'Oh, I'm sure Shug'll be doing his own thing.'

'As long as his thing is way out of the way of my thing.'

'You didn't exactly hit it off, did you? Pity, I thought he'd be a nice little friend for you.'

'Little? Nice? Mu-um!'

'Well, I guess he's misunderstood. It can't be easy having a megastar as a parent.'

'You're telling me!'

'Anyway, I think Oliver's kind of sweet, in an Englishy sort of way. Don't you?'

'Sweet?'

'But you do like him just the teensiest bit?'

'Teensiest at most.'

'So do I have your permission for him to call on me?' said Mum in a baby voice.

'Would it make any difference what I said?'

'Good, because he's coming round tomorrow to take us sightseeing.'

'So you are going out with him?'

'Depends what you mean by "going out".'

'Oh, Mum, honestly.'

Sunday 26th January, 0h45
La Vendôme Intercontinental

I can't sleep. I'm lying in bed trying to figure out a way to break the news kindly to Becky. She's had this mega-thing about Oliver Bream for like for ever, ever since he stripped off his chainmail in *Attila the Hun*. (Though now I'm wondering if maybe he used a body double – he didn't look that fit to me in real life.) I mean, each time we make up our Ultimate Wish List, a date with Oliver Bream is right up there at the top of hers after the Stradivarius.

This thought brought me on to my own list. Which has changed somewhat of late:

1) A pet (any kind): now down-listed because I currently have Thumper
2) Boobs (any size beyond AA)
3) A trip to Ranthambhore National Park in

Rajasthan to visit what's left of the Royal Bengal Tigers

4) Dad to record a hit — or maybe sell more than 100 white labels
5) Teeth that fit for Sister Marie-Agnes
6) Hair that doesn't frizz when damp
7) To pass maths GCSE with a grade C or above
8) That Gi-Gi lives for ever and ever — or a very long time at any rate
9) That beetroot had never been invented
10) That caged birds are banned

(So now I've got Thumper and they've all moved up one place, I can add: smaller feet!)

Anyway, apart from revising my U.W.L. I had the problem of how to compose an appropriate text message to Becky. You have to be careful when you break tragic news. Like when you're looking after your neighbour's goldfish, for instance, and they ring up, you don't say right out: 'Jaws is floating up-side down in the bowl stone dead.' You start with something like, 'Jaws was a little off his food this morning' and then work through things like 'He'll only swim sideways in one direction' until they kind of get used to the idea and the sad truth doesn't come as such a blow. So I had to think of some way to tell Becky gently that Oliver is not for her. In the end I came up with:

dream date quiz
re: night out with oliver bream

answer the foll:

O. B. is:

a) 23 years old?

b) 29 years old?

c) 39 years old?

HBWx

Sunday 26th January, 9h45
La Vendôme Intercontinental

I am woken by sun flooding into my bedroom. I go to the window and stare out. The rain has stopped, the clouds have disappeared, it's going to be a fantastic day.

What's more, when I climb back into bed and check my mobile I find there's a text from Becky:

Ans to dream date quiz

don't know/don't care

a)   is just old enough for commitment

b)   is ripe for settling down

c)   is a bit on the mature side but who cares, he's

still gorgeous

Bxx

Hmm. She really has got it bad. How on earth am I going to break it to her that her dream date is currently going-out-with-my-mum? Big problem. What's more, I've another sneaky little negative feeling lurking somewhere deep down.

Today 'we're' going sightseeing. How many people does 'we' cover?

I ring through to Vix to check on our schedule for the day.

The voice the other end of the line makes some incoherent croaking noises.

'Vix, is that you? You OK?'

'What?'

'It's me. I just wondered what time we were –'

'Holly, it's Sunday morning. It's God-knows-what time. I've just got to bed. This is Paris. Am I allowed a life?'

'Oh, right. Sorry.' I put the phone down. Vix must've been out clubbing all night, she sounded really wasted. I consider ringing Mum and decide against it. She can be very scary when roused from sleep. Instead I ring down for breakfast and order in my Very Best French: 'Croissants, brioches, jus d'orange et café au lait.' (See!)

'Would you like English newspapers with that, Mademoiselle?' Why do they always do that!

My breakfast arrives a few minutes later accompanied by a huge bundle of newspapers. I take a big sip of my orange – nice freshly squeezed, I note – and flip over the first of the papers.

ARE THEY OR AREN'T THEY?

screams the headline. Underneath are two separate pictures, one of Mum and the other a rather obvious press release photo of Oliver.

I read on in disbelief.

55

A secret rendezvous in Paris. Dinner à deux at the Chasse d'Or...

Some 'dinner à deux'. I mean, I was hardly inconspicuous. And neither was Shug.

...where the average price for a meal goes into three figures...

Oops! I feel really guilty. The mermaid alone must've cost a fortune and we couldn't even eat that.

I pick up the next paper. Similar headline but this time a photo of Oliver and Mum taken someplace else, getting out of a cab. I squint at it – looks like a yellow cab. When was she last in New York? I try hard to remember. Ages ago!

'I haven't decided yet.' That's what she said. But this thing with Oliver must have been going on for like months.

The rest of the pile of newspapers has much the same story, except that in the *Guardian* and the *Independent* it has been pushed on to page two by some boring political scandal.

And then I realise with a jolt – Becky! Will she have seen the papers? Unlikely, it's Sunday morning, everyone at SotR should be filing down to the chapel. But afterwards it's the mad rush down to the newsagent in the village to stock up on chocolate and doughnuts and she's bound to see the headlines. I have to warn her before she gets down there. Gently, though.

dream date quiz
re night out with o.b.
match the foll. into couples:

56

Madonna Posh Spice
Becks Kandhi
Guy Richie Oliver Bream
НВШ xxxxxxxxxxxx

After that I spread my croissant with butter and honey. It is heartless, I know, to eat at a time like this but remember I only had caviar and salad for dinner and I was positively salivating watching Shug dig into his burger and fries (and ketchup).

Hang on. SotR must be out of chapel. I have a text.

!!!!!!!!!!!!!!!!!!!!!!!!!!!!!!!!!!!!!!
B

Maybe I didn't break it gently enough. It's Sunday, so SotR is out of mobile curfew. I decide to ring her. She answers first ring.

'Becky?'

A muted snuffle.

'You OK?'

'. . . Glug . . . ummm.'

'It's probably only temporary . . . like a fling or something. You know my mum.'

'. . . Sniff . . . Sure.'

'Anyway . . . I mean he's far too old for you. You should see him close up.'

'Holly. Please realise. This is more of a mind thing . . . It's not just physical, you know.'

57

'No, I realise that. But, Becky. He's got a son who's older than us!'

Another snuffle. 'How old?'

'Must be 'bout fifteen, I reckon.'

'Fifteen! I don't believe you!'

'Yep. I met him last night.'

There's a silence while this sinks in.

'Is he like his dad?' (I hear a little glimmer of hope in her voice.)

(Oh my God. Shug like Oliver? I rack my brain for the faintest resemblance. Apart from ego size, that is.)

'They're about the same height.'

'Ummm?'

'Well, I mean he must be potentially. He has half his genes, after all.'

'Potentially?'

'Well, I think maybe, like right now, he's going through a kind of father-son rebellion thing. You know, wanting to be his own man. It's quite normal at his age.'

This obviously has a favourable impression on Becky because her next question is: 'Do you think you could get me a photo of him?'

'I thought this was more of a mind thing.'

'It is.'

'I'll try. OK?'

'Thanks. And Holly?'

'Umm.'

'You could still maybe get me Oliver's autograph?'

'OK.'

'You promise?'

This is like totally uncool – to ask someone you know personally for their autograph – but I promise anyway.

11h00

Mum rang through eventually to say we were all going to meet in the lobby. I arrived to find Sid and Abdul in deep conversation with two guys who were clearly bodyguards too, and who I assumed must be Oliver's. The four guys had their heads together, obviously discussing security tactics for the day, so I didn't like to disturb them. I went and sat on one of the Vendôme's big squishy leather sofas and flicked through a magazine.

Then who should arrive, swinging his way down the main staircase, but Shug.

'Seen my dad?' he said without so much as a 'Hi' by way of greeting.

I waited a fair moment, licked my finger and and turned another page of my magazine before I deigned to say, 'No.'

He slumped down on the couch opposite and propped his filthy trainers up on the arm.

The concierge was watching him with a pained expression but didn't say anything. I concentrated hard on my magazine, homing in on an article, but I could still feel Shug's eyes focusing uncomfortably on me.

'Interesting, is it. Your magazine?' he asked.

'Yes, very,' I said. Realising too late that I was deep into a double-page spread about how to tell whether or not you have cellulite.

Shug took some gum out of his mouth and placed it in the middle of one of the Vendôme's pristine ashtrays. Instantly, a gloved hand swept it away and a new ashtray appeared.

'Nice service,' said Shug, taking another piece of gum out of his pocket. He hesitated, and then tore it in half. 'Want some?' he asked.

'No thank you,' I said.

He smirked at this. 'Didn't think you would.'

He chewed thoughtfully for about five chews and then took the gum out of his mouth and shoved it in the new ashtray. The gloved hand reappeared and took it away.

'Just kills me how they do that,' said Shug.

I'd had enough at this point. I put down my magazine and looked him full in the face.

'How would you like it if you had to clear up after people like you?' I demanded.

Shug shrugged. 'They're paid to do it, aren't they?'

'That's not the point.'

'Oh, so what is the point?'

'Frankly, I don't think it would help to try and explain,' I said.

There was silence for a while apart from Shug fidgeting. And then he asked, 'So what time we meant to be leaving?'

'We?'

'Oh, maybe you're going spend all day reading magazines?'

'I wouldn't have thought sightseeing was exactly your thing. Surely a guy like you must have something better to do than go trailing around after his daddy?' I countered.

'Better than going out with Kandhi the megastar round Paris? Now come on.'

'Anyway, your guess is as good as mine. I haven't the faintest idea when we're leaving.'

'Depends what time the prima donna gets her image fixed, I guess.'

'You talking about my mum?'

'Are there any other prima donnas round here? You, maybe?'

I thought the coolest thing to do was to ignore this remark, particularly since I couldn't think of a cutting enough reply. I got to my feet. The time had come to interrupt the important security discussion going on behind us.

'Yeah, well,' Sid was saying. 'If he hadn't transferred to Real Madrid . . .'

'Excuse me, guys. Does anyone know what our schedule is?'

All four of them immediately fell into security mode, doing a load of watch synchronising etc., which was totally unnecessary since it was only me.

But it was just as well, as there was an audible gasp from everyone in the lobby as the elevator doors opened to reveal . . . Mum.

SO-OO unfair. She was dressed in the Armando Mezzo black leather bustier and matador pants that had been judged highly unsuitable for me. She'd added a scarlet-lined cloak and three-inch-heel boots and had her hair scraped back from her face in a chignon. June had done wonders to her face. Today it was her pale look – ivory skin and sculpted cheekbones, accessorised by a single black beauty spot off centre on her chin. A bit overdressed maybe for sightseeing, but I 'spose she had to impress Oliver.

'Hollywood Bliss, babe,' said Mum, giving me a fussy public display of affection. 'And my, it's Shug too.' She looked as if she was about to kiss him and then stopped herself just in time and said instead, 'I can see you two are getting along just fine.'

Neither of us responded to this.

'Well, whatever,' said Mum. 'I wonder where Oliver can be?'

Right on cue the elevator doors opened again and Oliver stepped out.

He made a big thing of saying, 'Good morning,' to Mum and kissing her on both cheeks.

Shug seemed to think this was a great joke. 'What's so funny?' I hissed.

'Frankly, I don't think it would help to try to explain,' he said in a silly mock version of my voice.

13h00, on board a 'bateau mouche'

It should have been a perfect day. We'd left by the rear exit of the Vendôme so had given the press the slip.

We had an entire Seine 'bateau mouche' to ourselves. It had a domed glass roof that gave an all round view of the river. Our 'bateau' was a luxury version of course, complete with red carpets, banks of flowers and six uniformed waiters lined up in a row to greet us as we came on board. And there was a buffet large enough to feed half of Paris laid out for our lunch.

As the boat set sail from the quay I couldn't help thinking that in spite of present company this wasn't a bad way to spend a Sunday morning.

There was an open part of the deck where you could sit on benches in the sunshine. I positioned myself up at the very front, looking back down the boat, enjoying the warmth of the sun on my face. It was sending dappled light through the plane trees and Paris was all misty and glittery in the January light.

'Heaven,' said Mum, leaning against the rails and smiling her sweetest smile at Oliver. Oliver sent a besotted smile back. (How many times have I seen guys look at Mum like that?) Shug didn't seem to have noticed. He was spending his time alternately lounging on deck smoking and sneaking inside and helping himself with his fingers from the buffet.

All was pretty well perfect until we reached the part of the Seine where the riverside walk dips down so that pedestrians can enjoy a stroll at river level. Then things got somewhat less perfect. In fact, all hell broke loose. Out of nowhere, the air was filled with shouts of, 'Kandhi, over here.' 'Oliver, give us a smile.' And all of a sudden the world's press was escorting us along the riverbank on an assortment of bikes and roller blades and even some weird kind of three-wheeled electronic scooter thingies. At any rate, a couple of hundred zoom lenses were focusing in on us close enough to capture a hangnail.

Mum instantly turned on her Dazzling Press Smile. I tried to hide beneath my hair. Oliver leapt to his feet and shouted at them to go away and leave us alone. And Shug just stared at Mum with an odd sort of smile on his face.

'How's about we have some lunch,' suggested Mum and got to her feet and walked inside. We followed her to the table. It was quieter inside but there wasn't much more in the way of privacy seeing as the bateau had this all-round glass roof.

As soon as we were seated the waiters leapt into action. Reverently, they carried over the centrepiece of the buffet – a vast silver dish on a stand, piled high with crushed ice and just about every form of shellfish the sea could offer, laid out with geometric precision.

'Oh, oysters. Yumm,' went Mum. (Her ultimate diet food, not just raw but live.)

'What I don't understand,' said Oliver, piling oysters on to Mum's plate, 'is how the press knew we were here. I mean, I booked the bateau under a false name and we were really careful to use people who up to now have been totally trustworthy . . .'

'Yeah, that's true, Dad,' said Shug. 'I really wonder how they got on to it. Don't you, Kandhi?'

Mum seemed far more interested in her oysters. 'Yumm, yumm,' she said, making little slurping noises as they slid down her throat. 'Come on, Oliver, see how many you can eat. Holly, please try one. They won't bite you.'

'And come to think of it, it was kind of odd about how they sussed out last night,' continued Shug.

Oliver stopped in the middle of squirting lemon on an oyster. 'Last night?'

'Oh, Dad, haven't you seen the papers yet? No, I guess you were too busy.'

'What do you mean?' said Oliver, starting to lose his cool.

'Well,' said Shug. 'Seeing as I thought you two might have missed them, I just happened to bring a few key pages along . . . I know how Kandhi hates to miss out on anything concerning her . . .'

Mum's eyes narrowed and she glowered at Shug, but she said nothing.

Keeping his eyes on Mum, Shug leaned down slowly and groped in the big baggy pockets of his combats, bringing out a series of torn-off front pages. He carefully smoothed them out on the table.

OFFICIAL! AN ITEM screamed the last one over a picture of Kandhi and Oliver together at some awards ceremony.

Oliver stared hard at Kandhi. She said nothing but I saw her lips do that little quiver thing they do when something's really getting to her.

'So how did they know?' asked Oliver in a threateningly level voice.

'How the hell should I know,' snapped back Mum. 'They probably use clairvoyants!'

'Oh, sure,' retorted Oliver. 'Like you dressed up today for the weather!'

'Any other guy would give his right *whatever* to be seen with me,' hissed Kandhi.

'I reckon Dad already has,' interrupted Shug.

'And you can keep out of it,' snapped Mum.

'But I thought we agreed,' stormed Oliver. 'No press coverage. You promised . . .'

'I promised! Do you think I can control the press? Who do you think I am? Even God Almighty doesn't have a say in what they do.'

'No, not when they're being tipped off . . .' slipped in Shug.

Mum shot him another look that could kill.

'Tipped off?' said Oliver. He stared hard at Mum. 'Are you trying to say they're being fed stuff?' His voice was cold with anger.

'Well, what do you reckon, Dad?'

Hot angry tears filled Mum's eyes as she stared back at Oliver. Her lips narrowed. 'Fed stuff? I'll show you who's being fed stuff . . .' she snarled.

And with that, Mum summoned strength that I didn't know she had, lifted the giant silver seafood platter from its stand and flung it straight at Oliver.

It hit him full in the chest and tipped its contents right up into his face just like custard pies do in the movies.

Oliver stood up at that point. Not a good move actually, since he was facing the riverside where the reporters were gawping at him. A barrage of camera flashes like strobe lightning caught the moment. As crushed ice and seaweed and various random forms of marine life slid down his front, Oliver, with icy-cold dignity, did his incredible smile and frown charm thing and bowed to the cameras.

Mum was totally bawling by now and heading downstairs to the loo.

'Well, I hope you're satisfied,' I said to Shug and started to follow her.

'Looks like it did the trick,' said Shug.

Mum had locked herself in and I could hear her tearing off tissues and scrabbling in her handbag.

I tapped gently on the door.

'Mu-um?'

'What?'

'You OK?'

Sound of nose-blowing. 'Yep. I'll be out in a sec.'

I waited. Within two minutes the door was thrown open and Mum reappeared. Magically her make-up was totally repaired. She literally looked as if nothing had happened. Sheer professionalism, you have to admire her for that.

'Right, Hollywood. We're going back to London,' she said.

She strode up the stairway ahead of me, two steps at a time.

I hurried after her. 'But Mum, we only just came, last night. I mean, I haven't even seen the Eiffel . . .' Mum paused at the top of the stairs and turned. The expression on her face made me fall silent.

'Hollywood,' she said. 'We've done Paris, OK? We've done shopping. We've done dinner.' And, waving her hand in the direction of what I think was Notre Dame, she added, 'We've done sightseeing. So we've done Paris. Period.' She turned to Oliver. 'Tell the captain or the driver or whatever you call the guy that drives this damn thing to turn it round. Hollywood and I are going back to London.' And with that

67

she sat down at the table again. 'Now, do you think I could have my lunch in peace?'

We all sat down in fact. The waiters must've worked flat out. There was a new clean tablecloth on the table and the buffet had been rearranged. Everything seemed totally back in order.

Shug gave up making rude gestures at the press and joined us. Even he seemed subdued by the display of cool-headedness on the part of Mum. He actually started to use his knife and fork.

With threatening composure, Oliver refilled Mum's water glass. Like a perfect English gentleman, he behaved with silent dignity as if nothing had happened. An impression that was somewhat marred by the king prawn hanging from his breast pocket, but still.

As the boat headed back at a speed fast enough to produce a wake, we finished our lunch in silence.

The only good thing that occurred to me on the way back was that I now wouldn't need to sneak a photo of Shug for Becky. Pictures of the lot of us would be bound to be all over the papers by tomorrow morning.

Monday 27th January, 9.00 a.m.
Suite 6002, The Royal Trocadero Hotel, London

On waking the following morning back in my suite, I compose a suitable text message for Becky.

Re: dream date quiz
tick one of the foll:
O.B. and K. are currently
a)   engaged
b)   married
c)   history!!!!!

Then I ring down and ask for the day's papers to be brought up with my breakfast. I might as well know the worst.

I know the worst.

It is a picture of Mum snarling at the camera with the headline: SWEET AS KANDHI!

Then another entitled: IN SEINE SCENE with Shug making rude gestures.

BATEAU BATTLE with me with my hair in my eyes – all of us looking like the family from hell.

THE ICE MAN COMETH? featuring an ace shot of Oliver dripping with ice and seafood.

And finally THAT'S ALL FOLKS with a shot of Mum and Oliver bawling at each other. Underneath this came six paragraphs on the ins and outs of the on-off affair between Mum and Oliver – ending with the statement that it was now well and truly OFF.

I folded the papers, thinking, well, at least one good thing has come out of it. That's the last we'll see of Shug and Oliver.

As you can imagine, the next most urgent thing on my agenda was the retrieval of Thumper. I rang through to Vix, who must still have been recovering from her Saturday night in Paris, and left a message on her voicemail to the effect that I was taking Sid and Abdul and the limo on a very important mission. We'd ring in at intervals and keep her updated.

Then I got on to the RSPCA and established Thumper's whereabouts. Due to the generous cheque Mum had signed for them, he had become a V.I.B. (Very Important Bunny). The nice kind lady who answered the phone said that he was going to have front-page coverage on the RSPCA newsletter. So you see, once you're with Kandhi, even being a rabbit won't save you from the press.

10.30 a.m., The Hatton Cross branch of the RSPCA

So Sid and Abdul and I took the limo out to Hatton Cross, where Thumper had spent the weekend. I wondered on the way if he'd recognise me, but thought it unlikely as my *How to House Train Your Rabbit* book had warned me that rabbits have very short memories.

He didn't. In fact, when he saw me, he burrowed further into the wood shavings at the back of his cage. I'd been right about his neighbours. On one side he had a feral-looking cat who hissed at me when I approached and on the other a black-and-white mongrel with yellow teeth and a deafening bark.

Anyway, once I'd scooped him out and zipped him back in his holdall, he went quiet. I held him on my lap all the way back in the limo and I could tell he'd gone to sleep because he felt like a little warm bundle inside.

11.00 a.m., The Royal Trocadero lobby

So all I had to do now was slip through Reception, and zoom up in the elevator to my suite. But, as luck would have it, who should I bump into as I passed through the lobby but THE MANAGER.

'Oh, Miss Winterman,' he said, doing his almost-curtsy-bow thing. 'We are so glad to have you back.'

'Thank you very much,' I said, clutching the holdall. 'I'm glad to be back too. I'm just in a bit of a hurry to –'

'It won't take a moment,' he said. 'Just a formality. Your school trunk has arrived by Red Star. We need you to identify it before it can be sent up. Security, you know. You can never be too careful . . .'

'Oh, right. OK. Errm. Where is it?'

The manager led me to a side room where my trunk stood covered in its familiar stickers and scuff marks.

'Yep, it's mine all right.'

'Fine. As long as you're sure. Now if you could just sign here . . .'

The manager was holding out a clipboard and pen.

Signing a clipboard is a two-handed affair.

'Oh, let me take that for you,' he said, indicating the holdall.

'No, I'm fine. Just give me the pen.'

But, in the end, I was forced to put the holdall down. Whereupon Thumper, feeling solid ground beneath him, must've woken up.

OK, so you get the picture. Holdall is doing self-propelled skippity-jumpy things across the floor. Manager's

71

face is registering amazement. Manager is asking would I mind opening said holdall ... Shock, horror, disbelief on both Thumper and the manager's faces.

It's so unfair. 'Cos in spite of the fact that he's a very small rabbit and practically house-trained and even taking into account the fact that we are V.I.P.s and he's a V.I.B., the manager is still enforcing the Royal Trocadero's 'no pets' rule (except for guide dogs).

Sid and Abdul were watching all this from a safe distance by the entrance, not wanting to get involved. The limo was still standing outside. So I zipped up the holdall and sadly made my way back to it, wondering if I could bribe the lady at the RSPCA to put Thumper's cage between two less frightening neighbours. Oh, this was so unfair. He was my very first and only pet and I wasn't allowed to keep him.

But then, all of a sudden, I had a brilliant idea – Gi-Gi!

Gi-Gi's such a softy I knew I could persuade her to look after Thumper until I found a better solution. So Sid and Abdul and Thumper and I got back into the limo and headed towards Maida Vale.

12.30 p.m., Flat 209, Hillview Mansions, Maida Vale

Soon as I ring on the doorbell I can hear Gi-Gi's slippers scuffing across the hallway. I breathe in the heady perfume of sauerkraut, lemon air freshener and cinnamon sugar, not forgetting those low notes of communal rubbish shaft that I always associate with Gi-Gi's apartment.

I can tell she's peeping through the eye-hole and then she throws open the door.

'Holly! My leetle pet one. What a surprise!' I am engulfed in folds of cuddly warm Gi-Gi. 'Come inside. I am making stroganoff and sesame dumpling for Karl. You will have some . . . and pie?'

'Umm, that would be nice.'

'The boys, they want to come in? I have plenty.'

'No, Gi-Gi. Sid and Abdul can go grab a burger. You can't keep feeding everyone.'

'Not proper food. No good to them.'

'Well, whatever. They could probably do with a break.'

'If you say so. But Karl. You should see him. Now he eats good. He's so strong. Look.'

I look. Karl, who is Gi-Gi's bodyguard (provided and paid for by Mum) is stretched out on Gi-Gi's couch with a can of lager in one hand and a pack of chilli Doritos in the other, watching Eurosport on Gi-Gi's vast TV (also provided by Mum so that Gi-Gi can watch Mum widescreen on MTV).

Gi-Gi holds a finger to her lips so as not to disturb him. 'We eat in the kitchen, OK? Is Munich playing. He no like when people talk through match.'

I consider trying to tell Gi-Gi for the umpteenth time that Karl is working for her and should be standing outside the main entrance of the block checking who goes in and out, not lying full out on her sofa stuffing his face. But I know it's no use. Ever since that first night she had him, when it rained and she allowed him inside, she's been spoiling him rotten.

73

The fact that she's rapidly turning him into a pale, bloated version of his fit, trim athletic self with virtually nil life expectancy seems to have totally passed her by.

I place the holdall gingerly on her kitchen table.

'What's that you've got there?'

'Look, Gi-Gi,' I say and gently unzip it.

Gi-Gi peers inside. 'Hmm,' she says. 'A rabbit. There's not much on it. But I suppose I could fatten it up.'

I stare at her in horror. And then I remember Gi-Gi's epic stories of her great walk through the frozen wastes of Siberia – or was it Poland? Anyway, hundreds of them had to walk miles and miles through the icy cold with nothing to eat for days and days on the way to get to the refugee camp. I mean, rabbit to her must still mean 'stew', or even 'furry hat' – although rather a small one in Thumper's case.

'No, Gi-Gi,' I say firmly. 'Not to eat. He's a pet.'

'Hmm – is pet,' says Gi-Gi with obvious disapproval.

'Please, Gi-Gi. You will look after him for me? Otherwise he's got to go back to the RSPCA where they'll keep him in a cage and there are loads of horrible vicious-looking animals there.' I can hear my voice going all husky at the thought of it.

'What does he eat?' asks Gi-Gi, clearly softening.

'Practically nothing. Rabbit mix from a packet.'

'Tsk, tsk,' she says, taking him out of the holdall and having a good look at him. 'He will have nice fresh salad and maybe sweetcorn. Won't you, my pet?' Thumper snuggles up to her warm and ample body. 'Well, maybe I could have him for little while.'

So that's OK. I just hope she doesn't start killing him with kindness like she is Karl.

4.00 p.m., Suite 6002, The Royal Trocadero

After a very heavy lunch, I left Gi-Gi studying *How to House Train Your Rabbit* with Karl and the help of a Russian/English and a German/English dictionary.

Back at the Royal Trocadero I found my trunk had been taken up to my room.

When I opened it, it suddenly brought home to me how much I'd left behind. Here were the remnants of another life lying before me. It was barely a week since I'd left SotR, but already my possessions felt as if they belonged to someone else.

I took them out one by one. My hockey stick – a fat lot of use that would be now. My school books. I opened the top one (maths) to check my latest mark and saw that I'd got a D– in red and a 'Please see me' for it. Sigh. They'd packed my textbooks too. I wondered what Mum had done, if anything, about finding me a tutor. Then came my clothes, mainly school uniform which I could now bin. I'd have grown out of it by the time they'd let me back, if ever. But, hang on, here were my favourite flannel Winnie the Pooh pyjamas. I took them out and put them under my Royal Trocadero pillow, where they looked so incredibly shabby that it would be too shameful for them to be seen by the chambermaids so I binned them too.

But what was this? A shoebox with 'TO HOLLY' done in bulbous graffiti writing on top. I opened it. Inside were a load of little parcels and envelopes. I opened the first one. It was a home-made friendship bracelet from Jamila with a tag attached saying: 'I'll never forget you, Holly.'

I felt a lump come in my throat as I found a little note or present wrapped in tissue from other people at school, not just those in my class but from all over.

There was a card made with pressed flowers from Marie, who hardly ever talks to me. A poem that rhymed but didn't scan too well from Portia (who wants to be a writer). A bottle of home-made scent made from the school lavender from Candida. And a tape from Becky. There was even a bookmark with a religious painting on it from Sister Marie-Agnes. The last thing I opened was a tiny origami plane from Lim-Ju with little windows drawn on the sides with me looking out and waving.

I decided to re-christen the shoebox and wrote carefully on top in felt tip under 'To Holly' – 'My Personal Private Collection of Very Precious Objects'. Then I packed each item back in its tissue paper and stowed them away in the box.

Everyone at school was clearly wondering what had happened to me. But I suppose Reverend Mother must have felt she had to explain my sudden disappearance. Now I'd left, of course, she could actually tell them who my mum is.

And then I felt really miserable as I had another thought. Which was that maybe people were only being nice to me because now they knew who I was. And I realised that this was one of the most horrible things about fame. It means you can never tell who really likes you or whether they simply want to know you because you're famous. And it must be like this for Mum all the time.

And then I put Becky's tape into my Walkman.

'Hi, Holly . . .' came her familiar voice. 'I realise that by now you must be really missing us all so I thought I'd take you on a prestige audio tour of a day in the life of SotR. Starting of course with . . .' There followed the inimitable noise of slamming doors, water rushing, squeals and sleepy grunts . . . You've got it – the washrooms!

The rest of the tape was a sound recording of a day in school packed with mini-interviews with girls and people like Peggy our cook – even the school cat supplied a grumpy miaow. And then finally there was a bit with Becky playing her violin. It was her exam piece, which had some really tricky slurs which had been bugging her. But this time she played them brilliantly. I don't really listen to classical stuff much. I guess you wouldn't expect me to, my mum being who she is. But with all the hassle Becky has had to take from people at school saying classical stuff is totally uncool, I reckoned she deserved some solidarity. And the funny thing was – the more I listened to it, the more this piece of Becky's really got to me.

At the very end her voice came in again. 'There. Told you I'd get it right, didn't I? Oh, and by the way, if you're wondering, I made the tape on Saturday – the day before Reverend Mother told everyone who your mum was. So they weren't sucking up – just in case you thought they were. We really do miss you, Holly.'

I put the shoebox back in the trunk after that and sat staring at it, wondering whether I was going to cry or not. And decided I wasn't. Then I started going through my books and realised with a jolt that they would all be hard at work right now and I was missing all this stuff I'd have to catch up on sometime if I was ever going to pass my GCSEs.

That's when I rang Vix and asked if I could come up and see Mum because I really had to sort my life out. Vix said, Yes, she thought she could fit me in at ten past three tomorrow afternoon.

'Tomorrow afternoon! But this is important.'

'Holly, you've got to understand. Your mum is a very busy woman. She's got a charity show tonight. Tomorrow it's the Kandhi Store financial review all a.m. That's followed by a through-lunch press briefing. Then there's –'

'OK, OK, I get the picture. I'll see her at three.'

'Three-ten. She won't be back before then.'

Tuesday 28th January, 3.10 p.m. precisely, The Penthouse Suite (sorting my life out)

I arrive to find Mum's suite deserted. She's given me this second pass key to her door so that I can 'pop up and see her whenever I like'. A fat lot of use that is when she's never in.

I wait for what feels like for ever, fuming at the unfairness of it all. Just because I've got a mum whose mega-famous, I hardly have a mum at all. How many people in the world actually have to make an appointment to see their own mother?

At around four Mum breezes in. She's wearing a pinstripe suit with a bustier under it. Her hair is scraped back and she has on a pair of Gucci spectacles which I know for a fact have got clear glass in them. Like everything else about Mum, her sight is 20–20 – absolutely perfect.

'Hollywood, babes! What are you doing here?'

'I came to see you. Don't you remember? Vix said we could meet at ten past three.'

'Well, Hollywood, you can't expect me to remember every single teensy detail when I've got so much on. Now I've got to get changed and out of here in five minutes. What is it you want?'

Mum is walking into her bedroom and opening the closet. I follow her.

'Five minutes. Is that all you can give me?'

'Well, maybe ten. Is it important? She is taking out various outfits and holding them up against herself, staring at her reflection with her full mirror face on.

'Important? You drag me out of school without so much as consulting me. Then you simply forget I exist! All you seem to be interested in is yourself and your life.'

Mums puts down the jacket she's holding and turns to face me.

There's no need to use that tone with me, Hollywood. You've got my full attention now, haven't you?'

'Mum, you've got to understand. I'm not some sort of possession you can just pick up and stash away for safe keeping. I've got to sort my life out. I'm missing loads at school and you don't even care. What about this tutor you promised?'

'Oh, if that's all. No worries. I've put Vix on to it. She's going to ring some agency that has a load of teachers they hire out by the hour. Now what do you think? The black or the cream?'

'Mum, will you stop staring at yourself in the mirror and concentrate on me for a moment?'

Mum glances at her watch and starts frantically to dress.

'I am concentrating on you, babes,' her voice comes in a muffled sort of way through the dress she is dragging down over her head. Then her head emerges saying, 'And while you mention it, I think we should get Daffyd to sort your hair out.'

I give up. 'What, precisely, is wrong with my hair?'

'Baby, when did you last have it cut?'

'Errrm . . .' Actually Becky had cut it and I didn't think she'd done a bad job.

'And he could do something to the colour maybe. Just brighten it up a bit.'

'We're not allowed to at school.'

'You're not at school now, babes.'

'But what if I go back?'

'Why don't we worry about that when the time comes. Now can you zip me up?'

Before I know it, Mum's swept out of the suite in a heady cloud of her own personal designer perfume 'K' and Daffyd and June have been summoned.

So now I'm clamped to a chair with Daffyd taking chunks of hair and sliming gloop on and wrapping it in tinfoil. June has

80

grabbed one of my hands and is trying to find enough nail to file. As soon as they get to work they seem to forget I exist.

Daffyd is updating June on the never-ending saga of his wedding to fiancée Bronwyn in Bangor.

'Yes,' says Daffyd. 'Bronwyn's finally decided on cyclamen.'

'Isn't that a bit strong for bridesmaids?' wonders June.

'Since it's a March wedding, she thought it'd brighten the place up. Rather an exotic touch, don't you think?'

'I've always thought of bridesmaids in pastel. You know, to set off the bride.'

'Well, Bronwyn's dress is oyster satin. Not that I've seen it, mind.'

'Of course not.'

I try to remember how long Daffyd's been planning this wedding. Which is like for ever. Each time he and Bronwyn set a date, he has to postpone it because Mum insists on taking him off somewhere.

'What do you think?' Daffyd asks June. 'Just a natural sunflashed look, or should I add a third tone?'

'She's pretty pale-skinned. I'd go for the natural look.'

Excuse me, do I get a say in this? Isn't it my hair? But they carry on regardless.

'A little individual basket for each guest, with sugared almonds wrapped in tulle inside. That's what the French do, you know.'

'Will they understand that, in Bangor?'

'It's not the end of the world, June. Only Wales.'

'Umm.'

'Anyway, the whole problem is, she's set her heart on silver and cerise. They already do the almonds in silver. But she's been on the net trying to find a supplier who'll do the cerise.'

'Hmmm. Tell me, have you been biting these nails, Holly?' cuts in June.

'No. At least, not any more.'

'I might have to go for extensions,' says June. 'Cut down maybe, so as not to look too obvious.'

'No way!' I exclaim. 'I'm not going around with stuff glued to my fingers.'

'Well, it would stop you biting them,' she retorts.

I glare at her, and then Daffyd wants my head tipped back so I have to be content with glaring at the ceiling.

Wednesday 29th January
Suite 6002, The Royal Trocadero

When I wake up next morning my hair is all over the place. I try to smooth it down some with my hairbrush and that makes it worse.

I'm just hacking at some bits that are falling in my eyes when Mum rings and asks me to come up to her suite right away as she has something important to give me.

Give me? I wonder what it is?

I throw on my clothes and make my way up there.

'Oh yes, I like the hair,' she says as I enter the suite.

'Do you? I'm not sure –'

But before I have a chance to continue she says, 'Listen, babes. I know you were really disappointed we had to come back so soon from Paris. So I've got you a little present, to make up.' She's holding out a watch that looks a bit like a Swatch.

'Oh, thanks, lovely. But you shouldn't have, Mum. I've already got a watch.'

'Not like this one, you haven't.'

'Errm no . . .' Actually, no one at school is wearing Swatches any more.

'You see this one has got a little bitsy chip in it which means wherever you go, you can be tracked on a compu—'

'Tracked?'

'Umm. On a computer. Isn't it clever? So even if you did get kidnapped your mama could find you, just like that.'

'Mum, you can't mean this! You want to tag me, like some wild animal?!?'

'Only because I want to keep my one and only baby safe.'

'No way!' (No way! My freedom, such as it is. Little forays, like my trip to Harrods, for instance, are important to me.)

So I go on at some length about my right to a degree of personal liberty. Like not being tagged like some violent and possibly perverted prisoner.

Mum pouts at this and says, 'So if you won't take a simple little precaution to please me . . .'

'Mum, I'm always doing things to please you.'

'Like what?'

She's got me there. I can't think of a single thing.

'So what are you doing today? Couldn't we do something together?' I counter.

'Well, my meeting's been cancelled so I thought I'd spend the day at my health club having a body wrap and a de-stress massage. I think I can feel just the teensiest bit of tension coming on in my neck.'

'Oh. I see.'

'Hollywood, babes – you could come with me and have one too.'

For your information, I do not fancy being wrapped in wet bandages soaked in mud or to have some person pummelling and stretching my naked body. For someone like me, with my least impressive measurement, it is just too humiliating.

'No thanks. I might drop over and see Gi-Gi. She rang and said she hadn't heard from you for ages and was everything all right.'

Mum puts on her wounded expression. 'Well, if you'd prefer to be with your great-grandmother than your very own mother . . .'

'It's not that I'd prefer. I just don't want to spend a boring day at the health –'

'No, it's OK. I understand. You do your own thing. I won't mind spending the day on my own with no one to talk to.'

So I go over to Gi-Gi's and invest some time in putting Thumper (who is gaining grams by the minute) through an intensive session on his circuit training course. The only problem is he will only go though each obstacle if I put a tempting morsel of sesame dumpling the other side, which kind of defeats the purpose.

When I get back that evening, Mum is in a post body-wrap state of relaxation. She's laid out on her bed propped up by big fat satin cushions.

'How was Gi-Gi?' she asks sleepily.

'Fine. She might kind of appreciate it if you dropped by.'

'Vix. Send Gi-Gi some flowers,' Mum calls out. 'With a note. You'll know what to say.' She turns back to me with an angelic smile. 'So it's all settled, babes. Vix has been on to the agency and she's got two teachers starting tomorrow. We'll get the most important things sorted first.'

'Two?'

'Well, you can't expect one teacher to know everything.'

'No, I guess not. Tomorrow?' Suddenly starting work doesn't seem so totally urgent.

Thursday 30th January, 8.30 a.m.
Suite 6002, The Royal Trocadero

I wake to hear an odd clumping noise from the suite next door. And I roll over in bed. Then I remember what Daffyd's done to my hair and I rush to the bathroom mirror to see if it's still like it was yesterday.

It is. It's hardly grown out at all. I just look so non-me. I tug at random shafts of multi-coloured hair. The bits I had a go at with the nail sissors are now sticking out straight, looking even more obvious.

When I get back to my room, I can hear more furniture moving sounds from the suite next to mine. There's a communal door beween us and up until now it has been locked. Gingerly I turn the handle and to my surprise it opens and I come face to face with – a grand piano.

So that's what they were doing, moving a piano in. I wonder who could possibly need a grand piano in his suite. Maybe some famous musician is going to be staying there and he's going to have to practise. Something to tell Becky. Odd, though, that they've unlocked the door.

An hour later, just as I am finishing my breakfast, there's a brisk knock on the door in question.

'Hello-oo,' I try tentatively and the door swings open.

'Could this be the suite of Miss Hollywood Bliss, by any chance?'

The voice is American. New York American. Leaning through the doorway is this big tubby guy with nice twinkly blue eyes and a totally shaven head set off by one earring.

I nod and swallow a lump of croissant.

'Well, hello. I hope I haven't interrupted your breakfast. Uh-huh, I have. Any coffee going?'

He doesn't look much like a famous concert pianist. But these days you can never tell.

'No. Yes. Sure, I think so. Though it may be a bit cold.'

'I like my coffee cold, so be a star and pour me a cup and then we can start. I'm Jasper, by the way.' And with that he goes next door and seats himself at the piano and plays three chords:

Thrumm … 'Jasper.' Thrrrummm … 'Fernando.' Thrrrumm … 'Garcia.' Thrumm te Thrumm … And I'm here to teach you, if I'm not mistaken.'

'You're my tutor?'

'At your service.'

'Oh, right. I better get my books.'

'No books,' he says. 'Sit down and tell me all about yourself.'

'What do you want to know?' I put his coffee down on the piano and pull up a chair.

'Errm. Well. Let me see. For a start. Can you sight-read? Have you any particular repertoire? Anything you'd like me to work on? Or shall we just start with a few scales?'

'Hold it right there,' I say. Suddenly I have a sinking feeling that Mum has her own ideas about my 'education'. 'What is it precisely you've been hired to teach me?'

'Why, singing of course. Music theatre is my specialty. But I can do you the odd operatic aria if that's your thing.'

'I'm sorry, I don't think so.'

'I beg your pardon.'

'For a start I'm hopeless at singing.'

'But surely with Kandhi for a mother, and if I've got my facts right Pete Winterman's your father, jeez, you must have music running though your veins.'

'Oh no, not me. I'm rubbish at music. I reckon I could even be tone deaf.'

'No worries,' says Jasper. 'I'm telling you. I can teach anyone to sing. You should hear some of the cases that have been sent to me.'

He turns back to the piano and plays a note. 'Right,' he says. 'Sing that.'

I sing it.

'Well, we've established one thing. You're not tone-deaf, Hollywood. But we're going to have to teach you how to breathe.'

I point out that I think I've managed pretty well so far, like since birth – but Jasper goes into a long rigmarole about how you have to learn a particular kind of breathing for professional singing.

'But I don't want to be a professional singer.'

'You don't?' says Jasper. 'What do you want to be?'

'I don't know. But whatever it is, it's not a singer. For a start I don't want to be anything like Mum.'

Jasper cracks up at this.

'What's so funny?'

'It's just that I teach all these kids. And they idolise Kandhi. All of them are burning to be like her. To be mega-star famous. They spend their whole lives working for auditions. And when they don't get the parts it breaks their hearts. Practically kills them. But you say you simply don't care?'

'No. I don't.'

'Well, I think that's wonderful. But I don't know what we're going to tell your mum. She's set her heart on you learning to sing. Besides, Kandhi, she pays well. I need the money.'

'You do?'

'I do.'

'Can't you find anyone else to teach?'

'Not at the rate Kandhi pays. The thing is, I'm flat broke. No, worse, I owe loads.'

'I see.'

'Umm.'

'Maybe you could teach me something else?'

Jasper shakes his head.

'All right, then, I guess I'll give it a go. But just for a while. Until I go back to school.'

'Right,' says Jasper, swinging round on the piano stool. 'Let's get down to work.'

Friday 31st January, 11.30 a.m. Suite 6002

I am standing in front of the mirror with my hand on my diaphragm, trying to push my hand out simply by breathing. I didn't know lungs went down that far. Jasper says he reckons he can improve my range by at least half an octave. (See, I'm already mastering the jargon.) I decide to text Becky with the news.

> **are there any duets for**
> **soprano and violin?**
> **If so I'm booking the royal albert hall**
> **for us next season.**
> **HBWx**

After that I check my voicemail. Vix has left a message to say that Mum and her whole team are out on location for the day and Tutor Two is arriving at 12.00 sharp.

I range my books into piles, wondering which subject Tutor Two will start on. I'm hoping it's not maths because that 'D– Please see me' is not the ideal introduction to a new teacher.

Twelve o'clock comes and goes and nothing happens. I'm just about to ring down to reception and complain when a call comes through for me saying that someone is waiting for me in the ballroom.

'The ballroom?'

'Yes, Miss Winterman, she's been there a full quarter of an hour.'

I take a stack of books and go up in the elevator. The ballroom is on the top floor. I make my way through the debris of last night's ball – sad deflated balloons, wilting flowers and glasses full of cigarette butts – to find my new 'Tutor' standing waiting for me.

She's in the centre of the ballroom floor doing some stretches. She's dressed in a leotard and tights and leg-warmers and has a little pink fluffy angora bolero wrapped round on top. Maths tutor most definitely NOT.

'We'll get the most important things sorted first.' That's what Mum has said. And I guess on her scale of one to 100, singing and dance must be way up top and schoolwork way down at the bottom. I mean, to quote her on geography: 'If you want to know where somewhere is, you ask the way.' Or history: 'History, it's all so passé.'

Tutor Two turns at that point and catches me standing there. She walks over with long swift steps.

'Hollywood. I'm Stella. I thought you'd got lost. My goodness, yes. Lovely long legs.'

I dump my books on the floor. 'Don't tell me. My mum wants you to teach me . . . dance?'

'Is something bothering you?'

'I just thought . . . No, forget it.'

There's no point in arguing. I might as well get on with it.

It takes us a while to get organised. Like, I have to go back down again and get kitted out in some Kandhi dancewear. But within half an hour or so I am standing mid-ballroom facing Stella with my feet in what she calls 'first position'.

Stella is looking tall and straight and somehow impossibly relaxed at the same time while I'm looking tense and stick-like and I'm all legs and arms and feet. (Mostly feet.)

We start with some barre work and then Stella takes me through a couple of step routines. And I'm telling you this is absolutely nothing like school aerobics. I'm using muscles that have lain dormant since birth.

When I land up on the wrong foot for the fifth time, we pause.

'I'm not much good, am I?' I pant.

'You'll be fine. Just relax.'

'Mum's a really good dancer, isn't she?'

'She's a natural mover. But she hasn't got your height.'

'Are you a proper dancer? I mean, like on the stage?'

'On and off. I trained for ballet. But I guess I hadn't got what it takes.'

'But that's impossible, you're brilliant!'

'Like hundreds of other girls. In ballet, even if you're brilliant, there's always someone a bit more brilliant than you. Mostly, you have to settle for being in the troupe. I was in the back line.'

I stare at her. I mean, I've always taken success for granted. That some people naturally get to the top, like Mum had.

'Well, you'll be relieved to hear, the last thing I want to be is a dancer.'

'It's a pity, you've got the right body. And having a mum like yours could be an advantage.'

I shake my head. 'Look at the way I move. My legs and arms and feet are all over the place.'

'We can sort that out.'

'I wish.'

'Look,' says Stella, glancing at her watch. 'That's all we've got time for today. You're going to feel stiff in the morning, so do a few of those exercises we started off with and take a hot bath.'

I watch as she packs up her CDs and heads off.

'I'll be back the day after tomorrow,' she says. 'Don't forget the stretches.'

The ballroom is silent after she's left. It's a vast room with mirrors all round and a glass ceiling that lets the sun through in a great shaft like a spotlight. I hang around for a while, making private surreptitious attempts to do one of those neat turns that Stella did with such ease, one leg thrown nonchalantly in the air.

Then as I turn I freeze in shock. I've caught sight of my reflection in one of the full-length mirrors. And for a split second, I take myself for Mum.

I stare at my reflection in its brightly coloured Kandhi dancewear. That's what she's doing, I realise. Mum – she's turning me into another version of her. It's like the ultimate in reinventing yourself. She's turning me into a Kandhi clone.

6.00 p.m., the Penthouse Suite (facing Mum up with it)

I caught Mum alone for once while she soaked in the tub. She was up to the neck in Charles of the Ritz bath foam. It was puffing up all around her like little fluffy clouds.

'So how do you like your tutors?' she purred before I could get a word in.

'They're lovely but –'

'You were lucky to get Jasper, he's really in demand. He's even done some of my backing tracks. Ages ago, of course, but –'

'Mum?'

'And how did the dance lesson go? I wish I'd had a teacher like Stella at your age –'

'It was fine but –'

'Stella's brilliant, isn't she? She turned down Festival Ballet, you know, to do workouts with me –'

'That's not what she –'

'You are just so-oo lucky, Hollywood. Most girls would give their –'

93

'Mum, would you listen to me? PLEASE . . .?'

Mum's eyes widened. 'OK, I'm listening.'

'Mum, I can't go through life only knowing how to sing and dance.'

'Oh, well, I know that. We'll find someone to do all that boring school stuff with you in the afternoons.'

'When? I'm already missing loads.'

'Vix is on to it. She's got a pile of CVs and she's lined up interviews with some agency, starting from tomorrow. So we'll have a tutor for you in no time, don't worry.'

'Good. And they better be smart at maths and chemistry 'cos those are my weak subjects. And maybe biology.'

Mum frowned at me and said in a baby voice, 'I don't want my treasure doing all those nasty old dull subjects.'

'Well, you better get used to it because . . .' That's when I came right out with it without even thinking. 'I've decided. I want to be a vet.' Somewhere deep down I knew this was what I had always wanted to do.

'A vet?' Mum nearly shot out of the tub.

I faltered. I mean, the idea had just come to me and it was pretty new.

'Yes, a vet.'

Mum was staring at me in horror as if I'd said that I wanted to become a mortician or a prostitute or something.

'But you can't possibly want to be a vet. All that mopping up after sick animals. And cutting out stuff. Yuck.'

'I won't mind if it helps the animals.'

'Hollywood. Any other girl would give their . . . their . . . I don't know what they'd give, to have the opportunity I'm

94

giving you. It's the chance to really make something of yourself.'

'But, Mum. You don't understand. It's not what I want to do. It's what you want.'

'How can you possibly know what you want to do at your age?'

'Didn't you?'

Mum was somewhat taken aback by this.

'Well, sure. I felt I had like a mission. You have to be pretty focused to get to the top.'

'I just don't want to be a singer, that's all.'

'You'll thank me for it in the long run.'

'Oh no, I won't.'

'Hollywood, you are beyond me. I simply don't understand you.'

'No, you don't. You never will.'

'I do so much for you and you're so ungrateful.'

'Ungrateful! You expect gratitude for ruining my life. All you do is interfere.'

Mum's eyes narrowed. Two hard frown lines appeared on her brow. I knew this look. It spelt danger.

'Well, I suggest, Hollywood,' she said between clenched lips, 'that you get on with your singing and your dancing and think how lucky you are. And you give this wild career idea of yours a little bit more thought. Now I'm getting out of the tub. Pass me my robe.'

I was being dismissed. Mum was really wild at me. I hadn't seen her this angry since . . .? Yep. Since she flung the seafood platter.

She snatched her robe and swept out of the bathroom.

I was left staring at the hole in the bath foam where Mum had been. How is it that your mother, the person you're meant to be closest to in the world, can turn your life into hell? I watched as, caught in the up-draughts of the air con, the bath foam floated off in great slabs . . . What did it remind me of?

Like detergent off a polluted river.

Saturday 1st February through to Monday morning

I spent the whole weekend at Gi-Gi's in order to avoid Mum.

Gi-Gi thinks me being a vet is a brilliant idea – so there! Thumper is not so sure as I have been practising on him. One thing I've learned so far is that rabbits do not like having their temperature taken, even if it's only under the forepaw.

Monday 3rd February, 9.30 a.m.
The Penthouse Suite

Mum is having a lie-in. She is seriously not to be disturbed for any reason. So I'm having a sneak preview of those CVs. Vix is busy on the phone booking Mum's lunch appointment and making sure her tickets for some gala dinner are near enough the front to get her within range of the TV cameras.

I make three piles out of the CVs. 'Too old', 'Too dull' and 'To interview'.

I notice that a couple of my 'To interview' candidates have also been ticked by Vix. In fact, according to her scrawled biro notation at the top, they are due in this morning.

The first is Harvey Dare – hmm, sounds cool. His CV has all the right subjects too. He majored in maths, I note, so he shouldn't have any trouble sorting out my D minus problem. The other is Rupert Smithers – yucky name. I check his birth date again. Could that be right?

'Vix?'

'(Can you hold a minute?) What?'

'This Rupert Smithers, he's only like five years older than me!'

'So? Look on the bright side. It's all still fresh in his mind. (No, the third row won't do. You'll have to move Ambrosia round. Look! She's only a frigging model.)'

I read further down the page. Accepted English Oxon. A levels: Classical civilisation A. English AA. Latin A. Greek B. Not a single science subject. And he'd only got a D in maths GCSE. This simply wasn't on.

'Vix?'

'(Can you hold again?) YES.'

'You better cancel Rupert Smithers. He's rubbish.'

'Too late, I've told the agency he's on the to-see list. (Look, if you can't seat Kandhi in the first or second row she's not coming. Umm. You'll see what you can do? Good.)'

Mum wanders in at that point, still not dressed. 'Did you sort the seating out?' she asks Vix. 'And did you book my table at the Ivy?'

'They're on to it, don't worry. And yes, your usual table.'

'Mum, in case you've forgotten, this is a very important morning. Like, you've got people to interview?'

'Oh, them, that. Yes. Umm. Vix can deal with them.'

'Mum, this is my future.'

'I'm sure Vix will manage. I've got so much on this morning. I'll just pop in and give a nod or a headshake at the end of the interview, OK?' She swans off. I hear her on the phone in her bedroom asking Daffyd and June to come up.

Oh well, I guess with Mum's attitude to education her non-interference could be a good thing.

10.30 a.m.

Harvey Dare is not the tall bronzed fit guy suggested by his name. He is short and, I can't help noticing, mainly nose. He has so much nose that it makes you wonder why he doesn't overbalance forwards. My eyes keep resting on it. I can't stop myself.

Vix is asking all the usual questions about what he's been doing lately and when he's available etc. But she has noticed it too. She keeps her eyes down studiously on his CV and I can tell she doesn't dare catch my eye.

Mum wanders in towards the end of the interview, takes one look at Harvey's most prominent feature and I can positively feel her from behind me mouthing at Vix, 'No way!'

After that Vix races through the last questions and tells him, 'We'll let you know.'

I feel sorry for Harvey as he leaves.

'It's not his fault,' I protest as the door closes after him.

Mum looks at me pityingly. 'Typical of you, Hollywood. I remember when I took you to *The Hunchback of Notre Dame* – you wanted to marry the Hunchback.'

11.30 a.m.

We are waiting for Rupert Smithers. He's late, twenty minutes late. And anyway, he sounds so lame.

'Well, that's it,' says Vix. 'I'll ring the agency. If he can't even turn up on time. And as you say he's too young.'

She lifts the phone and at the same moment there's a buzz on the door buzzer.

I raise my eyebrows at Vix and go and open the door.

There are moments when time does a little whirry thing all of its own and then stops. The lights in the hallway brightened by several megawatts and the vases of flowers sent out tidal waves of yummy perfume. The hotel muzac switched to a symphony of strings and even that sounded kind of OK. Because standing before me was the most perfect human being I have ever seen.

I stood glued to the spot in the doorway and said, 'Hi!'

'Hi!' said RUPERT SMITHERS. 'Can I come in?'

'Oh, yeah, sure,' I said, taking a step or two back.

'Errm, I hope I've got the right suite. Umm, you must be Hollywood. And you must be Mrs Winterman?' he said, taking a lunge towards Vix to shake her by the hand.

'No,' said Vix, virtually bristling. 'In actual fact her mother is Kandhi.'

'Kandhi?'

'Kandhi. The singer?'

'Oh, *Kandhi*! They didn't mention it at the agency.'

'A job tutoring at the Trocadero? They probably didn't think they needed to,' said Vix dryly. I could tell she thought Rupert was a total waste of space.

'Please sit down. Would you like a coffee?' I asked, realising that I was going to have to take things into my own hands. 'Vix, do you think you could get some coffee sent up?'

Vix glared at me and snatched up the phone.

Then in my best interview manner I asked, 'So tell me all about yourself.'

Rupert started telling us how he was filling in time before going up to Oxford. Doing a gap year, as he put it. I could hardly listen. I was too busy watching his perfect teeth and the way those little smile lines played around his mouth. And how he kind of squeezed up his eyes in such a cute way when he laughed.

'So what is it you actually need me to do?' he asked as the coffee arrived.

'Errm, yes. Right,' I said as I came back to my senses. 'Now, it's really easy. I'm meant to be doing my GCSE's in like two years, so we've got loads of time. (Two whole years together!) And I've got all my books. I just need someone to kind of take me through bits I don't understand and set essays and mark stuff. Which I'm sure you can do, easily.'

'Well, English is really my –'

'But you can do maths and science and stuff, I mean, 'cos I can see on your CV that you passed them at GCSE.' (I mean, who really cares about a D grade in maths?)

'Well, I suppose –'

'And you're free to start right away. Which is really important, because I'm missing loads –'

Vix was giving me warning glances.

'And let's face it,' I glared back. 'You have a big advantage because it's all still fresh in your mind.' I stared at her meaningfully.

'Of course, the final decision is up to Hollywood's mother,' interrupted Vix.

'Did somebody mention me?' came Mum's voice. She appeared out of the bedroom, dressed for lunch. She was looking stunning, wearing what I call her 'Marilyn look', very pale with thick lashes and bright red lips. She was dressed in a tight white suit and scarlet strappy stilettos.

Rupert instantly leapt to his feet.

Mum looked him slowly up and down.

'Hi, I'm Kandhi,' she said. 'When can you start?'

Mum is a STAR yet again. I've totally forgiven her for her cruelty over me wanting to be a vet. She's hired Rupert. All of a sudden I can see how, deep down, she is kind, concerned, insightful and above all a brilliant judge of tutors. I rush down to my room – I have to text Becky.

I am totally in L.O.U.E.
Holly ❤ Rupert

He's my tutor
He's per-fect.
I'm so-oo happy
HBШxxxxx

Tuesday 4th February, 8.30 a.m.
Suite 6002

I wake up with this soft fluffy feeling as if my brain has turned into candyfloss. And I try to identify why. And then I remember what happened yesterday. I can't believe it. I've got a tutor. I have the most gorgeous delectable tutor anyone has ever had. And he's starting this afternoon.

Rupert Smithers. Who was it who said: 'What's in a name?' I mean, Rupert Smithers, it's kind of musical, it scans, it's got a rhythm. I could sing it over and over again. Ru-pert Smith-ers. Ru-pert Smith-ers.

I've even had to revise my U.W.L.

It now reads:

1) A dream date with Rupert Smithers
2) Boobs (any size beyond AA)
3) A trip to Ranthambhore National Park in Rajasthan to visit what's left of the Royal Bengal Tigers
4) Dad to record a hit — or maybe sell more than 100 white labels
5) Teeth that fit for Sister Marie-Agnes

102

6) Hair that doesn't frizz when damp
7) To pass maths GCSE with a grade C or above
8) That Gi-Gi lives for ever and ever — or a very long time at any rate
9) That beetroot had never been invented
10) That caged birds are banned

(So now they've all moved down one place, I'll have to delete Smaller Feet.)

9.30 a.m., Suite 6003

Jasper had turned up for my singing lesson.

'Hey. You're looking happy. What happened? Something good?'

'I've sorted my life out. That's all.'

'Well, I sure wish you could sort mine out for me.'

I looked at Jasper seriously.

'It sounds to me as if your problems are merely financial.'

'Yes, well. But "merely" doesn't come near to describing them.'

'How did you get so broke?'

'Long story.'

'Go on.'

'I did something stupid. I wrote this musical. And then I needed loads of finance to put it on. And the guys who were backing me pulled out. So I mortgaged my house to work-shop it. Small time, like in the provinces. And it bombed. End of story.'

'What's it like? Your musical?'

'My musical, Hollywood Bliss Winterman, is brilliant.'

'So why did it bomb?'

'Lots of reasons. Wrong time. Wrong place. Wrong contacts. Wrong publicity. Or not enough of it, at any rate.'

I thought about that for a moment. I mean, living as I was with Mum, it was hard to imagine having the problem of not enough publicity.

'I'd like to hear some of it.'

'You would?'

'Go on. Play me something.'

'You're sure?'

'Sure I'm sure.'

'OK, I'll take you from the top. So the overture starts and it sounds like this . . .' He began to play strumming notes.

'Sounds like a train.'

'You've got it! It's an old old train. An old old train in the States. 'Forties time. You can hear it wailing here. That's meant to be played on a sax. Then the curtain goes up and we're in a train station. Big one, could be Grand Central. But it's night and it's creepy and there's this girl all alone centre-stage and she's homeless – she's got nowhere to go. There's a single eerie spotlight on her. She starts singing . . .'

At this point Jasper started humming in a funny high-pitched imitation of a girl. He added some words and then hummed on again. It was a really sad song but with a beat to it. As the last notes faded I could really feel what it was like – being all alone at night in a big empty space like that girl.

'But it's really great! That song's brilliant. Do you think I could sing it?'

'Do we have some interest here? From that person who doesn't want to be a singer?'

'OK, so I don't want to be a professional singer. That doesn't mean I don't want to sing, ever. Like in the shower, maybe.'

'Well, I've never coached anyone to perform in the shower before. But here's a first. You're going to have to work hard to get those top notes, though.'

The song was called 'Home is Where Your Heart is'. We worked on it for an hour. Then after that I couldn't get the tune out of my brain. I was even humming it when I went up to see Mum.

'What's that?' she asked. 'Catchy.'

'Just something Jasper's teaching me.'

'Uh-huh,' she said. 'Glad to see you taking an interest.'

Friday 7th February, 1.00 p.m.
Suite 6002

I've had a text back from Becky. She can be SO unfeeling sometimes.

r u really in love?
a) how long have you known him?
b) is he in love with you?
c) am I wrong or r u still only 13?

However, Rupert – R.U.P.E.R.T. – is due at two thirty, so

I have a whole hour to prepare. I decide to wash my hair to try and tame it down some. I give it three shampoos and gloop on loads of conditioner, then I set to drying it. But it doesn't dry like my hair does when it's all the same length. And it doesn't dry all smooth and shiny like when Daffyd did it. It's fluffy and sticking out. I am going hot all over when I look in the mirror. This is SO NOT the moment to have a bad hair day.

There's nothing else for it. I have to call Daffyd on his mobile.

'Hi, Holly. What's up?'

'Daffyd. What are you doing right now?'

There is a chewing and swallowing noise. 'I'm halfway through a tuna mayo baguette.'

'Please, please, Daffyd. You've got to do something about my hair. This is an emergency.'

'What's happened?'

'I washed it and it's taken on a life of its own.'

'Uh-huh. Bit unruly, eh?' There's more chewing. 'OK, I'll be over soon as.'

'How soon is that?'

'By the end of the day.'

'End of the day! Daffyd, you don't realise how much depends on this. You've got to come now.'

'I'll try, but I can't promise anything.'

'Daffyd. You must. You don't understand. You've got to.'

There's a bit of a discussion the other end of the phone at this. Then Vix comes on the line.

'Holly, what is this? Daffyd's got a whole restyle for your mother this afternoon. You've only got lessons. What's the panic?'

I wasn't going to admit to Vix that it mattered what I looked like for Rupert. So I just said, 'There isn't a panic, I guess.'

I return to drying my hair. I'm making it worse. And to top it all, what with the heat and the panic and everything, a pimple has appeared on my chin. And I shouldn't have touched it. And now it's so much worse that even Coverstick – which says on the pack is designed to disguise ALL unsightly blemishes – doesn't cover it.

I decide to call Vix to cancel the lesson and dither over my possible menu of excuses.

a) I've developed some rampant infectious disease in the past five minutes (I've a pimple to prove it).

b) The chambermaid has binned all my exercise books (she thought they were rubbish. She was right).

c) The lock on my door has mysteriously jammed so no one can get in or out.

I decide that c) is the most credible candidate and am about to attack the little pixilated plastic credit card thingy that acts as a room key with my nail sissors.

It's at that point that the buzzer on my door buzzes. I leap to it, thinking that Daffyd has had second thoughts and has taken pity on me.

It isn't Daffyd. It's Rupert. He's early.

Mortification doesn't come in half doses. You are either totally mortified or you're not.

The Royal Trocadero has provided two desks, one positioned facing the other. Like a teacher's desk facing a class. Except that this class only has one pupil. So the entire attention of this teacher is focused in on me. Or to be more precise – my chin.

As a distraction I start feeding my textbooks to Rupert. He receives them, giving little grunts of recognition or surprise. 'Uh-huh, *The Metaphysical Poets*,' he says and then: 'Shakespeare's Sonnets – good.'

He doesn't make any comment about my chemistry book but flips through a few pages and puts it to one side. Maths joins it with a cough and a frown.

'So how about starting with a sonnet?' he says at last. 'Which one have you been working on?'

I'm not wild about Shakespeare's sonnets. In fact, of all the stuff we were studying at school, I found Shakepeare the most BOR-ING. I mean he's so kind of old and out of it. But I was glad to be able to focus on something apart from my pimple. I riffled through the book. I'd left a Post-it in the page.

'Errm, yes, I remember. It's number one hundred and sixteen . . .'

'Ah . . . "Let me not to the marriage of true minds . . ." ' says Rupert – like he knows the whole lot off by heart.

'Umm, that's the one.'

'So . . . How about you reading it?

'Aloud?'

Rupert nods and does one of his wonderful smiles, then suggests I stand up to read.

I get to my feet, feeling weak at the knees.

' "Let me not to the marriage of true minds",' I start hesitantly.

' "Admit impediments; love is not love

Which alters when it alteration finds,

Or bends with the remover to remove." '

Rupert interrupts there. 'What do you think Shakespeare means? "Bends with the remover to remove?" '

'I don't know.'

'Well, have a guess. What do you think?'

'Erm, well, I guess . . . it's like love shouldn't be pushed around by someone else. Not bent or removed by anything that might be like . . . removing things . . .?' I falter. This answer seems really dumb.

'Exactly. True love isn't influenced by anything outside itself. The next line goes on to reinforce this. So go on reading.'

' "O no it is an ever-fixéd mark

That looks on tempests and is never shaken,

It is the star to every wandering bark,

Whose worth's unknown, although his height be taken." '

I feel more confident now I've got something right. In fact, I'm warming to this sonnet.

Rupert interrupts again. 'So what do you think those last two lines mean?'

'Errm . . .'

'You must have some idea.'

'Errm, well. It makes me think of, like, dogs, maybe, wandering around in the night. Not special dogs like pedigree or anything 'cos their worth's not known, although their height be –'

Rupert is shaking his head sadly.

'No?'

'No. I'm afraid not. A bark is another word for a ship. From the French – *barque* with a q, u, e.'

'Oh.' That time my answer didn't just seem dumb. It was dumb. Really dumb. Rupert tactfully goes on to explain about ships and stars and navigation in Shakespeare's time.

I sit down behind my desk again. I can hardly listen to him. All I can think of is that I have fluffy multicoloured hair. I have a pimple the shape and nearly the size of Mount Fuji on my chin. And I have made myself sound totally brain-dead.

Mortification by the bucket-load.

6.00 p.m., Suite 6002

I am lying flat on my back on my bed staring at the ceiling and trying to work out how I can erase from my life the hideous events of this afternoon. I have only come up with three solutions:

a) To build a time machine and travel back to yesterday so that this afternoon hasn't happened yet.
b) To book Rupert into a Harley Street clinic and

110

have his memory cells permanently wiped. (Mum
might be able to fix this, though it will probably
cost a bomb.)

  c) Throw myself off London Bridge.

I text Becky hoping for comfort.

> **disaster!**
> **a) he thinks I'm stupid**
> **b) I am stupid**
> **c) I'm too stupid to think what to do next**
> **НВШx**

Her reply comes back straight away. She must be in the prep
room with her mobile secreted under the desk.

> **impress the shit out of him**
> **by turning into mega brill**
> **student, stupid.**
> **Вxxxxx**

She's right, of course. It is almost possible that I will live to
look back on this day with something resembling calm.
With hair re-grown and dyed back to normal colour of
course. Pimple, no doubt, will take its own personal route to
recovery. Self-esteem may take longer to heal. Besides, I've
just remembered that London Bridge isn't in London any
more. Some American guy bought it and took it back to the
USA. So that wasn't an option anyway.

At that moment there is a buzz on my door buzzer. I open it to find Daffyd standing outside with his bag and hairdryer.

'Accident and Emergency?' he says.

'Hi, Daffyd.'

'Hey, what's up?' He's bustling into my room.

'Nothing.'

'Sit yourself down. Oh my, you did go to town, didn't you? We're going to have to wash this hair again.'

'It doesn't matter any more.'

Daffyd plugs in his dryer and then stands looking at me with his head on one side.

'Now, Holly, you can tell me about it. It's all part of the service. We're trained to take personal confessions. It's in the hairdresser's manual.'

'No, it's nothing.'

'Oh no, it's not.'

'It's just that I had my first tutorial with my new tutor this afternoon. And basically, I loused up.'

'Well, he's being paid to teach you, isn't he? That's his problem.'

'I guess. But I said something really stupid and now he thinks I'm an idiot.'

'Look at it from his point of view. What an advantage. He's got something to work on. It's like people who come to me with really terrible hair. I get so much more job satisfaction when I sort them out.'

'But when you make a bad first impression, I mean, that never goes away.'

'Rubbish, you should hear what I thought of Kandhi the first time I met her.'

'Mum? What did you think?'

'Well, don't tell her I said so. But I thought she was about the most selfish, egotistical prima donna I'd ever met.'

'Umm, I guess lots of people do.'

'And then you realise, that's just your mum on the surface. Those are the vibes she likes to put out. Underneath she's a really lovely person.'

I look up at Daffyd gratefully. 'But she's not always easy to have as a mum.'

'No mum is.'

'She thinks she has a right to run my life.'

'Got ambitions for you, has she?'

'No, worse. She wants me to be exactly like her.'

Daffyd has meanwhile washed my hair and is now massaging conditioner into it in a soothing manner. 'You should've heard what my dad said when I told him I wanted to be a hairdresser,' he says.

'What did he say?'

'I wouldn't want to repeat it. He practically took his belt to me. He was a coal miner, see. I had my way, though. And they closed the pit soon after, so I'd've been on the dole right now.'

He towel-dries my hair then sets to blow-drying. 'You've got to believe in yourself, Holly. And go your own way.'

'I wish I knew which way that was.'

'Just be yourself and you'll be fine.'

While Daffyd has been talking he's been doing masterful things with my hair. Suddenly under his dryer it has become all straight and soft and shiny again. And in that magical way that hair has power over mind – I feel loads better.

Saturday 8th February, 8.00 a.m.
Suite 6002 (being myself)

Saturday is a very good day for being yourself. For a start there are no singing or dancing classes, which minimises the opportunity for others to turn you into something you're not.

In bed I decide to spend this Saturday visiting those I love most in the world, i.e. Thumper and Gi-Gi, roughly in that order.

I haul myself out of bed and get dressed in my most 'being-myself' clothes. Pale blue T-shirt, jeans and Converse trainers. I even manage to flatten my hair down some with gel and squeeze a ponytail band on the little tufty bits sticking out at the back so I vaguely look like myself too.

I ring Vix and ask if I can borrow Abdul or Sid to take me over in the limo. She says no go as Mum needs them but that she will get Karl to come over and fetch me, which is epic because he'll come over on his Golden Wings and I'll get to have a ride.

'Before you leave, though, can you pop up and see Kandhi? She's got something for you,' finishes Vix.

'A present?'

'Uh-huh!'

I go up to her suite wondering. What could Mum possible have bought me?

Mum is standing by the window, all smiles. Whatever she's got is in her hand and it's very small.

'Hollywood, babe. Look what I've got you. I thought you ought to have the latest.'

She's holding out one of the newest, smallest, coolest mobiles, one that takes video.

'Brilliant. Cool. Thanks, Mum. What did I do to deserve this?'

'Do you have to deserve it? Mothers give their daughters little presents sometimes, don't they?'

'I guess. Only, I'll have to transfer all my numbers.'

'But you're going to have new friends now.'

'Umm, I suppose. But thanks anyway.'

'Call me up soon as you get to Gi-Gi's, so I can see how she's keeping.'

'Why don't you come too?'

'Baby, I'd love to, but I've got lunch.'

'You could cancel, she's always asking to see you.' Mum never cares if she blows people out.

'This lunch is kind of important.'

'Who with?'

'Oh, you know. Contacts.'

So I go alone on the back of Karl's bike and it's brilliant. It's even got stereo speakers in the helmet – only thing is he's playing Mum's latest single, which I've heard so many times I feel like it's stuck on perpetual replay.

I hardly recognise Thumper. You wouldn't believe how much a rabbit can grow in a few days. (Even at Gi-Gi's.) He's not exactly laid out on the sofa with a can of lager in his paw, but he already bears a striking resemblance to Karl.

In the kitchen I find his bowl filled with dandelion leaves, sweetcorn kibbles, popcorn and the weeniest bit of sesame dumpling (nibbled).

'Gi-Gi, you can't possibly give him all that to eat. He'll burst.'

'He's growing rabbit, aren't you, my pet,' says Gi-Gi. 'And he loves my sesame dumplings.'

'He's starting to look like a sesame dumpling. Honestly, Gi-Gi. He'll have to go on a diet.'

Gi-Gi won't hear of this. We spend the next ten minutes trying to make Thumper pose for my camera phone with his ears up. Each time he sees the phone his ears go down in alarm. We get some footage in the end but the clip has a serious red eye problem.

I am starting to have doubts as to whether I'm truly fitted for my second fall-back career choice of 'wildlife photographer'. But I guess Thumper isn't wild. And he knows he's being filmed. Whereas wild animals only get filmed when they don't know. Which must be easier.

Mum is unimpressed by the footage I send via mobile of Thumper and is more interested in asking Gi-Gi whether she's been watching out for the video of her latest single on MTV.

Gi-Gi is answering guardedly. For a start she's hardly had time to view because Karl has been tuned non-stop to Sky Sport. Also I know for a fact that she prefers the Nostalgia Classics Channel where she can tune into her beloved Vienna waltzes.

As Mum delves deeper, asking detailed questions about her video, Gi-Gi deftly turns the tables by asking where Mum is right now and could this magical telephone receive pictures as well as sending them. Mum is evasive.

I interrupt. 'Oh yes, you know it can, Mum.'

Mum says she can't remember which buttons to press, which is odd because I've seen her sending shots to her press agent with no trouble at all.

I spend the rest of the day lazing around Gi-Gi's apartment and helping her make poppy-seed marble cake. In the afternoon the sun comes out and Gi-Gi and Karl and I take Thumper down into Gi-Gi's communal gardens with a big flask of sweet Russian tea and the cake, which is still warm. We all sit on the grass and stuff ourselves, including Thumper who gets his first taste of proper green growing grass.

And then we spend the next hour trying to locate him since he has responded in true rabbit fashion to a taste of the wild by tunnelling inside the communal gardens' clump of rhododendrons.

I am SO relieved when we get him safely back upstairs to the apartment. Thumper is not so pleased. He takes one look at his litter tray and does a single resentful rabbit poop in the middle of Gi-Gi's best Persian rug.

I wake up and lie in bed wondering what to do today. At school every minute was crammed. I've never had so much time on my hands. I daren't ring Mum for hours yet to ask what she's doing.

I decide to go down to the hotel's health centre in the basement and have a swim. I don't expect they've ever seen a navy regulation SotR swimsuit down there before.

I'm just doing my fifth length when I notice a little huddle of Trocadero guests has gathered and is staring through the glass window that separates the pool from the gym. They're on the swimming pool side, and whatever it is they're staring at is in the gym.

I haul myself out of the pool to check out what it is.

I don't believe this.

It's Mum. She's laid out like a prisoner on a rack doing amazing stretchy things. There's a guy standing by who looks like he's just dropped out of a Mr Atlas Contest. He has a permatan and his biceps are so well developed I swear he can't get his arms down by his sides.

I force my way through the huddle and enter the gym.

'Hi, Mum.'

'Hollywood, babe! Meet Gervase, he's from Argentina. Isn't he wonderful?'

Gervase ripples his muscles in my direction and conde-scends a smile. 'Please to meet you.'

Gervase, it appears, is Mum's new personal trainer

118

(Mastermind of the Raw Food Diet). Mum's really worried because she overdid it just a little yesterday at lunch (she had half a glass of dry white wine instead of water) and thinks she may have gained a few grams. She is busy working these off. It seems Gervase actually has a system for working out how many calories Mum can burn per minute per machine. She still has half an hour to go on this one.

The machine leaves her just enough breath to speak.

'So what have you planned for today?' she pants.

'Nothing.'

'Oh.'

'I thought maybe we could do something together?'

'Umm . . .' Pant. 'Sure.' Pant. 'What?'

'Oh, anything. Nothing special. Just spend Sunday like ordinary people.'

A frown passes across Mum's brow. She obviously hasn't the faintest idea what ordinary people do on a Sunday.

'Like?' Pant.

'Like, I don't know, maybe visit the zoo, or a museum. Have a burger. Or just maybe take a walk.'

Later that day (spending Sunday like ordinary people)

At around eleven thirty I meet up with Mum and Sid in reception. Mum has dressed down, i.e. no stilettos, no designer labels, no Gucci sunglasses. I think she must've borrowed some stuff from Vix. She's wearing jeans, sneakers and a lime-green fleece. No one in their right mind would confuse her with Kandhi. Sid is wearing similar casuals. We look for all the world like a mum and dad and daughter on a day out.

Our ordinariness is somewhat marred by the fact we leave in the limo. But when we arrive at Madame Tussaud's (because that's what Mum's chosen) we leave it discreetly round the corner and head for the Waxworks on foot.

Mum pauses as its familiar dome comes into view.

'Oh-my-God there's a queue,' she exclaims.

I shrug. 'So?'

'Do you mean to say we have to stand in line?' she asks. I don't think Mum has ever queued for anything. Well, not since she's been famous anyway.

'That's what ordinary people do, Mum.'

'But it's starting to rain.'

Sid offers to go and get an umbrella from the car.

'No need,' says Mum. 'Just go to the head of the queue and tell them I'm here.'

'No, Mum. What did we agree? We're going to have an ordinary day. Besides,' I lower my voice. 'Do you really want to get mobbed?'

'No, I s'pose not,' Mum agrees grumpily.

Mum and Sid and I huddle under the umbrella for half an hour while the queue inches forward. Mum is starting to fume. She is making hissed asides about the inefficiency of the museum and how they ought to sell priority tickets like a kind of Museum Queue Club Class.

At last we get in. Sid and I get a brochure and are taking a polite interest in dull, famous people like President Nixon and Margaret Thatcher and Winston Churchill while Mum steams ahead hardly looking from side to side.

We catch up with her as we approach the 'Stars of Stage and Silver Screen' section. This must be where she's been so keen to get to all along. But she hasn't exactly lingered there. No, she's now heading back towards us at some pace, shoving her way through a little clump of people who have stopped by Marilyn and Fred Astaire. For some reason Mum's furious. She's far madder than she was in the queue. She's even madder than she was when she flung the seafood platter . . .

I about-turn and fall into step beside her.

'Mum, what is it?'

'Just go down there and look for yourself,' she snaps. 'I'm going to see if I can find someone who's in charge of this pathetic charade.'

Sid and I dutifully go and look.

We make our way past Cher and ABBA, Madonna and Michael Jackson, Kylie Minogue and Britney Spears. And then Sid stops and says, 'Uh-oh.'

I home in on the problem. There's Kandhi looking large as life and dressed to kill but pushed right to the back. I mean, she's hardly in the limelight, she's hardly in the light at all. No wonder she's mad.

Sometime later (grabbing a burger)

Nobody from the management was available. Not on a Sunday. The girl behind the ticket counter and the guy in the little back office who manned the phones each had quite an

121

experience that morning. Mum didn't actually say who she was, but I think they must've had a strong suspicion. (After this I reckon they'll be eternally grateful the other celebs they deal with are made of wax.)

But now it's lunchtime. We don't go to McDonalds. No, this 'ordinary' family goes to 'Sunset Strip Diner' – London's most exclusive American-style restaurant where the walls are made of video screens and for the cost of a burger you could buy yourself an average cow. But the burgers are yummy and Mum actually eats meat for once. She settles for steak tartare and a rocket salad.

'Well, anyway,' she says eventually through a mouthful. I reckon maybe starvation must've contributed to her anger. I mean, one whole hour burning off calories? 'At least I was in there,' she continues as she wolfs down another huge mouthful. Then something resembling a smile appears on her face. 'Apparently they've put Sheherazadha into the back room. She's now in their reserve stock.'

I ought maybe to explain here that Sheherazadha is Mum's pet hate. She's hated like only one superstar can hate another. (Bloodcurdlingly.) They came into the charts about the same time. And to start with, every time Mum had a new single out, Sheherazadha like pipped her to number one. Thankfully, in recent months, Sheherazadha has been building up her film career and she's kind of disappeared from the music scene. I'm just praying she doesn't make it in films or Mum will be unliveable with.

Later still (taking an ordinary family walk)

Round about three o'clock the rain stopped and the sun came out so we decided on the walk. Except Mum said just walking with nothing to look at was boring, like you might as well be on the walking machine at the hotel – which actually does have something to look at because it's got a video screen which allows you to walk your way through a choice of the Grand Canyon, the Pyramids, or, if you really want to burn calories, the Himalayas.

Anyway, we took the limo out to the Royal Botanical Gardens at Kew.

At the ticket booth, they gave us a map of the gardens and Mum spent quite some time talking to the man at the gates as he pointed out the various things there were to see.

'Right,' she said with a smile. 'I'll lead the way.'

'Can't we go inside the greenhouses?' I asked. 'They've got one with a tropical climate.'

'Hmm, hothouses,' said Mum. 'So stuffy. Maybe later.' And set off at a considerable speed with the map.

Sid and I followed.

'What do you think she's looking for?' I asked Sid.

He shrugged. 'Search me. Never known your mum to take an interest in plants.'

Mum shot round the lake and disappeared between two vast hothouses. We caught up with her standing in front of a big round flowerbed covered in mulch. A gardener was at work hoeing between the plants.

'Can you tell me where I can find the roses?' Mum was asking.

The gardener leant on his hoe and waved an all-encompassing hand. 'Take your pick,' he said.

'These are roses?' said Mum incredulously.

'Unless I'm very much mistaken,' said the gardener.

'OK, so roses are your thing. Can you show me which is the one called "Kandhi"?'

Sid and I exchanged glances. 'Last Chelsea Flower Show,' said Sid. 'I remember now. Someone named this rose after her.'

The gardener put down his hoe and led Mum to a far bed. There was a rather small plant whose leaves were going brown at the edges. It looked as if it had been pruned to within an inch of its life.

'But what's wrong with it?' demanded Mum. 'It should be covered with all these huge pink blooms.'

'Not at this time of year, miss.'

'Well, can't you put it in a greenhouse or something? Look at its leaves. They're all kind of droopy. I reckon it's being attacked by something.'

The gardener straightened up and looked at Mum side-ways. 'Well, if you look at it this way, miss. In the world of nature, you can't all be blooming all of the time. Summer comes, that's the time for your roses. Other times is the turn of other plants. For everything there is a season, as they say.'

'Well, I sure hope you know what you're doing,' said Mum.

'Mum,' I whispered, pulling at her sleeve. 'Of course he knows. He's a gardener. At Kew.'

'I wouldn't worry about it,' said Sid. 'My gran grows roses. They're not much to look at at this time of year.'

We started to lead Mum away before she could make more of a scene.

'Oh, and by the way,' said the gardener, as we were leaving. 'My daughter's a great fan of yours. You wouldn't sign an autograph for her would you, Miss Kandhi?'

Later still

'What I don't understand is how he knew who I was,' said Mum in the limo when we were on our way back.

Sid and I both cracked up at this.

I lay in bed that night thinking about our day. Mum has this phrase she trots out:

'You can't be a bit famous, babes. You're either famous or you're a nobody.'

That's what it is, I suddenly saw. All the time, she needs to prove to herself how famous she is. She can't be just 'ordinary' like everyone else – or 'nobody' as she puts it. That's why she has to keep sizing herself up against every other celebrity.

And then I realised that I was part of it. She couldn't let me be 'ordinary' either. Everything Kandhi touched had to be glossy, glitzy, out of the ordinary. Above all me, because I was a part of her. Sooner or later, if Mum had her way, I'd have to be a star too.

I thought about this for a long time into the night and then fell into an uneasy sleep in which I dreamt that I was a waxwork in Madame Tussaud's all dressed up to look like Mum. But inside I was really me. But since I was made of wax, I couldn't speak or move. I couldn't escape from inside, or tell anyone I was there. I just had to stand rigidly glued to the spot while all these people filed by staring at me.

I woke with a start and lay there wondering what it meant. ???????????????????????????

However, I didn't dwell on it too long because I quickly realised it was now MONDAY and after my singing and dancing lessons I'd be spending the afternoon with RUPERT and if I was going to erase the terrible impression I'd made last week, I'd better do my homework (you see I'd been far too busy to get down to it over the weekend). So I got up really early and lay in the bathtub learning the sonnet he'd set me.

Monday 10th February, 12.00 p.m. The Royal Trocadero ballroom

I have just finished my dance class. Or to be more precise I have just finished an hour of agonising exercises.

Stella is not happy with my progress. In fact, she is SO not happy that she has called Gervase up to the ballroom to advise her.

They are both now standing staring at my feet.

My feet. (My least favourite bodily feature.)

'Well, I think that's the problem,' says Stella.

Gervase nods sagely. 'I sink so too.'

'I'm afraid we both think. You've got a problem with your feet, Holly.'

I know I've a problem with my feet. They're size nine, for God's sake.

'The problem is, you've got fallen arches.'

'Fallen arches?' This sounds like some architectural disaster.

'Or flat feet if you prefer.'

I do NOT prefer flat feet. For me flat feet come under the heading of unmentionable disabilities alongside nits and piles and halitosis.

'I mean, it's nothing to worry about,' Stella continued. 'Especially at your age. But we'll need to get you along to a specialist to get them sorted out.'

'A specialist? Sorted out?' I have lurid visions of being operated on. Or maybe strapped and buckled into leg irons.

'I'll get your mum to book an appointment for you. But till it's sorted out we better leave off dance lessons.'

'Oh, you're not going to tell Mum, are you?'

'Holly, it's only flat feet.'

'But Mum'll be so cross. I mean, she expects everyone around her to be so perfect, specially me.'

'It's not your fault, Holly. They should have noticed this at school.'

2.30 p.m., Suite 6003

Rupert has arrived wearing a navy polo neck. He looks so-oo cute. In fact, doubly cute because he's like totally unaware of it. I forbid my skin to blush. I'm just being totally matter-of-fact, like he's any other teacher. I try hard, and unsuccessfully, to pretend he's Sister Marie-Agnes.

'OK, shall we start on another sonnet? You ready, Holly?'

'Yeah, sure.'

'Holly, your book. The other way up, maybe?'

'Oh, right!'

We read a couple more sonnets and then Rupert asks me to recite the one he set me for homework.

All is going well (with maybe a little prompting). I hurry through the 'bark' bit, which unfortunately brings to mind last Friday's fiasco. And I still manage to stay composed.

After that my brain goes totally blank.

' "Love's not time's fool . . ." ' prompts Rupert, ' "though rosy lips and cheeks . . ." '

It's the rosy cheeks that does it. Oh, pl-ease, skin, DON'T! But no, I can feel a mega-blush flushing up my neck and over my face. I try to bury myself in my book.

'Head up, Holly, I can't hear you,' says Rupert. 'Maybe you should begin again from the beginning.'

'You want me to start over?'

'I think it would be a good idea.'

'Right.'

So I do it again. Same sonnet. Same blush. Same mortification.

So that about sums up today's lesson.

I'm sure I'm not the first person to have a crush on a teacher. And I certainly won't be the last. But what I'm telling you now, is that if it ever happens to you – it is the most agonising and humiliating experience. Made worse of course by the fact that the teacher considers you to be nothing more than a kid, who is no way old enough to have illicit feelings like mine. Sigh.

Tuesday 11th February, 11.00 a.m.
Mr Crookes's waiting room, somewhere in Harley Street

Mr Crookes, Mum's consultant osteopath, said he could see me right away. So my feet and I are here waiting to be seen, with Sid and Abdul for company. The room is silent apart from the ticking of a geriatric grandfather clock. A receptionist in a white lab coat has told us we have to wait and we all sit on velvet-covered armchairs and read from the selection of magazines and papers on offer on the coffee table.

Sid is reading *Autocar* and Abdul has *The Times* open at the sports pages. My magazine is called *Country Matters*. I've chosen it because it has a picture of a hare on the front which reminds me, in a comforting sort of way, of Thumper.

We have to wait some time. I've been through all the pictures of people at race meetings and shooting parties and I've read up on how to double-dig your veggie patch ready for spring and I've got to the back, which is full of small ads for 'Saddlery by Appointment' and 'Custom-Made Riding Boots', when my eye is caught by a picture of a very sad donkey. It's an old donkey with its head hanging down in an Eeyore-ish way. As I read the text it gets worse. The ad is asking for funds for a retirement home for working donkeys, some of whom are picked up by the side of the road too exhausted to carry on.

My feet are forgotten. What do my flat feet, or rather 'fallen arches', matter in comparison with the fate of these poor suffering donkeys? While the receptionist isn't looking, I surreptitiously tear the ad out and hide it in my pocket.

I go through the 'consultation' in a haze. I have my mind on far more serious matters. While my feet are flexed and examined and made moulds of, I am searching my brain for a way to get my hands on enough money to 'bring comfort to the last days of these poor suffering beasts'.

Personally, I don't have much money. In fact, any money. I have a second credit card on Mum's account which I can use for 'Essentials and Emergencies'. I doubt if Mum would rate a large donation to a 'Twilight Home for Distressed Donkeys' as either of these. If only I had something to sell or auction. I did pretty well on eBay with the signed photo of Kandhi. But a donation to a cause like this needs to be way more substantial.

While staring at my feet I have a sudden inspiration.

Shoes. Mum's got hundreds and hundreds of pairs of shoes she never wears. There are two whole trunks of them that go round the world with her wherever she goes. She wouldn't notice if just one pair of the oldest ones went missing. I mean, she has to pay so much excess on her baggage I'd be doing her a favour really.

9.00 p.m., the Penthouse Suite

Mum's out all evening doing a run-through of her song for the Brit Awards. I've told Vix that I need to have a little search through Mum's shoe trunks to see if there's a pair that is worn enough to have a decent imprint of her feet. Mr Crookes says maybe my foot problem is genetic and he'd like to have a look at a pair of Mum's shoes to prove it. (Well, it's true in a sense, he does think maybe it's genetic.) He also thinks he can cure it. All I have to do is a half hour of exercises every morning which includes such riveting ways of passing the time as picking up pencils with my toes and flexing my non-existent arches. The other exciting news is that from now on I'll be wearing these big clumpy things inside my shoes. Which means I may need to get a larger size of shoe. A larger size! This is SO not fair.

Delving deeper into the trunk I rake around for shoes that have a real Kandhi look to them. No one is going to want to put up a grand for a pair of cheesy sneakers. There's a pair that is absolutely perfect. They have diamante straps and razor-sharp heels and MB embossed under the instep. (Hmm, not Mum's initials. Still . . .) BUT, the shape of Mum's feet can be seen clearly as a slightly darker shade on the pale buff leather. The true imprint of the sacred foot – I should get a bomb for these! They look totally impossible to walk in. In fact, they're shoes I've never seen her wear.

Now all I need do is to photograph them with my new digital phone, send the shots to my email address and pop down to the hotel's Executive Infotec Suite and set up the deal on eBay. A reserve of a thousand pounds? Would that be too steep?

I wrap them in a hand towel and I am making for the door when I hear Vix coming down the corridor. Somehow I don't think it would be a totally good idea to let Vix see which shoes I've selected. I shoot out of the door.

'Did you find a pair?' she asks.

'Oh, yes. Thanks. See you.'

Down in the Executive Infotec Suite I log on to eBay. Maybe that career as a photographer would be possible after all. The shot of Mum's shoes came out really well.

Thursday 13th February, 12.30 p.m.
The Royal Trocadero Executive Infotec Suite

I pop down to check on how the bidding is going, and SUCCESS! Competition for Kandhi's shoes is extremely fierce. They reached their reserve and then bidding went mad. I have made £2,640 for the 'Twilight Home for Distressed Donkeys'. Having double-checked that the donation has been paid direct to the charity by credit card I have mailed the shoes to the lucky bidder through the Royal Trocadero postal system.

I am now basking in the after-glow of a virtuous deed well done.

Friday 14th February, 9.00 a.m.
The elevator, the Royal Trocadero

I can hardly get into the elevator. The whole area is taken up by a huge basket of fat peach roses trimmed with glossy ribbons. It is actually taller than the bellboy who's accompanying it.

He gets out at Mum's floor and I follow the basket down to her door.

'Another delivery for Miss Kandhi,' announces the bellboy through the intercom.

'Oh, not more,' says Vix as she opens the door.

I follow the basket in. Mum's suite looks like the interior of one of those totally over-the-top Hollywood funeral parlours. There are flowers everywhere. The air is heady with their scent. The ceiling is practically obscured by pink and silver heart-shaped balloons.

Mum wanders out of her bathroom in her robe.

'Hollywood Bliss, Happy Valentine's Day, baby. Come and give your mama a kiss.'

It's Valentine's Day! Oh God. Great.

There is one huge bouquet of pink roses that has been given the place of honour as the centrepiece of Mum's table. It has a little card with the letter 'O' and a heart on it.

'"O"? . . . Oh!'

'Mum, who are these from?'

'Just people. Aren't they sweet?' She takes the card from the centre of the pink bouquet and a little secret smile plays across her lips. Where have I seen that smile before . . .?

'Mum, tell the truth. Are these from Oliver?'

'Oliver? How ridiculous. Whatever makes you think that?'

'How many people have names beginning with "O"?'

The door buzzer buzzes again and an armful of red roses is passed in. Mum glances briefly at the card and hands them to Vix, then she says to me, 'Do you want some balloons? You

133

can take them down to your room. And flowers if you like. I've got so many.'

'No thanks. It's OK.'

I do not want balloons. I am not some kid. And I do not want second-hand Valentine gifts, thank you very much.

Mum reads my expression.

'Oh, your turn will come, baby.'

'Sure.'

'So what are you doing today?'

'The usual – lessons.'

'Wonderful, because I'm going to be busy practically all day. You know it's the Brits tomorrow and I've got to really concentrate on my acceptance speech. It's important how I come over.'

(I just hope she isn't being over-confident.)

'You don't feel left out, do you, babes?'

'No, of course not.'

I go to my dance class. Stella is looking all kind of pink and fluffy and she asks me how many Valentines I got this morning.

(As you know – for I would most definitely have mentioned it – I did not get any Valentines. I didn't even get the token joke Valentine card Dad usually sends to the school – I guess it's still in the post.)

I counter by saying, 'How many did you?'

'Five,' she says.

'Hey, cool. Do you know who they're from?'

We spend the next ten minutes in a long gossip-session

going through all Stella's admirers. Happily she seems to have forgotten her original question.

Jasper seems blissfully ignorant of the fact it's Valentine's Day and we get through my singing class without a humiliating mention of it.

Still Friday 14th February (unfortunately),
2.30 p.m., Suite 6003

But!

Now I am totally floating. I am practically stuck to the ceiling like one of Mum's pink and silver balloons.

Because, when I arrived at RUPERT'S class, waiting for me, on top of my maths exercise book which RUPERT had taken home for marking, there is this little chocolate heart wrapped in pink foil.

I think it's the kind of chocolate that has pink strawberry cream stuff inside. But this fact will never be verified. For this one will stay wrapped in its pink foil in its central place of honour in My Personal Private Collection of Very Precious Objects until the cream has turned to rock. This one may even be found in some old trunk in the attic, like the photos in *The Bridges of Madison County*, by my children and wondered about.

RUPERT has come back into the room.

'Just checking my bike lock, it's been playing up.'

'Thanks Rupert . . . for the . . . errm . . . chocolate.'

'Aren't you going to eat it?'

'Oh, no. Not right now.'

'It might melt.'

'No, no. I'll keep it till later. Don't want to spoil my appetite for . . . you know, dinner.'

'But dinner's hours away.'

'Sure, but you know, eating between meals?'

'You are just so disciplined, Holly. I admire that.'

'Do you?'

Saturday 15th February, 1.00 p.m.
Flat 209, Hillview Mansions, Maida Vale

Tonight is the Brit Awards so Mum's busy all day. She has a freelance voice coach in. They're hard at work rehearsing her acceptance speech to ensure it sounds really astonished and off-the-cuff. You'd be amazed at how many different ways there are of saying: 'And I also want to thank . . .'

I am not expected to attend the event. I have a sneaking suspicion that this must be because I'm so tall now. At 5′ 6″, she really can't keep pretending I'm just a baby. But Mum's excuse is: 'We just can't rely on the security.'

So I'm going round to watch it with Karl and Gi-Gi on TV. You can't get safer than that I guess, unless I fall off the couch.

Karl and Gi-Gi and Thumper are already installed on the couch when I arrive.

There are some boy bands on. Karl has the volume on full blast and is nodding to the beat. He waves a lager by way of greeting.

Gi-Gi and I shelter from the noise preparing supper until the solo artistes come on. We get the cold salmon mayonnaise ready just in time to catch Mum's song.

It's called 'Sex Kitten'. I've seen the video so many times I know it backwards. It's the one in which she appears curled up in a basket dressed in a variety of very skimpy fluffy things with a load of males with well-greased torsos looking on. Which I guess is all very sexy if it's not your mum doing it. And you don't know that she's done umpteen takes and been sitting round and joking with the blokes between them. And that most of them are gay anyway. And that she's not really singing at all. That's all been pre-recorded so she can go totally overboard miming to it. I mean, in the video she's actually chewing gum in one frame. I know 'cos if you put the video on pause you can see a tiny corner of the gum if you look really carefully.

Anyway, for the Brits she has to do all this for real – live. Except for the singing of course – which everyone tries really hard to pretent is not pre-recorded.

Seeing your mum writhing across the screen is kind of embarrassing to watch with your great-grandmother. I glance at Karl but he's drinking his lager with an unreadable expression on his face. At the end of her song there's loads of applause and whistling.

Anyway, after Mum Sheherazadha came on with a single she made before she set off on her film career. She and Mum are both up for 'Best Single Solo Female Artiste'. Sheherazadha's song was called 'Oh Boy' and on stage she out-writhed Mum. I mean, it was verging on disgusting actually.

'Has the woman no shame?' tuts Gi-Gi.

'Not a lot,' I agree.

'If your mother doesn't win she won't be worth living with,' says Gi-Gi, taking up the empty plates and scraping off the leftover mayonnaisy salmon bits in a totally matter-of-fact manner.

Sunday 16th February
The Penthouse Suite

It's OK, she's won. But Mum is still not liveable with. She's been holed up in her suite giving telephone interviews all day.

I popped by but she didn't have time to talk to me. In fact, her ego is so inflated that she can't talk to anyone unless they're put through on the phone on speaker, so that no one in the room feels left out.

More flowers have arrived than even on Valentine's Day. And some boxes of chocolates which I prudently take down to my room for safe keeping. (Mum would simply chuck them.)

Monday 17th February
The Penthouse Suite

Mum has actually remembered I exist. Vix must've reminded her. She's asked me up to have lunch with her. We're having it in her suite so it can be 'just the two of us'. Apparently, she has something important she wants to discuss with me. I'm wondering with a horrible sinking feeling what this could possibly be.

I decide to come in with something to make her feel good about herself before she starts in on me.

'Hi, Mum. Congratulations. It's so great about the Brits.'

'Thank you, babes. Come and give your mama a kiss.'

I lay it on a bit. 'You must feel very proud of yourself.'

'Mmmm. But did you see what Sheherazadha was up to?'

'Well yes, she was pretty obvious –'

'Obvious! She was completely copying my style.'

Hang on. Who was copying who? This could be looked at more than one way.

I point this out. 'Maybe she thinks you're copying her.'

'Me? Copying a cheap, trashy act like Sheherazadha's!' Mum's eyes are blazing.

'No, but it's just that your acts are a bit, like, similar –'

'Similar! Mine's nothing like Sheherazadha's.'

'So what are you fussing about, then?'

The logic of this is completely beyond Mum.

'I'm going to have talk to Mike to see if we can sue.'

'But Mum.'

'Yes?'

'Can't we have lunch? I'm starving.'

'Oh, well, yes. I suppose so.'

Mum leads me over to a table that's been set for us by the window. She's had a light lunch sent up. And when I say light I mean micro-light. I has been prepared by Thierry – her personal French chef who travels everywhere with her. Because Mum has found to her cost that Thierry is the only person who truly understands how she likes her food prepared. He's got radish carving down to a fine art. The light lunch consists of raw fish, seaweed, grated carrot, nuts, cocktail tomatoes, slivered celery, shredded lettuce, sculpted radishes and chicory. (You don't as a rule eat beetroot raw, thank God.) I stare at the table wondering whether I could ask for a bunny bag to be made up for Thumper.

'Yuum, yumm,' says Mum as if she's about to dig into a thick juicy steak. She helps herself to a few strands of watercress.

'Couldn't I have just maybe one bread roll with mine, Mum?'

'Bread is cooked, Hollywood,' says Mum and she starts on her standard spiel of: 'The diet according to Saint Kandhi'. I switch off while she trots out the familiar phrases. 'Now I really believe in this one.' 'And I've tried everything.' 'It's for your own good.' 'You simply don't know what's in processed foods.' 'All the diseases of modern living.' 'Beauty starts from the inside.' Finishing with: 'And I've really been worrying about your diet, Hollywood.'

'But I have a brilliant diet now compared with at school,' I protest. (I haven't eaten chocolate, chips, muffins, biscuits, marshmallows, ice cream, crisps or one single Monster Munch in a whole week.)

'Hmm. I do believe I can see just one teensy little pimple . . .'

OK, yeah, it's made a comeback. Or maybe this is

son-of-pimple. I cover my chin with my napkin. I've totally camouflaged it with Coverstick. Mum must have X-ray eyes.

'Anyway, whatever. I just want to go through these appointments Vix has fixed up for you.'

'Appointments? For what?'

Mum glances down at one of Vix's printed schedules. Ominously, it's got 'Hollywood' printed at the top. I crane over but can't manage to read it upside down.

'Well, for a start there's the dentist . . .'

'No problem. I've just had my check-up with the school's dentist. A clear round. No fillings.'

'Hollywood. I'm not talking about fillings. This is Mr Evans. My own personal cosmetic dentist.'

'Cosmetic dentist? What's wrong with my teeth?'

'I'm just worrying that you might have the teensiest bit of an overbite.'

'Overbite! No way. Not after three years of a fixed brace!'

'Well, I want to be totally sure that he can't make an improvement.'

'I'm not going back into a brace.' Imagine the humiliation of having a brace in front of Rupert.

'Then there's your nutritionist.'

'My nutritionist? But I'm skinny as anything.'

'Diet is not about skinny or not skinny. You are what you eat, Hollywood –'

I break in before she gets back into the groove of the Saint Kandhi Sermon.

'OK, I'll see a nutritionist, if it'll make you happy.' Maybe he or she will allow me some decent cooked food.

'Then on Friday there's the dermatologist.'

'It's only one very small pimple.'

'I know that, but there's your whole beauty routine to set up. You can't start on skin care too young, you know.'

'Mu-um.'

As she continues down her list, my heart sinks. It seems that Mum is intent on having every part of my body toned, honed even reboned if necessary. At least she's stopped at cosmetic surgery. But I have a sneaking suspicion that this is because surgeons won't do cosmetic surgery on someone who's only thirteen, so she's saving that treat up for later.

Wednesday 19th February, 9.00 a.m. Suite 6003

Jasper has brought in the whole score of his musical today. He says he'll teach me two of the songs he's written for the principal character, the homeless girl, who's called Tyger. Naturally, I think it's a really cool name, and he says it comes from a poem about a tiger in the night with eyes burning bright.

Anyhow, we are well into the first song, the catchy one that Tyger sings at night-time in the station, when Mum bursts in wanting to know how my singing is 'coming along'.

When she's completely disrupted the lesson and Jasper has got up and kissed her on both cheeks and they've spent half an hour catching up on all the people they know in the music scene in New York, Mum says, 'Don't let me disturb you. I'm going to sit here quiet as a little mouse.'

Jasper settles back on the piano stool. I clear my throat. My mouth has gone dry. Can I possibly sing in front of Mum? I start on a false note and Jasper stops me and sends a reassuring smile over to Mum. Then we start again.

Actually, it's such a great song that I really get into it. Jasper is nodding and smiling and adding bits in the accompaniment that make it sound extra good and then suddenly Mum says, 'Hold it right there. Listen, Hollywood. It's not like that. Look, Jasper, can you take it from the top?'

Her 'little mouse' act is totally forgotten. Mum's basically muscled in between us and now she's leaning over Jasper and tapping her heel to the beat.

'Now there, you see – if you come in here just a half beat earlier with . . .' Mum starts singing. 'Home is where your heart is . . . da de da de . . .' She's not getting the words right or anything, but she's belting it out and suddenly I see the difference between what I call singing and what she does.

Jasper leans across his score with a pencil. 'You're right. That gives it a bit of a whahhhr . . .'

'Hmmm. Imagine lots of doubling. We should try it in the studio. And maybe echo to zonk it up . . . I like it, Jasper. I like it a lot. But it needs orchestrating.'

'Oh, that's done. The whole score, I've got it right here.'

'The whole score? What's it from?'

'Oh, it's just some musical that –'

I interrupt. 'It's not just some musical, Mum. It's a musical Jasper wrote himself. It's called *Metropolis* and it's brilliant.'

'You wrote it?'

'Well, er . . .'

'You mean, like you've got copyright?'

'Well, yes, I guess . . .'

'And nobody else is using it?'

'Well, not right now, but . . .'

'But there's load of people after it,' I butt in.

'Jasper, I'm getting an idea here . . .'

'You are?'

'Yeah. I'm still not totally convinced by the intro number Mike's talked me into for the Heatwave.

The Heatwave is this really massive concert tour that Mum's planning to take round the world. It's the biggest thing Mum's done in ages. They've booked Wembley for the opening and the Sold Out signs went up on the very first day. And when you consider that some of the tickets are like £150 each, you can see that it's going to be some event.

'You're not?' This comes out as a kind of wheeze. Jasper looks as if he's about to explode. If he seems too keen he's going to blow it. I can see his hands shaking with the suspense.

'But I thought you said that Sheherazadha was interested . . .' I said to Jasper, giving him a meaningful look.

Mum cuts across me, her eyes narrowed. 'Listen to me, Jasper. I really like this number. Will you promise me one thing. You won't sign it over to anyone else until you've spoken to me?'

'You want to option it?'

'I can't promise anything. I've got to talk to Mike. Look,

you just continue with Hollywood's lesson, right. I'll get back to you.'

With that Mum sweeps out of the room.

Jasper and I stand for a moment staring at each other. And then he gives a whoop of joy and hugs me.

'Hollywood Bliss. You are one genius!'

'But she hasn't promised anything yet.'

'I've worked with your mother. I'm telling you, baby. She is hooked!'

Later that morning

Between my singing and my dance lessons I popped up to Mum's suite to see how things were progressing.

Mum was on the phone to Mike Dee, her manager.

'OK, well, Mike, yeah, so he's a nobody. But everybody's a nobody before they're somebody . . . What do you mean, not enough time? I'm telling you, the orchestration's done . . . Well, maybe we need to work it up a bit but . . . So, change the publicity. It's only a reprint . . . OK, so you do that. You think it over.'

Mum slammed the receiver down.

'Vix, get me Harold.'

Harold is Harold Schwarz, the head of DBS, the recording company with which Mum is signed. This means she is going right over Mike's head – as usual.

'Hi, Harold. It's Kandhi . . . Yeah, well, I'm fine too. Now, listen, this may be a long shot. But Mike's really enthused. We want to change my intro number for the Heatwave . . . No problem, he's taking care of all that . . . Yeah, sure there'll

145

be cancellation fees. But this could be a big one. Listen, it's called "Home is Where Your Heart is" . . . No, no way. Not cheesy or folksy. Look, believe me. This is right for me, right now. I just feel I'm finding myself, Harold. This is the new me. It's a woman thing. I mean, now I've got Hollywood with me . . .'

?!

Mum reaches out an all-encompassing arm and drags me towards her.

'Umm, right here now. Do you want to speak to Harold, Hollywood, babes?'

I guess I have to.

'Hi, Mr Schwarz.'

'Hey. Hollywood! You sound grown-up.'

'Thanks.'

'What's this number like? You heard it – this "homey" thing . . .?'

'IT'S BRILLIANT. It's like the best thing I've heard Mum sing in ages.'

'It is?'

Mum grabs the phone back from me.

'Listen, Harold, the time's right. All those troops coming back from, you know. . . . that whatsisname place . . . Yeah, wherever. This number, Harold. Trust me. It's got NOW vibes . . . OK, so we'll make a demo track. And if anyone needs convincing, they'll be convinced.'

Mum leans back in her chair. 'Vix, will you ring through to Mike and say that Harold wants him to get a contract drafted for Jasper. Right now.'

146

Smug? Do I feel smug? DO I FEEL SMUG. I do!!!!!

Thursday 20th February
The Penthouse Suite

Vix rings down at 8.00 a.m. to say can I pop up to see Mum so that she can say goodbye.

'Goodbye?'

'Yeah, she's leaving for the States at ten.'

I head up there right away.

'Hey, Mum. What's all this about you going to the States?'

She should be working on 'Home is Where Your Heart is' if she's to get it ready in time for the Heatwave.

'I need to be there for the Grammys. I do have to work you know, babes.'

'But the Grammys are not for a week. How long are you staying?'

Mum looks evasive. She's fiddling around with the little pots of cream on her dressing table. 'About ten days, probably.'

'Ten days! Why do you have to stay ten whole days?'

'I've got loads of people to see in LA. And besides, I do have to top up my tan.'

Los Angeles. It must be really hot and sunny there right now. I glance at the continuous rain lashing against her vast ceiling-to-floor windows. Hang on, Mum's tan is spray-on, she can top that up wherever. I point this out.

'But it's for the Vitamin D. I have to consider my bones too, you know.'

'Can't I come too?'

'Not this time, Hollywood.'

'But you did say I could go everywhere with you . . .'

'No, I think it's best if you just keep up with your studies, and besides Vix has booked all those appointments for you.'

The dentist. The nutritionist. The dermatologist. Oh, lucky me!

'But Mum, shouldn't you be working on Jasper's song?'

'One thing you'll learn, Hollywood, is that in show business, when push comes to shove you can fit anything in . . . Now Vix, can you get me Mike on the phone? No, on second thoughts, get me Harold . . .'

Mum clamps her phone to her ear. She's forgotten I exist – again.

Friday 21st February
(Mainly) Harley Street

The entire day is spent visiting umpteen random surgeries where people have been delving into my innermost private life.

Mum has called me twice. First call was to find out the verdict of Mr Evans, the cosmetic dentist. He's suggested something called veneers. This means rubbing down my perfectly healthy teeth and sticking false fronts on. I had a sneaky feeling that while he was examining my teeth he had a model of Kandhi's up on his computer screen and he was trying to make mine into an identical copy. (Hers are, of course, one hundred per cent perfect, so you can't really blame him for using them as a guide, but still . . .)

Second call was rather fraught as it was when I was at the dermatologist, Mr Crick. Mum was freaking out because she was by the pool at the W Hotel LA (sigh) and had just noticed the teensiest mole which she hadn't remembered being there before. She wanted Mr Crick to get her total body plan up on his screen to check out if he had this one already mapped, or not.

He had. It was OK. She didn't have to fly back straight away.

Saturday 22nd February, 6.30 p.m.
Flat 209, Hillview Mansions, Maida Vale

Thumper has put on another twelve grammes since last week, which is worrying. I have looked through *How to House Train Your Rabbit* to see what the average weekly gain is for a growing rabbit, but it's not covered. However, he is making good progress with his house-training regime. Karl has hardly had to bring out Gi-Gi's dustpan and brush this week, which means that his work-load is back to normal, i.e. changing the channels on the remote control.

Gi-Gi has cooked a special dinner for Karl because Dortstadt Wanderers are playing, and if they win this game they'll get into the running for the European Cup. It's all in Dortstadt Wanderers colours, which are a particular shade of burgundy, so everything she has cooked is in burgundy or white.

We are having a weird kind of burgundy soup which has taken Gi-Gi two whole days to make and has had to be strained through egg white, followed by some kind of meat in white sauce, spiced red cabbage, white rice, black cherry tart and sour cream.

Gi-Gi has said that we are allowed to eat it in front of the TV as the match is really important for Karl.

While eating, or rather drinking, our soup, which has sour cream and chives on top, Karl sits sighing and moaning as it seems that the Wanderers are not 'doing so good'.

'What is this soup, Gi-Gi?' I ask. It tastes kind of weird.

'Borscht,' she says, bustling off into the kitchen to fetch the meat course.

We're in the middle of the second course when we get to half-time. Barcelona are now two goals up and Karl is so depressed that he says he'll have to go down to the corner shop to buy another six pack of lagers.

While Karl is out I do some random zapping with the remote control and what do I come up with? The Oscar Ceremonies. I'm glued to the screen, as I really want to witness the great event of Oliver NOT getting Best Actor in a Leading Role Award.

Karl has been gone three minutes and I fume as we are given flashbacks of the guests swanning down the red carpet into the Kodak Theatre in Los Angeles. These are followed by tedious fill-in facts and figures – like there are one thousand five hundred journalists present! But now we've cut back to Claire Danes, looking dazzling in this kind of silvery shimmery evening gown, who is about to read out the nominations for Best Actor.

I pray that Karl has run out of cash and had to go to the cashpoint, or tripped or got stuck in the elevator, or run over, whatever.

'And the nominations for Best Actor in a Leading Role are Oliver Bream for Antoine in *Loyal Subject* . . .' The floodlight zooms round and rests on Oliver, but I don't hear the rest because WHO is beside him, in her latest cream satin Armando Mezzo off-the-shoulder number, but MUM. And WHO is beside HER with his hair all gelled up in spikes like a stegosaurus but SHUG.

'Oh,' says Gi-Gi. 'What a pity Karl missed seeing your mother. Mind you, I never did like her in cream.'

I swallow a great lump of meat as I hear the fateful words: 'And the winner is . . .' And see Oliver leaning over and giving Mum this massive kiss on the lips. And now he is making his way accompanied by all that schmaltzy music up on to the stage to claim the award. He kisses Claire Danes too, but only on the cheek.

Oliver is well into doing his smile-and-bow-charm-thing when Karl arrives back and we have to switch channels. Dortstadt Wanderers are still losing.

Karl notices my down-at-the-mouth expression and assumes it's because of the match. He sympathetically passes me a can of lager and without thinking I take a sip. It's yukkk!

So that's why Mum was so vague about how long she was staying in LA. She wanted to be there for the Oscars. How long has she been back with Oliver, I wonder? And now he's got Best Actor. I know Mum, she's attracted to fame like wasps are to jam. There'll be no holding her back now. I better get used to the idea – Kandhi and Oliver are an item.

Later that night, Suite 6002

I am sitting in the bathroom feeling really queasy. This has been the very worst night of my life so far. I've discovered what was in the soup – beetroot. I've discovered what was in the stew – veal. I've accidentally drunk lager (only a sip but that was enough). And I've discovered that if things go the way things usually go with Mum, I could shortly be stepsister to my least favourite person in the entire universe.

Sunday 23rd February, 7.00 a.m. Suite 6002

I am woken by the phone ringing.

It's Mum. (Mum at this hour!) But then I remember that in LA they're eight hours behind so she hasn't gone to bed yet.

'Hollywood, are you all right?'

'You woke me up to ask?'

'Oh, were you asleep, babes?'

'It doesn't matter. I'm awake now.' As I surface, last night's Oscar ceremony comes back to me in vivid detail, so before she can continue, I blurt out, 'Mum, admit it. You didn't go to LA for the Grammys. You went for the Oscars.'

'Oh, you saw us. I just happened to bump into Oliver and he had absolutely no one to sit at his table so I guess I took pity on him –'.

'No one to sit at his table! I'm not a baby, Mum.'

'Well, whatever. I was the only person he really wanted.'

'Exactly! He wants to be seen with you because you're so mega-famous. He just wants to get pictures of you and him together plastered all over the papers.'

'We stars do these little things for each other.'

'So you're not going out with him?'

'Oliver? No way.'

'You're sure?'

'Wasn't his acceptance speech just brilliant?'

'Mum, tell me the truth. Are you or aren't you?'

'Of course not. It's just as you say – all for publicity, babes. Don't take any notice.'

'As long as you're sure.'

'Would I lie to my one and only baby?'

I consider this and decide, 'Yes, quite possibly.'

But when the Sunday papers come up with my breakfast, shots of Mum and Oliver together have spread across them like some disease.

IT'S ON AGAIN! shouts the *Sunday Times*.

TINSELTOWN'S TWOSOME says the *Sunday Telegraph*.

SHE'S NAMED THE DAY! claims the *Sun*.

KANDHI'D CAMERA adds the *Sunday Sport*, showing a shot of Oliver's hand steering Mum's Armando Mezzo'd bottom along.

Then – ooops! I have a text from Becky. (She must've seen the Oscars.)

Re: dream date with o.b.
Why didn't didn't you tell me he was back with your mum?
B

I text her back:

sorry i didn't know
HBWx

She texts me back:

don't you two ever talk?

I text her back:

not about anything that matters

Her reply comes back as one word.

s.a.d.
Bx

Did Mum and I ever talk? Well, sure we talk. But Mum never listens. And now she'll have Oliver to talk to, so she'll have even less time for me.

This thought makes me feel very small and insignificant, so I bury my face in teddy and indulge in a vast all-engulfing tidal wave of self-pity.

8.00 a.m.

It's Mum on the phone again. Can I get no peace to have a decent attack of self-pity? She wants to know if I've seen the papers.

'Yes I have! And they're all saying that you and Oliver are practically married.'

'Babes. Would I get married without consulting you?'

'You did the last time.'

'Yes, well, that was different. Fernandez was a mistake. Never trust a polo player. I'd've known if I'd been able to speak Spanish.'

'Didn't he speak Portuguese?'

'Well, whatever.'

'I worry about you, Mum.'

'I worry about you too, babes. But remember, whatever happens, your mama's always there for you.'

That's rich from someone who's the other side of the world.

'So when are you coming back?'

'We've got the Grammys tomorrow. And then there'll be all the post-publicity. You know, when you win – you've got to be there for the fans.'

'You can't be sure you'll get a Grammy.'

'Harold reckons I'll get several.'

'Well, don't stay too long.'

'What's the hurry?'

'You've got Jasper's song to prepare for the Heatwave. Remember?'

'Oh, that. Well, as a matter of fact, I met up with Gerry Oldman over here and he's got an amazing new song . . .' Alarm bells are ringing. Jasper will be absolutely devastated if she backs out.

'Mum. You can't change your mind now.'

'Umm, well, maybe Mike was right. Jasper's number is a bit "homey".'

'No, no way. Look, believe me. This is right for you, Mum, right now. It's like you're finding yourself. It's the new you. It's a woman thing. I mean, now you've got me with you . . .' I have the oddest sensation as I am saying this that I've heard it before.

'You really think?'

'Mum, I know.'

'Maybe you're right.'

'I know I'm right.'

'OK. Ask Vix to e me the contract to sign.'

PHEW!

Tuesday 25th February, 9.00 a.m.
Reception, the Royal Trocadero

I've had another card from Dad. This one has a picture of a Barbie doll on the front in full wedding gear.

On the back, Dad's scrawled handwriting reads:

Holly-Poppy

What's all this about your mum getting spliced again?

Tell her Oliver Bream is:

a) a cold fish

b) a stuffed shirt

c) a joke

B-C-N-U

Your ever-loving DADx

I needed to tell him I was totally in agreement, so I popped down to help myself to a free postcard of the Royal Trocadero from reception and I found the whole place in chaos!

Toppling stacks of little gold chairs were being carried into the main conference room. Deliveries of flowers were arriving by the minute. It looked as if there was going to be some sort of massive party. Or society wedding. Maybe royalty was about to drop by.

I asked the concierge what it was all about.

'It's for your mother,' he said. 'Press conference, all day tomorrow. We've been asked to prepare the main drawing room and the two side rooms for round-table forums. They're starting as soon as she flies in. It's going to be a big one.'

I peeped into the conference room. A massive video screen had been erected, fronted by a long table set with a row of mikes. Down the sides of the room people were busy pinning posters of Mum on boards. Buffet tables with snowy cloths already had pyramids of champagne glasses and a battalion of ice buckets was lined up at the ready.

Wow. Mum was taking this publicity thing seriously. But I guess when you win the Brits and the Grammys – maybe even several Grammys – you've something to celebrate.

I take my postcard back up to my suite and compose my reply.

On the front, I mark the windows of my suite and Mum's balcony with a cross. I then add a speech bubble to each. Mum's says: 'Oliver, Oliver, wherefore art thou Oliver?' Down from below comes a bubble: 'I'll be up in a minute.' And from mine comes: 'Not if I have anything do do with it!'

On the back I simply write:

> I agree totally.
> I'm on to it.
> H-Px

Wednesday 26th February, 8.00 a.m.
Suite 6002

I've woken up in the middle of a terrible nightmare in which I'm hearing a message on my answerphone.

I grope for the button and replay the message. It wasn't a nightmare. On my voicemail there's a message from Vix, in her full-mourning voice, saying they're waiting in the hotel for Harold and Mike to come for an emergency meeting, but she can't talk loud because Mum hasn't got a Grammy.

This is SUCH NOT GOOD news. Mum's never not got a Grammy before.

I lie in bed thinking of the waste of it all. All those gold chairs set out waiting for no one. Those banks of flowers starting to droop, going brown at the edges. All those ice buckets with their ice turning to water. The canapés laid out on their trays in the kitchen going so sadly soggy.

I decide to spend the day working as hard as I can at my classes, trying to make it up to Mum somehow.

When Jasper gets in the whole thing gets worse. Apparently not only has Mum not got a Grammy, Sheherazadha has. This is even badder bad news.

I ring Vix to ask how Mum is coping. But I'm told by the woman on the phone that she can't talk because they are currently involved in a 'damage-limitation' conference in which they are 'reassessing Mum's image projection parameters', whatever that means. I sure hope it's effective.

I'm also informed that Mum will be arriving back late tonight, which means I won't have to face her till tomorrow.

Thursday 27th February, 6.00 a.m.
Suite 6002

I'm woken yet again at some unearthly hour. Can't I ever get a decent night's sleep? But this time I think I'm hearing the strangest sound of gongs beating gently in the dawn. I turn over, telling myself I'm imagining things, and go back to sleep.

Half an hour later I am convinced I can totally hear a gong beating. Boom. Boom. Boom. In the Royal Trocadero? Weird!

I can't hold out any longer. I slip on my robe and creep to the door and peep out. The bodyguards have given up patrolling my floor because ever since I've been here absolutely nothing has happened. From the security point of view, the nasty threat thing seems to be a bit of a disappointment. The guys tend to hang around downstairs instead. But in place of them – now this IS weird – walking down the corridor is a totally shaven-headed monk in a saffron robe. He has bare feet and is swinging a small woven basket with a lid.

He comes to my door, holding his two hands together as if praying, and bows his head.

'Er, hi!' I try.

Silently, he holds out his basket.

I peer inside to find a cheese sandwich and a peach melba yogurt.

'Errrm?'

He bows again. The penny drops. Of course. He's Buddhist. A monk. He's asking for food.

'Hold on. I'll be back.'

I head for the mini-bar, wondering if anything inside will be suitable for a Buddhist's breakfast. I present him with a packet of luxury salted cocktail nuts, a Coke and a Kit-Kat.

He bows again in acceptance and moves on down the corridor.

I go back to bed thinking ?????????

9.30 a.m., the Penthouse Suite

All is revealed. I have summoned up the courage to go up and see Mum and found her deep in meditation on a prayer mat opposite my mystery monk.

Vix holds a finger up to her lips.

'How is she coping?' I whisper.

Vix casts a glance towards Mum's bedroom. 'Well, she's stopped flinging things around.' Mum's door is open. The room's a tip.

Vix then takes me aside and gives me the low-down in an undertone.

The monk's name is Sit (which suits him, I later find, since that's what he spends most of his time doing – admittedly with his legs in a very uncomfortable sort of cat's-cradle position, but still).

Sit is Mum's new 'spiritual adviser'. It seems she's now done Roman Catholicism – period. Or as Mum told me later: 'Let's face it. What has it done for me? All that praying and I didn't win a single Grammy.'

She now thinks an Eastern religion might be more 'her thing'. She picked up Sit early one morning when she was jogging at Venice Beach. Apparently, he's doing a kind of Buddhist version of our 'year out', i.e. a 'year in' a Buddhist temple.

'It seems to be helping,' whispered Vix. 'To cope, you know.'

I nod. They've just got to the mumbly-chanty bit. I creep off to my singing lesson and leave them to it.

10.30 a.m., Suite 6003

I ask Jasper why he thinks Mum needs a 'spiritual adviser'.

'Oh, it's because she's so insecure,' says Jasper without a moment's hesitation.

'Mum, insecure?' Are we talking about the same person?

'Yeah, sure. Imagine what it's like being at the top. If you're going to be going anywhere, there's only one direction. And that's down, baby. Now she's missed out on those Grammys she's scared rigid that her fame is suddenly going to fade away. She's going to slide down a slippery slope to nowhere and wake up one morning a has-been.'

I stare at Jasper disbelievingly. 'But, I mean, she's so famous, she's so rich, she's got all these people working for her. Like Mum says, she's an empire.'

'A house of cards,' says Jasper. 'One litttle pouff and it could all be blown away.' He turns to the piano and plays a few chords: 'Down . . . down . . . down . . . down . . .' he sings and then he continues with some lyrics.

'What's that?'

'It's a chorus from *Metropolis*. There are all these people in the subway, right? And they're going down. But it's also about the city. A city sinking under the weight of all the dirt that's going on.'

'Isn't that a bit gloomy?'

'Sure it's gloomy. So's life sometimes. It's not all nice, you know, Holly.'

'No, I know.'

After that I tell him about how Mum so very nearly changed her mind about 'Home is Where Your Heart is'.

'Typical insecure behaviour. She's too scared to commit herself. She has to keep changing her mind until it's a "fait accompli".

'What does that mean?'

'It's French for "too-late-baby-there's-no-going-back".'

We spend the rest of the lesson working on a couple more songs. I have been practising my scales and my breathing exercises and Jasper says I've extended my range by a couple of notes at the top of my register, whatever that means. But I feel pleased anyway.

I go back to my room thinking about what he said about Mum being insecure. Surely not.

Friday 28th February, 12.30 p.m.
The Penthouse Suite

I've gone up to see how Mum is dealing with the Grammy fiasco.

She's in black, all black. Even her hair is black.

'Hi, Mum. You OK?'

'Hollywood, we've all decided, it's time I had a complete change of image.'

'Sure, Mum, but . . . black? It's so kind of last year.'

'No. You don't understand. It's my whole image. My whole being. It's the inner me that needs changing.'

'Re-ally?'

'Umm. Come and give your mama a kiss, baby.'

I go obediently and note close up that she's not so grief-stricken that she's forgotten to put on a liberal dose of 'K' (her own personal designer perfume) and full make-up including a beauty spot. Black, of course, but still.

'You know what? People see me as this tough, hard person without a heart. But, believe me, I know what it is to be hurt.'

'Of course you do.'

'But I'm going to put all this behind me and start over again.'

'I'm glad to hear it. So are you going to start work on the Heatwave?'

'Not today. I'm just not up to it. Besides, I've got lunch . . .'

'Mum, lunch doesn't take all day!'

'Hollywood. This is a very special lunch.'

'Who's it with?'

'Well, if you must know, it's with Oliver. He was so sweet at the Oscars.'

'Sweet? Oliver? Oh Mum, you can't like him. He's so cold and calculating.'

'Not when you get to know him.'

'But he is. I know you can't see it. But believe me, he's using you!'

'Rubbish. You just wait and see.'

'Wait? For what?'

I can feel goosebumps coming up and the little hairs on my arms are standing to attention. So Oliver's in the UK.

And he's having lunch with Mum. A special lunch. Alarm bells are ringing!!! Is Shug with him? Oh my God, is a nightmare future with the step-brother from hell heading my way?

2.30 p.m., Suite 6003

At two thirty I manage to erase this horror scenario from my mind as RUPERT is here. He and I have at last got down to maths. Rupert is studying the page for which I got the 'D minus, please see me' with a look of concentration.

'Hmm. Hmm,' he says.

'Well?'

'It's clear where you went wrong.'

It is. It's marked in Sister Elizabeth's red biro, in fact double-underscored.

'Of course it's ages since I did, errm . . .' He checks the heading. 'Ahh, simultaneous equations.'

We both look glumly at the page.

'Look, maybe we should start out fresh with a new exercise book . . .' suggests Rupert.

As I'm getting out my pen and nice smooth new book of squared exercise paper, I catch him taking sneaky looks at the back of the textbook where the answers are.

'Yep, it's really simple. If the sum of two numbers is ten, what are the numbers?'

'Search me. They could be anything. One and nine, five and five, errm . . .'

'True.' Rupert pauses and nibbles thoughtfully at the top

of his pencil. Oh, lucky pencil to come so close to Rupert's lips. I'm lost for a moment.

'But you must remember something from the lesson. It was only last month, Holly.' Rupert is being quite forceful for once. With an effort I pull myself together.

'I seem to remember it's something to do with them changing their signs when they jump over the equals.'

I'd spotted this little scrawl in the margin of my old book with sheep turning into cows as they leap over a gate. It's what Sister Elizabeth calls a 'mnemonic', which is a really difficult-to-pronounce way of saying 'reminder'.

'Oh, RIGHT! That helps.'

Somehow, with the aid of the textbook and a lot of checking the answers at the back, we manage to get the whole page corrected.

In fact, I get the exercise I'd found so difficult in school one hundred per cent right.

Rupert marks it AA+. And I'm absolute rubbish at maths.

So you see, he is the most perfect tutor.

5.00 p.m. (after maths), the Penthouse Suite
I decide that I'd better check out how Mum's lunch went.

I enter her suite to find Mum striding back and forth like a caged panther. She hasn't seen me. She's raging at Vix.

'How dare he blow me out? Who does he think he is?'

'Maybe he was held up . . .' suggests Vix limply.

'Held up! No one gets held up when they're lunching with me. Not even . . . not even . . . not even if there's an earthquake and they fall down a crevasse!'

Vix is mumbling about traffic and taxis.

'Well, I got there, for God's sake!'

'And he didn't call to expl—?'

'No, he did NOT call. And if he does, not only am I NOT IN, I'm NOT EVER IN EVER AGAIN. Is that clear?'

I back out, not wanting to get involved.

So Oliver has blown Mum out! That figures. When she doesn't get a Grammy, she doesn't get lunch. Hmm. I told you so.

The whole thing has confirmed in my mind what I've always said about Oliver. As I pointed out to Mum, it's her fame he's after. When the teensiest bit of failure tarnishes her image, he's not seen for dust.

I'd better text Becky the good news.

re dream date with o.b.
o.b. was with k.
then he wasn't
then he was again
but he's not any more.
HBШx

I get another text back:

???????
Bx

I text her back:

> **to simplify:**
> **two egos won't go into one**
> **HBWx**

Saturday 1st March, 9.30 a.m.
The Penthouse Suite

I'm burning to know whether Mum has or hasn't signed the contract for 'Home is Where Your Heart is'. So I pop up to Vix's office to check her in-tray where I saw it a day or so ago. I flick quickly through her papers and, yes, sure enough, there it is. And triumph! There's Kandhi's signature on the bottom line with its inimitable flourish. I'm just about to creep back out when Vix's phone rings. I feel almost as if it's seen me. I stare at it guiltily.

Normally Vix would have picked up the call on her mobile if she's not in the hotel. But it continues to ring, which means Vix hasn't transferred it. In fact, it could actually mean that maybe she's somewhere loose on this floor and if she hears it she is bound to dash in and answer it. If Vix sees me going through her in-tray there is going to be a scene. So I snatch up the phone.

'Hello.'

'Is that Kandhi?' It's a woman's voice. It's a nice warm deep voice. American. It's the kind of voice a mum ought to have.

'No, she's not here right now.'

'Is that Kandhi's PA?'

'No, she's not here either. But I could take a message if you –'

'So who are you?'

'Errm, well, I'm Holly, Kandhi's daughter.'

'You don't say!'

'Umm.'

'Well. Aren't I the lucky one getting through to you?'

''Errm, well . . .'

'Because I've got a load of things I want to ask you.'

'Ask me? You have?'

'I believe you have some pretty interesting insights.'

She must've heard about my views on fur farming, caged animals, bio-testing, third world exploitation. Naturally, I'm flattered.

'Oh, well, I like to speak up for things that don't have like a voice. You know, animals and things.'

'Exactly. And I'm sure your mother shares your views.'

'Well, errm . . .' Of course there was that generous donation that Mum gave, anonymously, to the Twilight Home for Distressed Donkeys, but . . .

'She wouldn't be with Oliver Bream, by any chance?'

'Oliver Bream? No way!'

'Why do you say that?'

'That creep. Last time they were meant to meet he didn't show up.'

'No way. Blew out Kandhi?'

'Umm.'

'She must've been mad.'

For some reason I'm getting vibes that this person is not so interested in my ecological views after all.

'Could you tell me who I'm speaking to, please?' I remember, too late, to ask.

'Oh, just a friend.'

At that point the phone goes dead. And then I remember, even more too late, that I'm not supposed to talk to anyone about Mum. Certainly not the press. But this woman didn't sound like the press. Did she?

I don't have time to ponder on this. Because I can hear Vix coming down the corridor. If she discovers I've been talking to anyone about Mum she's going to throw an epi.

I'm out of here.

Sunday 2nd March, 10.00 a.m.
Suite 6002 (Black Sunday)

I've hardly got the heart to write anything as I am in total shock due to the report in the *Weekday News* under the heading:

GUESS WHO'S BLOWN OUT KANDHI!

The article below goes on about the fiery relationship between the two superstars. They've even raked out the old shot of Oliver covered in seafood. There are quotes from me that have been amplified beyond belief. And from somewhere they've unearthed a very ancient school photo of me, in uniform. (I even had my brace at the time.) Oh why, oh why did I talk to that 'friend' of Mum's?

There's only one consoling factor. Mum never reads the newspapers. She gets Vix to go through them for her so that she can cut out anything relevant. (And edit out anything negative.) Vix always has a pile of them waiting on her desk that she hasn't had time to tackle.

I feel it would be kinder to Mum to remove the *Weekday News* with the offending article and destroy it. I'm doing Vix a favour too because I'm reducing her workload.

Monday 3rd March, 9.30 a.m.
Suite 6002

Disaster!

Vix has had a call from Oliver, who must be signed up with some creepy underhand paparazzi press cuttings agency. He has just received the cutting from the *Weekday News* – with the 'Guess who's blown out Kandhi' article.

Vix has summoned me to her office and faced me up with it. I even have to admit to confiscating the *Weekday News* from her pile.

'Please, please, don't tell Mum,' I beg her. 'It's bad enough being stood up. But having the whole world knowing about it – Mum'll kill me.'

Vix has said that she and Oliver have agreed not to tell Mum because she's having a rough time at present what with the non-winning of Grammys, etc., and that even at the best of times she reacts so badly to negative publicity. But that from now on, I owe her one.

I have also had to promise on my word of honour never, ever to talk to the press again.

In fact Vix has cancelled both my singing and my dance lessons this morning and, much worse, my lessons with Rupert this afternoon. She's given me the job of catching up on her pile of press cuttings as a punishment.

11.30 a.m.

Just when I think I've reached my lowest ebb – newspapers can be SO depressing – I get a call through from Reception.

'There's a visitor here for you, Miss Winterman.'

'A visitor, for me? Who?'

'She won't say. Please could you come down to the lobby?'

I go down in the elevator with grave misgivings. If it's that no-good journalist lady I'll give her a piece of my mind.

But as I alight from the elevator – NO!

YES! Standing there in her grey SotR regulation coat and beret – is BECKY!!!!!!

I don't think the Royal Trocadero has experienced quite so many decibels for some time. We actually made one of their cut-glass chandeliers vibrate!

When we'd calmed down some I took her up to my suite.

We were both talking at once.

'So what are you doing here?'/'What've you done to your hair?'

Somehow, I managed to establish that it was half-term. She'd come up on a day return with Miss Symes, who had something to do at the British Library.

'She said she'd be about three hours. So we haven't got that long. Oh my God, is this your room?' finished Becky breathlessly.

'Well, yes. I guess . . .'

Becky was opening cupboards and checking out the balcony. She ended up in the bathroom. 'I don't believe it. You've got a bath *and* a walk-in shower. It's huge. An average family could live in here! You are so lucky!'

'Am I?'

'Honestly, Holly. Oh, look, the towels. Do you remember SotR towels?'

'Grey and scratchies?'

'Exactly.'

She came out and stood facing me.

'So . . .?'

'So?'

'So what about that hot tutor of yours?' she asked with her tell-me expression.

'He's OK.'

'OK!'

'OK, he's more than OK.' Suddenly I didn't really want to bare my innermost soul, even to Becky. I mean, it may be a crush, but it's a serious crush. So I changed the subject. 'So what's going on back at school?'

'Don't ask.' Becky threw herself on the bed and started to give me the low-down on every single member of Year Nine.

Oddly enough I found myself switching off. I mean, it wasn't so long ago I was one of them. But now school felt like lifetimes ago.

Becky slowed somewhat and stared at me. 'You're not really listening, are you?'

I'll swear Becky really does have second sight.

'No I am, honestly.'

'So how are things – really?'

'I guess they were kind of OK until yesterday morning.'

I told her about the *Weekday News* fiasco.

Becky burst out laughing.

'It's not funny. I'm in deep trouble.'

'Holly, brighten up. Everyone knows the *Weekday News* is total rubbish.'

'Do they?'

'Of course they do.'

'Well, maybe . . .'

'And who cares, anyway. It was only a lunch date.'

'I know, but Mum must have taken it seriously because she's dumped him.'

'Imagine dumping Oliver Bream. What power!' says Becky, rolling her eyes.

Suddenly I could see how I was overreacting. Becky always had this way of making me feel better.

'God, what's the time?' she suddenly exclaimed.

'It's around twelve. Why?'

'I'm starving. We had to get up at six to catch the train. You got anything to eat in here?'

'We can have something sent up by room service.'

'Like what?'

'Like anything you like. There's a menu around some-where.'

I fished it out from under a pile of books and handed it to Becky.

Becky's eyes widened when she read down the list. 'You mean, you can order anything from this?'

'Yeah, pretty much. Their omelettes tend to be a bit soggy.'

'Omelettes! Who wants an omelette when you can have . . . Smoked salmon and caviar bagels with sour cream . . . Or foie gras with truffles . . . Or, oh my God! . . . Stuffed quails with lobster claws . . .'

'I pretty much stick to the salads. Mum's got this diet idea that –'

'Salads! Holly! You are such a killjoy. I could practically eat the Royal Trocadero right now!'

'Go on, then. Choose something.'

Becky took ages making up her mind.

In the end we had crab sticks, eclairs and peanut butter and jelly bagels.

'I'm stuffed,' said Becky, licking the last of the chocolate sauce off her spoon. 'So what's this diet thing of your mum's?'

'Oh, she won't eat anything that's cooked.'

'Nothing cooked! What's there to eat?'

'Well, salads mainly, and fruit . . .'

'And she expects you to do the same?'

'Pretty much. She's got all these plans for my future.'

'Plans?'

175

'I'm having singing lessons, dance lessons, that kind of stuff.'

'Hasn't she noticed you've got two left feet?'

I kicked her. 'As a matter of fact I am making progress, I'll have you know.'

Becky rolled her eyes. 'Don't tell me you're going to be a superstar like her.'

'No way! Remember my terminal stage fright? And that was only the carol concert! But I'm kind of going along with it to keep her off my back.'

We spent the rest of the time swimming in the pool and lounging in the jacuzzi. I don't know where the time went but almost before we knew it Miss Symes turned up to take Becky back to school. We were having a big hug in Reception when Mum swept out of the elevator.

'Why, who's this?' she asked in surprise.

Becky blushed absolutely scarlet as I introduced her She was totally dumbstruck. I stared at her in disbelief. Even Becky – the one person who was completely unfazed by Mum as a singer – was totally in awe of her fame.

That's what fame does to you. It makes people act weird. They stare and they're lost for words. It's totally spooky. They can't treat you as a normal human being.

6.00 p.m., Suite 6002
But is Mum a normal human being? She doesn't eat like one, she doesn't dress like one, she doesn't do any of the things that normal human beings do. In fact, currently she spends

most of her life holed up in her suite meditating with a Buddist monk. Is that normal? I don't think so.

I ring Gi-Gi to get her view on the current situation.

'Maybe she's trying to get in touch with her roots.' Gi-Gi's voice is thoughtful at the other end of the line.

'Her roots?

'Her mother, dear. Your grandmother, Anna.'

I am all ears. This mysterious figure, Mum's mum, Anna (short for Anastasia), has been the subject of endless romance all my life. She wandered off to Morocco in a campervan with a load of people who must've included Mum's dad, my grandfather. A year later, she arrived back in London with a load of henna tattoos and a baby on the way. Soon after Mum was born, 'Grand-Anna' left her sleeping peacefully at Gi-Gi's clutching a good-luck crystal in her tiny fist, and ran away with what Gi-Gi calls 'those dreadful orange people'.

'Yes,' continues Gi-Gi. 'I saw her only a month ago. In Oxford Street. I was going to Selfridges' food department for some sesame seed. She was with a whole group of them. Gongs and bells. Shaven heads and sandals. You'd think they'd catch their deaths this time of year.'

'Did you speak to her?'

'Oh no, no. No, you couldn't stop Anna mid-chant. At least, best not to.'

'It must've been dreadful for Mum to be abandoned like that.'

'It could account for much,' says Gi-Gi. 'She's always felt she had to prove herself. So headstrong. Right from a tiny child. Had to have her own way. And look at her now.'

'She's not too happy about not winning any Grammys.'

'It could be a good thing,' says Gi-Gi.

'How do you mean?'

'We all have to learn to cope with failure.'

'Not Mum.'

'Yes, her too.'

'I don't think she likes learning to cope with things,' I say gloomily.

'Oh, she'll come back up again. You'll see.'

Tuesday 4th March, 8.30 a.m.
The Penthouse Suite, The Royal Trocadero

Gi-Gi was right. When I check next morning to see how Mum is 'coping with failure' she's right back up again. I've popped up intending to remind her that she's meant to be starting work on 'Home is Where Your Heart is'.

There's no need. She has. She's already on the phone lining up her production team.

When I go down to Reception to check for my post, I find that the whole of the Royal Trocadero has been swept into a frenzy.

A crisis press room has been set up in one of the side lounges. All mention of the *Weekday News* scandal has been totally forgotten as the media has gone into a frenzy over Mum's last-minute switch to a new intro song for the Heatwave. They've practically taken up residence outside

178

the hotel. A load of extra uniformed security guards have been hired to keep them at bay.

Mum is being sued, apparently, for a sum undisclosed, by the guy who wrote the song she dropped. No one is allowed to talk to the press, of course. But that doesn't stop them bombarding us with questions like: 'How much are they suing her for?' 'Is it true she could go to jail?' 'Who's she hired to defend her?'

I'm going frantic over this. I'm really worried. I mean, I know how expensive these court cases can be. But Vix brushes it all aside, saying, 'No sweat. It's cheap at the price. However else could we have got so much publicity for the Heatwave?'

1.00 p.m.

I'm meant to be lunching with Mum, but I find her deep in discussion with Victor, her personal stylist on the new look for the 'Home is Where Your Heart is' video. Vix is alongside taking notes on her laptop. Mum blows me a couple of air-kisses and shushes me and I go and sit at the lunch table and munch salad while I watch.

Victor has come armed with what he calls 'Concept Boards'. These are covered in an odd collage of scraps cut from fabrics, magazines, news reports, art books, etc., to give them inspiration.

They are studying one which has what looks like a load of garbage with a bit of torn sack and the cross-section of a wellington boot on it.

'Yeah, definitely too much of a message in that one,' says Mum. 'Sure, I wanna pull the heart strings, but I still want it vampy, Victor.'

'I get you. I get you. Now here's more of "the vamp" factor.' He brings out another board.

'That's not vampy, that's slutty,' says Mum.

'Yeah, but it's a slutty-vampy look that's sexy too,' says Victor.

'I want it slutty-vampy-sexy but with a little-girl-lost feeling. Feeling, Victor. Remember this is the new me. The big-heart me.'

'Then it's got to be long hair,' says Vix. Both she and Victor agree. Which could be a problem because Mum had it cut into a neat shiny bob for the Oscars.

'Yeah, "little girl lost" . . . What do "little lost girls" wear?' muses Mum.

'It's blue jeans,' says Victor. 'And maybe a cropped jeans top.'

They both stare at him as if this is the most original thing ever.

'Yeah, blue jeans,' says Mum. 'But cut really low . . .'

'So that maybe the thong shows . . .' says Victor.

'Are you thinking what I'm thinking?' says Mum, staring at Victor.

'It's rhinestones,' says Victor. 'Yes, it's the rhinestone thong thing that gives the little-girl-lost look the slutty-vampy-sexy edge . . . AND maybe bare feet . . .'

'Nope . . . not bare feet,' says Mum, searching through the pile of garbagy boards.

Vix has leaned over towards Victor and I hear her whisper, 'Sheherazadha had bare feet in her last video.'

(Sheherazadha is an ex-model which means she's like six foot five tall – while Mum's petite; and she's so-oo not happy with this.)

'I know, heels that are really high. I've got just the pair to give it that vamp thing,' says Mum. '. . . with rhinestone straps.'

At the mention of 'rhinestone straps' I choke on a radish. I have a terrible premonition. (It gets worse.)

'Vix, go and search through the trunks. I've got this pair of Manolos . . .'

LATER!!!!!

'You did what?' I haven't seen Mum this angry ever. It's like 'seafood platter' and 'wanting-to-be-a-vet' rolled into one.

Vix is sitting on the floor with two open trunks and the whole of Mum's shoe wardrobe covering the entire floor area of the penthouse suite. She doesn't look too happy either. In fact, she's staring hard at me with this totally guilt-making 'tell-all' look on her face.

'But, Mu-um, it was for charity,' I say.

'Charity!'

'Yes, and a very good cause.'

'What very good cause?' snarls Mum.

'Umm, well . . .'

'I'm listening.'

'A TwilightHomeforDistressedDonkeys,' I mumble very fast.

'You mean to say that you have auctioned my hand-made, custom-fitted Manolo Blahniks for a load of mangy mules!' screams Mum.

'They're not mangy. Just old.'

'You couldn't you find a better cause? Starving orphans? Limbless war victims? No, you have to auction my favourite Manolo Blahniks for some cracked-up nothing of a charity that no one's even heard of. I can't even use it for publicity!'

'I got an email saying they were very grateful.'

'An email! Grateful! You'll just have to get them back.'

'But Mum, I don't think I can –'

'That's enough, Hollywood. Go to your room.'

Wednesday 5th March, 5.30 a.m.
Suite 6002, The Royal Trocadero

I'm woken by Sit's gong again. I'm prepared this morning. According to what I've learned so far about Buddhism, donations to monks earn you favour with the gods and I certainly need that right now. Last night I ordered from room service a small side dish of saffron rice and two chicken kebabs along with my cold prisoner's supper.

Sit bows and accepts the food, stashing it away in his basket. Then he gives me a half-sideways look. He must be able to see I haven't slept and maybe have tear streaks down my face.

'You are not so happy, Howywood?'

'Mum's wild at me. I did something really bad.'

'You are in need of spiwitual ad-vice?'

'I guess.'

'May I enter?'

Sit comes and settles himself cross-legged at the far end of my suite. I can tell he's dying to delve into his basket (monks only eat like once a day). So this is really nice of him.

'What do you mean by bad?' asks Sit.

'Well, bad is bad, isn't it?'

'Not necessawily.'

'Well, I guess it was a little bit good too. For the donkeys, I mean. And maybe the guy who got the Blahniks 'cos he was totally knocked out when he came out top bidder.'

Sit nods sagely at this. 'So it was bad and good?'

'Kind of. But it can't be, can it?'

'Why not?'

'Well, it just can't be both.'

Sit then goes into a long spiel about what he calls 'Karmic Qualities'. It seems that according to his religion, things can be classified as good, evil or neutral. Which is one up on Reverend Mother and the Roman Catholics because they only have good and evil. And I've found to my cost in the past that it's not so easy to decide if some actions are one or the other.

It gets better. According to Sit, even good acts come in degrees. They can be 100% good (if all factors are good). But they can also be 75% good, 50% good or even 25% good.

Which is really logical when you come to think of it. How many times have you done something that's a bit good and a bit bad? Like, for instance, chaining your bike up to railings

183

which say 'Bikes strictly forbidden', but only because you're trying to help a blind person across the road – and then, maybe, it turns out, whatever they wanted was the same side all along . . . So it's less good than you thought?

Or take the shoe situation. The auction must be a little bit good because right now at the Twilight Home they're probably raking the ground and spreading new grass seed with my donation and I can imagine all these old tired donkeys looking over the newly mended fence and thinking of this wonderful lush green grass they are going to be eating come summertime. Whereas Mum can get some more Manolo Blahniks. I mean, she probably won't even have to pay for them because Manolo will provide a replacement pair totally free of charge as long as her press secretary gets them mentioned in her Heatwave publicity handouts.

I lose the thread of Sit's discourse as I try to juggle with the percentages of good or bad in my shoe auction. But he's made me feel better anyway.

Once he's left I text Becky:

> **Q: You auction someone else's shoes without them knowing and donate the money to the really needy.**
> **Is this action:**
> **a) 100% good?**
> **b) 75% good?**
> **c) 25% good?**

d) Not good at all?

e) Evil

HBШx

Later that day I get a text back from Becky.

a) or e)

there is nothing in between

Bx

I am now starting to worry that Becky has been totally brain-washed by the school. All those 'comparative religion' classes when Sister Clare tries so hard to be fair and even-handed about other faiths have been like totally wasted on her.

6.00 p.m., the Penthouse Suite

I've found Daffyd hard at work on Mum's new image. He's doing hair extensions.

Hair extensions! Hang on, I'm SHOCKED.

'Mum. You can't have hair extensions. That's human exploitation!'

Mum frowns. 'You're pulling, Daffyd. That's better.'

I continue, 'Do you know that poor girls in the Third World have to sell their hair so that you can flaunt it ?'

'Nuns, babes. They want to have it cut off. It makes them feel virtuous. After all, what are they expected to do with it? Throw it away?'

'It's not nuns, Mum. Nuns don't have their heads shaven these days.' (I know for a fact – Sister Marie-Agnes always

185

has two little kirby grips showing under her veil.) 'It's ordinary young girls, like me.'

'Well, if they want to sell it, it'll grow back, won't it? It's not like selling . . .' she pauses, searching for the right body part, 'those inside things – livers or whatever.'

'Oh, honestly. I don't know how you can do it, Daffyd.'

Daffyd pauses with a tuft and glue-brush midair.

'Well, how I see it is this. What's done is done. The original owner would only have to stick it back on themselves now, wouldn't they?'

'That's not the point,' I argue back. 'As long as there's a market for it, people will be exploited.'

'That's what I said to Bronwyn,' he said with a sigh. 'She was considering extensions. But, the way things are going, she'll have enough time to grow it long for the wedding herself now.'

He looks sulky at this. Mum's made him postpone the wedding yet again because of the Heatwave. After Wembley, she's planning a tour in the States.

We are interrupted by Thierry (who'll you'll remember is Mum's personal French chef). He burst in without even knocking.

'I'm not 'aving it,' he roars. (Thierry can be really fiery-tempered.)

Mum sits up all startled with her hair half long and half short.

'What is it, Thierry?'

'Zat beggar. Coming into my kitchen. Eesch morning. Juss as I am slipping. Boom boom boom. I tell 'im what 'ee can do with 'ees basket.'

'Oh, Sit.'

'Yez, Sheet.'

Vix breaks in. 'I'm sorry, I booked him into a suite on the seventh floor. But he wouldn't settle. He insists on sleeping on his bedroll in the yard by the rubbish bins.'

'And he wakes. At first I think eet's cats and I throw water . . .'

'Poor Sit.'

'But no, Sheet, 'ee comes in all wet on my nice cleen floor and Boom boom boom.'

Sit is not far behind. He arrives in the doorway looking sheepish.

'Sit, listen to me,' says Mum. 'From now on you have to sleep in your suite. And your breakfast will be sent up on a trolley. No wandering round at all hours. Understand?'

'But, Kandhi. I am men to be welinquishing all worldly pweasures.'

'Well, whatever. Think laterally. Order something you don't like from the breakfast menu. That should do it.'

Sit wanders off sadly. Thierry leaves with his head held high, vindicated.

Thursday 6th March
Suite 6002, The Royal Trocadero

I open my curtains to find it's a beautiful day. But there's an odd piece of rope hanging down past my window. Window cleaners? I lean out to find Sit has come to a compromise. His begging basket is hanging from his seventh-floor window with a note saying 'PLEASE GIFT'. Surprised Mayfair shoppers are stopping to inspect – I've even spotted a couple dropping something in.

At around eleven Sit comes to see me.

'Horry. I don know what to do. Look!'

He holds out his begging basket. In it there is around thirty pounds in cash and a Hermes silk scarf.

'That's nice of people.'

'No' when you are men to be welinquishing all worldly goods.'

'Hmm, I see. What if you give the stuff away?'

Sit shrugs. 'Maybe. As long as the gift does not give me personal pweasure.'

'Give it to someone you don't like then. How about Thierry?'

A slow smile spreads across Sit's face.

'Maybe, Horry. Maybe you have good idea.'

Later that day. OOOPs!

Sit has presented Thierry with a huge bouquet of red roses and the Hermes scarf. Thierry's masculine sensibilities have been deeply offended. He's now calling Sit a pervert and trying to get him thrown out of the hotel.

I am starting to worry about my classes with Rupert. I mean, I'm really pleased he's my tutor. (But let's try and forget my massive crush for a moment.) Because this is serious. I can't help noticing that whenever I get out my science books Rupert kind of flinches.

Today I've decided to take the initiative. I'm sitting with my chemistry book open in front of me when he arrives.

Rupert hangs up his mac and cycle helmet.

'Umm, now let's get down to . . . Oh! Was it chemistry today?'

'Yes, we didn't do any science all of last week.'

'No, really?'

'No.'

We work for about an hour.

It's more than a sneaking suspicion now. I mean, I was kind of worried when Rupert tried to check on the Periodic Table in my human biology textbook. But I caught him having a sly look inside his briefcase and there was a *Crash Course for Beginners Chemistry Study Aid*. He is most definitely only one page ahead of me in the chemistry textbook. In fact, I think he might even be on the same page. I'm wondering who's teaching who.

I'd better not let Vix get wind of this. She still thinks Rupert's rubbish. If she finds out he can't teach science he'll get fired straight away.

But of course he's brilliant at Shakespeare and Shelley and

Donne and all those other guys who were writing stuff like yonks ago.

I know I find them boring but that's not surprising really. When you consider that they didn't even have laptops. They had to make do with quills and ink and paper. If they didn't get it right first time, they'd have all this crossing out. So you can't blame them if their stuff is a bit kind of tedious. I mean, let's face it, if you had to write like they did, you'd stick with your first version, wouldn't you?

Anyway, I'm doing my best in English in order to impress Rupert. I can always catch up with all those other subjects that I need to get into a vet school later. As Rupert says, it's important to have a fully rounded education.

6.30 p.m., the Penthouse Suite

I find Mum deep into wardrobe test shots for the 'Home is Where Your Heart is' video. The photographic team have taken over her suite. They've set up great big white umbrella thingies to reflect the light. There are steel equipment cases open all over the floor. June is standing by with a powder puff to damp down the shine on Mum's face and Daffyd is there to keep an eye on his extensions.

'Hi, babes. Do you want to stay and watch?' calls out Mum.

'OK.'

I am always amazed by the way Mum can play to the camera. She's twisting her body from left to right as if mid-dance and then stopping stock-still and staring into the lens as if challenging it to come up with a drop-dead gorgeous shot. The photographer is egging her on to do more and more outrageous poses.

She's dodging in and out of her room coming back with refinements to each costume. The little-girl-lost look is tried with an assortment of raggy things tied round her head. Which rather defeats the purpose of the hair extensions.

I note that Manolo has come up with a replacement pair of the rhinestone stilettos which are higher if anything than the pair I auctioned. It'd be tough being a little-lost-girl out on the streets with those on. You'd do better to bin them and nick a pair of sneakers.

After the blue jeans and rhinestones Mum switches to . . . (Oh no, please, Mum. No!) Few people can have had the mortification of seeing their mother in:

a) a black lace bra under see—thru white blouse
b) a luminous miniskirt
c) fishnet stockings with suspenders
d) the ultimate embarrassment — a tiny frilly net apron

'What's this for?' asks Mum, holding up a rolling pin.

'It's for rolling out that pastry stuff. You're meant to be a homemaker, right?' says Victor, emerging from the shadows.

'You don't think we're being just the teensiest bit over the top, do you?' asks Mum.

Victor is insistent. New image is new image.

'Now, let's get on to the dungarees and lawnmower.'

I am trying to touch base with reality by visiting Gi-Gi. I am coming to the conclusion that life is more real on TV than out of it. At least mine. When I watch TV, all the people I see seem to have lives that include houses and families and hot meals and things. Mine has a manic superstar who can't even dress up to look like a mum.

But nothing seems quite normal at Gi-Gi's either. Thumper has turned into a monster version of himself. He is not a small fluffy angora rabbit any longer. He is huge. He is so big Gi-Gi has bought him a quilted cat basket and he kind of overspills that. I'm even getting slightly concerned as Hillview Mansions has an 'only small pets' policy and at this rate Thumper is going to exceed the limit.

'Gi-Gi, what are you feeding him on?'

It takes a bit of prompting before she admits that now his diet consists entirely of sesame dumplings. She has to make a fresh batch every day. He has been so spoilt that he will not touch anything else.

I decide to take him down into the communal gardens on a piece of string for essential exercise. However, Thumper is no longer interested in exercise. He takes the excursion as more of an extra meal break and starts munching on the Hillview Mansions daffodils that are bursting into flower on the lawn. We've been spotted by a ground floor resident who's been lurking behind her twitching nets. She bangs hard on the window. So I take Thumper back upstairs again.

Sunday 9th March, 10.30 a.m.
Suite 6002

It's raining outside. It's the kind of rain that only London can come up with. Gloomy, continuous rain that never seems to get things clean. The hotel is practically empty. Everywhere you go there are staff standing around looking bored.

The trouble with a luxury hotel like the Royal Trocadero is that there is absolutely nothing to do. If you need food, you're fed. If you need your bed made or your room tidied, it's done. Your clothes mysteriously disappear and come back freshly ironed on hangers. I reckon if I stopped breathing they'd have someone on the staff who'd come and do it for me.

I spend some time sorting through My Personal Private Collection of Very Precious Objects and reorganise them into order of preference with the little pink heart on top. After that I set off for a roam around the hotel.

Mum and Vix and Daffyd and June are at the studios, working round the clock on the Heatwave video. Sid and Abdul aren't around either as they accompany Mum everywhere. Sit seems to spend all his time meditating in his suite.

I pop down to the kitchens to see Thierry but he's still haughty and grumpy over the flowers affair.

I text Becky twice. But she doesn't reply.

So I swim in the empty hotel pool. I take a jacuzzi which I have all to myself. I even get to sit for a good half-hour in the prime bubbly bit. I stay in till my fingers have gone all wrinkly.

Monday 10th March (otherwise known as The Longest Day), 10.00 a.m. Suite 6003, The Royal Trocadero

I go next door for my music lesson, but no Jasper. When I ring down to Reception to find out what's happened to him, I'm put through to Vix. My lessons have been cancelled indefinitely. Jasper will be working with Mum for the foreseeable future. He's director/ producer on 'Home is Where Your Heart is'.

'But what about me? What am I meant to do?' I complain.

'I don't know. What do people usually do? Read a book,' suggests Vix.

I do this half-heartedly, followed by a half-hour of arch-flexing exercises. After this I can barely walk so I hobble up to the ballroom for my dance class.

Stella doesn't turn up for my dance lessons either. Apparently she's strained a tendon and has to keep her leg up till the swelling goes down.

So I stare out of the window and wonder what everyone at school is doing right now.

2.30 p.m., Suite 6003

To my relief Rupert has turned up for lessons.

He's sorted through the books and put all the maths and science books to one side and is insisting that we concentrate on English lit. Shakespeare in particular.

We are doing this play called *The Taming of the Shrew*. Naturally, I like the title. But I soon to find that the 'shrew' in question is not one of those sweet little long-nosed, velvety mouse things but a rather cross woman who argues a lot.

Rupert and I start out by reading the play through together. He reading the hero's part, this guy called Petruchio who's trying to 'tame' the heroine; and me the heroine, who's called Kate. I can't help noticing that Rupert is really brilliant at reading – honestly, he should be an actor. I'm kind of hypnotised by the way his lips move . . .

Sigh.

After we've gone through a few pages Rupert stops.

'Holly, could you put some feeling into it? You're meant to be angry, waspish. You're meant to hate me, OK?'

'Oh, right, sure . . .'

I try really, really hard to sound as if I hate Rupert. Believe me, this is not easy.

I muddle my way through a long speech which starts with:

' "Why, sir, I trust I may have leave to speak. And speak I will. I am no child, no babe . . ." ' (If only!)

Rupert stops me again. 'You've got to try and spit the words out, Holly. Think of how a person behaves when they're really angry at someone . . .'

Suddenly I have this vision of Mum with the seafood platter.

'OK, I'll try again.'

I get to my feet. I stand, knees slightly bent, like Mum did. I narrow my eyes. I imagine that Oliver is right there in front of me and the seafood platter is just within my grasp. Then I let rip. I can hear my voice in my head sounding just like Mum . . .

    ' " . . . My tongue will tell the anger of my heart;
    or else my heart concealing it will break,
    And rather than it shall, I will be free
    Even to the uttermost, as I please, in words . . ." '

'Errm, was that all right?'

Rupert is standing stock-still, staring at me.

'Wow . . . that was really good, Holly. Where did that come from?'

I glow all over. Praise!!! Praise from RUPERT, like he's really impressed by something I've done?!!! This is the best moment of my life EVER!

I shrug. 'Well, you know. We've all got it in us, I guess.'

The lesson ends in a kind of heady daze. Rupert thinks I can act. I can act Shakespeare!

5.30 p.m., Suite 6002

I'm back in my room taking a bath. I'm lying in the bathtub totally dreaming that Rupert and I are really famous, like we're in this movie and I'm acting really cool in front of the cameras with no problems at all.

No, not only am I NOT crippled by stage fright, I am actually enjoying being the centre of attention. Which normally, as you may have gathered, is SO NOT me. Seriously, I have a phobia about performing. It's like the phobias people have about flying, or spiders, or snakes. My phobia just doesn't happen to have a name, that's all. Maybe it should – like 'performaphobia', for instance: the irrational fear of making a complete dick of yourself in front of an audience.

But when I'm with Rupert this phobia's cured. In my bathtub fantasy we're walking down a red carpet to our very own world première and all these people are crowding in on either side applauding like crazy.

I get out of the bath and dry myself. I want to rush up to Mum's suite and maybe read that bit out loud to her to prove that 'Yeah, there is a bit of the performer in me after all. Like, those genes haven't totally passed me by.' So I ring Vix to see if Mum's free. I can hear from the bleeps that Vix's phone is still on transfer. She answers me in a hushed voice.

'Who? Oh, Holly, it's only you. No, I can't talk right now. Looks like we're going to be in the studios all night at the rate we're going.'

In the background I can hear Mum's voice being played back over and over, singing a phrase from 'Home is Where Your Heart is'.

'Oh, I see. Well, I guess I'll order up something from room service and get an early nigh—'

Vix has already rung off.

Same day STILL: 9.00 p.m., The Royal Trocadero
I've had my lonely supper and I'm wondering if I can find someone to talk to.

I peep out of my door. There aren't even security guards to talk to as they don't patrol my floor any longer. It turned

197

out that those 'nasty threats' were all from the same person – a madly obsessed prowler who had this 'thing' about Mum. He's been rounded up and put behind bars. So we've gone from 'High Alert' to 'Medium Alert' to 'Not Alert At All'. The security guys currently spend their time playing pool in the hotel leisure centre.

The hotel is really still, like there's no one left alive in it. Even the muzak's been turned off – there's only the steady hiss of the air conditioning.

The only other person who isn't involved in the Heatwave is Sit. I decide that even if he is meditating he could probably do with a break.

Sit's suite is on the seventh floor, which is not so grand as the sixth. The carpet is just that little bit less poumphy and their light fittings don't have little crystal bits hanging off them, but it's still pretty grand for someone who's meant to be 'relinquishing all worldly pleasures'.

The smell of joss sticks leads me to Sit's suite. The door has been left slightly open. But I guess if your only possessions are a bedroll, a faded saffron robe and a begging basket, you're not going to be paranoid about security.

'Sit?' I call out. 'Can I come in?'

There's no answer, so I push the door further open.

Sit isn't in the suite. I note that he has rearranged the place somewhat. He's pushed the couch to one end and up-ended the bed against it. The bedside rug has been laid out in front of a sort of altar where the joss sticks are burning.

But what grabs my attention – what totally stops me in

my tracks, what makes my jaw drop – is not a tubby smiling figure of a Buddha, like you'd totally expect to see on that altar. No, it's a blown-up photo of Mum. I now notice that there are more photos of her stuck around the walls. (I totally hope Sit has used Sticky Fixers or there'll be no end of a scene when he moves out.)

This confirms in my mind the niggly doubt I've had all along. Like, I thought he was too good to be true. It's clear now that Sit is just another fan.

Fans – they'll do anything to get close to Mum. There was even one who glued himself to the underside of Mum's limo with superglue. Luckily for him, security found him on a routine under-car body search. But it just shows how obsessed they can get.

I creep out of the room and pull the door to behind me, wondering what to do about it. I mean, it's not as if I think Sit is dangerous or anything. Maybe it would be kindest to keep the whole thing to myself.

10.30 p.m., Suite 6002

Still nothing happening. I've done my homework and I'm not even tired. I check my mobile.

Hey, there's a text from Becky!

you'll never guess what!
i've been selected for:
a)   miss world
b)   pres bush's new mars mission
c)   young musician of the year !!!!!!!!!!

199

Young Musician of the Year – it's like this talent competition for all young people who play classical stuff. Win it and you're lauched on a career as a top international performer. It's like coming number one in the charts in the States and the UK simultaneously – in fact worldwide. Wow! Becky! So all that dedicated practising has paid off! I am so proud for her. Forget SotR no late calls ruling. I ring her straight away. She answers immediately.

'Becky! You are a genius!'

'Hi, Holly!' comes the whispered reply.

'You must be over the moon!

'Shhhh!'

'Becky, you still there? You sound all muffled.'

'I'm under the covers. Someone might hear.'

'You're in bed?'

'Holly, it's after lights out.'

I had totally forgotten that SotR has this obsessive regime. The girls are meant to be asleep by ten thirty because they have to be up at 6.00 a.m.

'But you're going to be on TV and everything.'

'I'm only shortlisted. There are loads of us in the violin trials.'

'But I know you're going to win.'

'Honestly, Holly, I'm happy just to get on the shortlist. I've got to go now. Keep texting me, OK?'

She rang off. I was left thinking how different this was from Mum. If she wasn't the best at something she wasn't worth living with. ('There's only one number one, Holly. If I don't get that I know I've failed.')

200

There are so few guests in the hotel the bellboys have been given the month off. I have begun to take the elevator down to the hotel pool in slippers with my towelling robe thrown over my swimsuit. Suddenly the elevator makes an unscheduled stop at the ground floor and who should climb in but SHUG!!!!!

He is SO NOT the person you want to bump into at an unholy hour of the day when you are feeling totally fragile and you are half undressed.

I can feel myself totally blushing all over. I never knew feet could blush before.

Shug is really lapping this up. He closes the elevator doors and then stands leaning against the buttons, looking me slowly up and down. He kind of snorts.

'Hi.'

'What are you doing here?' I ask.

'This is a hotel, isn't it? Or has your mum bought the whole place as a private residence, maybe?'

'No. But I thought you were in LA?'

'Been checking up on me, have you?'

'I just saw you looking totally dumb at the Oscars, that's all.'

'Sweet of you to take an interest. What are you doing by the way? On your way out?'

I do a big fake smile. 'Very funny. Can you stand aside please so that I can get to the elevator buttons? I'm going down for a swim.'

'Oh! I thought the way you're dressed might be a fashion statement.'

Shug makes no move so I am trapped in the elevator with him. I'm not going to let him see I'm fazed. I step back and lean, in a manner I hope looks nonchalant, against the far wall.

'So? What are you doing in the Trocadero?'

'I came to see you, as a matter of fact.'

'I'm flattered.'

'Don't be. I'm not about to ask you out on a date or anything.'

'Oh wow, where did you learn your charm from? Your dad, maybe?'

Shug rolled his eyes. 'It's my dad I've come about. Have you seen him lately? Have you any idea what's going on between those two?'

'Not a lot, I imagine. You don't stand up the richest megastar in the universe and get away with it.'

'Yeah,' said Shug with a grin. 'Must've been pretty tough on Kandhi being blown out like that.'

'Must be pretty tough on Oliver being dumped.'

'Oh, she's dumped him, has she?'

'What do you think?'

'I reckon your mum's crying her pretty little self to sleep every night.'

'You must be joking. Do you think Kandhi actually cares about some stuffed shirt, cold fish . . .' I was running out of insults.

'Do you think my dad cares about some overdressed, overrated bimbette who can't even sing?'

I paused for breath. So did Shug.

'Why does it matter to you, anyway?' I asked.

He shrugged. 'I was just trying to track down my dad, that's all.'

'Running out of pocket money?'

'Oh, very funny.'

'Well, there's no point in looking for him here, that's for sure. Now, could you kindly get away from those elevator buttons and let me go on my way?'

'You only had to ask nicely.'

He stands aside. He even presses the lower ground button for me.

When the doors open I walk out with as much dignity as someone dressed in a bathrobe and pink fluffy slippers can muster.

Wednesday 12th March, 11.00 a.m.
The Penthouse Suite, The Royal Trocadero

Shug has sown the seeds of doubt in my mind. Has Mum really dumped Oliver? Or NOT? She's been very quiet about the whole thing. In fact, she hasn't mentioned his name in days. This usually means she's up to something.

So I've popped up to her suite to see if there's any evidence lying around. Oliver's photo in her bedside drawer, love letters in her mail tray, shaving foam in the bathroom, that kind of thing. There's nothing. There's not so much as the negative imprint of a biro on a Post-it slip.

I've still got Mum and Oliver on my mind when Rupert arrives for our lesson.

I guess I'm not concentrating as much as I should. Rupert has actually started to lose his cool.

'Holly, are you listening to me?'

'Yes, sure I am. What was it you said?'

'Look at you. You look grey. When did you last get outside?'

'Thanks, you've really made me feel better.'

'No, but seriously. When did you last go out?'

I shrug. 'I don't know. Sid and Abdul are always with Mum. I'm not allowed out alone.'

'Well, I don't think that's fair on someone your age. I mean, here you are living in the very centre of London and you've hardly been anywhere.'

'No, I guess not.'

'Tell you what. Why don't we plan an educational outing. I bet you've never visited the Globe.'

'The Globe?'

'It's a full-size replica of Shakespeare's original theatre. You must've heard of it.'

'Well, yes. I guess.'

'They do a tour of the theatre. We should give classes a miss one afternoon and go on one. You know, to feel the atmosphere of the theatre Shakespeare actually wrote for.'

A trip out to a theatre with Rupert! I mean, wow! It'll feel like a date. Except it won't. Not if we take Sid or Abdul with us. But Sid and Abdul are like totally busy right now. And if

I'm with Rupert I won't really need a bodyguard, will I? And it's only in the afternoon. I mean, it's a lesson really. Essential study.

'Yep, I'd like that. When?'

'How's about tomorrow?'

'Brilliant!'

Thursday 13th March, 12.30 p.m. Suite 6002

I've spent the entire morning preparing for the afternoon. I am in a turmoil about what to wear. I've taken every single thing out of my closet and tried it on and put it back again. Oh, indecision!

I consider ringing Abdul and getting him to drive me to Harrods' young fashion department. I've still got a kilo of blueberry jelly beans. But Mum might need him and want to know where where he's going and this could ruin my plans.

In the end I've got dressed in a white Kandhi Store miniskirt 'cos it shows off my legs and a loose top that disguises the fact that I don't currrently have boobs worth mentioning. (Recently, these have moved nearer the top of my U.W.L.) A belt around the loose top so that I don't look totally shapeless and a black crochet poncho thingy that is really cool in spite of the fact Gi-Gi made it for me from a pattern.

Rupert has said he'll meet me in reception at 2.30 p.m. I have kind of avoided mentioning this trip to anyone. I mean, I know Mum would just put up stupid objections.

2.30 p.m.

I go down in the elevator to Reception and to my horror Sit is standing at the elevator entrance as I get out.

'Hi, Horry. You look, er – nice. Where you going?'

'Nowhere.'

'Is not possible,' says Sit.

'Oh, stop being philosophical for once, pl-ease.'

'OK. Have nice day,' he says.

He gets into the elevator and I get out.

'And Sit . . .'

'Yes, Horry.'

'Don't tell Mum you saw me, OK?'

'But I must, if she asks,' says Sit. (His blessed vow of truthfulness again!)

I narrow my eyes. 'Look, Sit. If you tell Mum anything, I'll tell her about the pictures you have of her plastered all over your suite, right!' And with that I push the 'doors close' button and Sit's amazed face disappears from view.

Sit may be her spiritual adviser, but he's also a fan. If Mum gets the slightest whiff of the fact that his devotion is greater for her than for Buddha, he'd be out of here faster than he can say 'plawn clacker'.

Rupert is late as usual, so I have to hang around Reception reading the leaflets for various random tourist attractions. If one more member of the Royal Trocadero staff comes up and asks me if they can help me, I'll belt them one.

At last, I see the figure of Rupert in the street outside, fast approaching the circular doors. I dash out to meet him.

'Oh, sorry. Traffic was at a standstill,' he apologises.

But I don't care that he's late. He's here now. And it's raining. He has an umbrella up which means we have to stand really close.

'Er, Holly,' he says, eyeing me curiously. OK, so I know now. I've overdressed. I look a freak. No, worse, I look like a total dog. 'Haven't you got a mac or something? Are you going to be warm enough?'

'I'm fine,' I say, wrapping the poncho firmly round me. 'Let's go.'

But Rupert doesn't lead me to the taxi rank. He's heading across the street to the underground station.

Now this may sound really weird to you, but you haven't led the kind of life I have. For me, going down into an actual underground station packed with strangers is really scary. The steps down to it are kind of slippery and greasy and people are pushing past me. I can feel panic rising in my throat. But I stay really close to Rupert, which calms me down some.

Down at the bottom, Rupert stops by a machine thingy and gets us two tickets. Then he pushes a way through to a gate, with kind of barriers in it to stop you going through. Rupert steps aside politely to let me go first. I'm causing a logjam of people while I'm wondering how to get through.

'Go on,' he says.

'What am I meant to do?'

'Holly. Don't tell me you've never been on the underground?'

'No. I've always wondered what it was like.'

'You put your ticket in that slot.'

'Oh, right.'

'I don't believe it,' says Rupert when we are on the escalator going down. 'You mean to say you've never been on public transport?'

'Well, maybe, when I was a little kid. Too early to remember. Before Mum was famous.'

We have to wait on a crowded platform. This is really freaking me out. A good half of the people look like potential kidnappers. But when we get into our carriage I feel better. The people on this train look more like families on outings.

All the way to the Globe, Rupert keeps up a non-stop commentary about Shakespeare, who you'd be surprised to know was way less famous than Mum in his lifetime. He was even quite poor when he died. But something tells me he had somewhat more lasting power than Mum. I mean, could you imagine anyone quoting Kandhi lyrics, like three centuries on?

4.30 p.m., SAME BLISSFUL AFTERNOON

It had stopped raining when we emerged from the Globe. The sun had even come out. So we walked along the Thames for a while. For once I wasn't doing anything grand or smart. I was just taking an ordinary walk along with loads of ordinary people. Nobody was staring. Nobody was shouting. Nobody was trying to take photos. Nobody was interested in me. Heaven couldn't possibly be nicer.

We mingled with the tourists who stopped in little clumps

around the street performers. There was a guy who pretended to be a statue and stood so still I really thought he was, till Rupert gave me a coin to drop in his hat and he bowed. There was another who was selling whistles that made a sound like a bird. But Rupert said he'd had one once and he could never get it to work. And a man dressed as a clown who made animals out of balloons. And there were loads of stalls selling old books.

By six o'clock I was ravenous and so was Rupert and he suggested having a burger before he dropped me back at the hotel.

So you see. It was like a real grown-up date. Theatre and dinner.

I was just about to take the first big juicy bite of my Big Mac when my mobile started ringing.

I could hear it in my bag.

'Aren't you going to answer it?' asked Rupert.

'I s'pose I better,' I said, reluctantly raking it out.

'Hi, Hollywood. Where are you?' It was Mum.

'Errm, I'm just having a bite to eat, actually.'

'I went down to your suite and you weren't there. I was really worried.'

'It's OK. I'm with Rupert.'

'With Rupert? Why aren't you in the hotel?'

'We've been having an essential educational outing. But it got kind of late. So we thought we'd have a bite to eat.'

'A bite. To eat? What kind of bite? Where?' A note of distrust had crept into Mum's voice.

'We're really close.'

'Where exactly?'

'At Piccadilly Circus.'

'Where *exactly*?'

Reverend Mother had said never, ever to lie.

'In McDonald's.'

'Stay where you are. I'm sending Sid and Abdul to pick you up straight away. And I want Rupert to come back to the hotel too. Do you hear?'

'But Mum –'

She rang off.

'What was all that about?' asked Rupert.

'It's Mum. She's being paranoid.'

'Didn't she know you were going out this afternoon?'

I shook my head. Suddenly I wasn't hungry any more.

6.30 p.m., the Penthouse Suite

We caused quite a stir leaving McDonald's. I guess not many people are escorted out by two seven-foot bouncers (who happened to get themselves a quick order of two Big Macs and double fries while they were about it).

When we arrived back at the Hotel, Sid said he had to take us straight up to Mum's suite.

Mum was standing at the far end, looking furious.

Rupert started. 'Look, I'm sorry Mrs Winterman –'

'Will you stop calling me Mrs Winterman. The name's Kandhi.'

'Sorry, Mrs Win— I mean, Kandhi. But seeing as Holly has such a talent for acting –'

'Talent?' interrupted Mum.

'Well, yes, she was doing this piece from *The Taming of the Shrew* that really impressed me.' Rupert was doing his best to get round Mum but her tone didn't change.

'*The Taming of* what?'

'*The Shrew*. It's by Shakespeare.'

'I don't care if it's by Andrew Lloyd Webber. Hollywood had no right to be out of the hotel.'

'But Mum, they caught that guy. There isn't even a threat any more.'

'You're my daughter, Hollywood – you're always under threat.'

'But Mrs W— I mean, Kandhi, I thought if I took her to the Globe . . . I mean, I assumed that Holly had cleared this outing with you.'

'Mum, you see. It was an educational trip –'

'Educational? McDonald's?' snapped Mum.

'Well, that was after the educational bit,' I said.

'So? Why didn't you clear it with your mother, Holly?' asked Rupert.

Suddenly, I felt about two foot high. Rupert was treating me like a little kid. This was SO NOT fair.

'Because I knew if I asked Mum, she wouldn't let me go,' I said miserably.

'She's right. I wouldn't. I can't believe this has happened. I take her out of a school that's way in the depths of the country, in order to keep her under better security, and then I find her at loose God knows where in London. Anything could have happened.'

'But it didn't, did it?' I retorted.

'Hollywood, I hope you realise what you are putting me through.'

Putting her through! I saw RED at that point.

'NO! I hope you realise what you are putting me through. I deserve a life as well, you know.'

'A life! Look what I do for you! You are SO ungrateful. Any other girl . . .!'

'Yeah, any other girl. Any other girl would maybe like being chained up and dressed up and trained to sing and dance and perform like some circus animal!'

Mum's eyes narrowed. 'Hollywood, go to your room. I'll talk to you later.'

Even Blacker Friday: 14th March
Suite 6002

Rupert has been suspended. Life is SO NOT worth living. I know I shouldn't say this, but right now, I actually think I hate Mum. One day, hopefully well before what Reverend Mother calls the 'Day of Reckoning', she will be forced to do penance for what she has done to me.

I lie in bed considering various options to register my revolt:

a) Not speaking to anyone ever again
b) Not eating or drinking anything ever again
c) Not leaving my suite ever again

I try the first for a good half hour and then I have to ring Gi-Gi to ask how Thumper is. So I have to amend a) somewhat.

a) Not speaking to anyone except Gi-Gi (and Karl, who happened to answer the phone).

Thumper is fine. Karl took him to the vet, who put him on a strict diet which does not include sesame dumplings (Thumper not Karl). (Though the diet might have been a good idea for Karl too.) He has lost two grammes.

I cancel my order from the breakfast menu and try b) for a good two hours. At around ten I amend b) to:

b) not eating or drinking anything except from the mini-bar: crisps, luxury salted cocktail nuts and orange juice, to be exact.

It is 10.30 and I have been staring at the ceiling for an hour. I reckon all my muscles are going to waste away if I don't do something. So I amend c) too.

c) not leaving my suite unless it's to go down to the leisure centre for a swim or maybe a jacuzzi or a sauna.

By lunchtime, I decide that my 'revolt regime' has been so watered down that it's not worth continuing and I have a lunch of steak and chips and fruit salad.

I do not feel quite so bad towards Mum or sad about Rupert on a full stomach.

Saturday 15th March, 9.30 a.m.
Suite 6002

Everyone seems to have magically erased 'my illicit afternoon out' from their memory, as tonight is the world premiere of the Heatwave.

The only communication I have had from the 'evil powers' above is a total rundown on what I must wear for the occasion. Apparently, I have a seat next to Gi-Gi in the VIP area where the cameras will be trained (when not on stage) and I have to wear a particularly nauseous Kandhi Store top that has a kind of iridescent daisy on the front. I am hoping the Special Gala Event Programme will be big enough to hide it. I have not been able to verify this as the Special Gala Event Programme has had to go in for a Rush Unscheduled Reprint due to Mum changing her mind about her intro song.

8.00 p.m., Wembley Stadium, The Heatwave
I am with Gi-Gi in this room buried underneath the stalls in Wembley Stadium which I think must normally be reserved for royalty. You can tell because there's a big royal crest stuck on the wall. The room is all lined with Tudor oak panelling and there are shelves stacked with sports trophies and loads of old black and white photos on the walls of football teams

in strangely baggy shorts. This place is so steeped in football heritage I'm starting to wonder if we've turned up for the right event.

However, Mr Schwarz and Mike Dee are here and they're drinking champagne in a little huddle with a load of other guys in suits who must be music promoters too 'cos they're all looking kind of tense. And then there are the other people who, like Gi-Gi and me, must be relations of people who are performing with Mum.

As I look around, the one thing that strikes me is how incredibly normal they all are. I mean, you wonder how any of those nice permed mums and those dads dressed in their uncomfortably new-looking casuals could have given birth to the kind of guys who perform with Mum. I mean, most are so ultra-cool they're scary. Like, they don't even talk to ordinary mortals.

I'm keeping an eye on Gi-Gi, who's way out of her depth – already looking flushed with the glass of champagne she's drunk, or it may be the reflection of her Kandhi Klub Klassics which are making her a luminous shade of cerise. She's having a one-to-one with the lady beside her about the problems of having a star in the family.

'Of course, she never eats a proper meal . . .' I can hear Gi-Gi saying confidentially.

'It's not what they eat that worries me,' comes the response.

My attitude softens somewhat towards Mum as I wonder how she's feeling right now. I know how important this is to her. Her whole future hinges on tonight. This is her chance to totally wipe what happened at the Grammys. It matters to Jasper as well. This could be a turning point for him. And to Vix and Daffyd and June, Thierry and Gervase, Sid and Abdul, because they could all be out of a job. And to Mr Dee and Mr Schwarz and everyone at DBS Records because they could lose all the millions they've invested. What if she louses up?

But Sit is with her. She'll be doing a bit of last-minute meditation before she goes on, which should help. (Sit must be in his seventh heaven. Relinquishing all wordly pleasures! A fan who's actually backstage at a real live event with the object of their fandom?)

But hang on, something's happening. A uniformed usher is taking us upstairs. We're being shown to our VIP seats.

As we emerge into the stadium we're hit by a wall of sound like a fleet of jumbo jets landing on your head. Instinctively, Gi-Gi grabs my hand. She clings to me, tottering slightly. I've never seen such a crowd. We're dwarfed by the size of it, deafened by it. I feel as if I've shrunk to the size of an ant, no, smaller, smaller than a minute grain of sand. I am just one grain in a great shifting mass of heaving life-forms. Gi-Gi is gazing speechlessly into the stadium. I drag her along until we collapse into our seats.

Suddenly there is an uneasy silence. There's a bit of an intro and then the warm-up band is announced. They come on stage and fling themselves into their first song.

I glance at Gi-Gi. She's looking on with disapproval.

'They are not good, yes?'

They are pretty good actually. But I say they're rubbish, to keep her happy. As we sit through their songs, I can feel my palms going damp with apprehension and my mouth going dry. At last the final chords of their last song fade out.

This is it.

A hush falls over the crowd. For a moment I think nothing is happening. But then I realise the lights are going down, very slowly. We reach almost total darkness. Nothing but the green Exit lights glowing. The fidgeting of the audience has stopped.

Silence. Respect. It's as if everyone is holding their breath.

Then in the darkness a spotlight comes on to a tiny, lonely, single figure centre-stage. And I remember Jasper's words the first time he described the song to me. It's night and it's creepy and there's this girl all alone centre-stage and she's homeless, she's got nowhere to go, and there's a single eerie spotlight on her . . .

And then, heart-piercingly, Mum's voice: clear, pure and unaccompanied, delivers the first few bars.

Despite myself – despite the fact that I've heard the song countless times, despite the fact that this is my mum singing – I've come out in goosebumps and big shivers are going down my back. And then the backing thunders in, and the dancers leap into formation behind her.

Suddenly every single person in the stadium is on their feet. The crowd has turned into a great waving, seething turmoil of frenzied bodies, arms up in the air, waving to the beat.

Up on the big screen, I can see Mum's face. She's responding to the crowd. Absorbing their love. Relishing it. It's running like electricity through her body and she's dancing like she's never danced before. Her body is slick with sweat, gleaming like an electric eel while those little glints of rhinestones are picking up the light and fracturing it into a million rainbows.

And then I glance back down on the stage. The other dancers have faded into the shadows. It's just Mum again. A tiny figure. Dwarfed by the arena. A mere speck on the stage. And it is on this tiny speck that the entire attention of thousands of people, in fact, millions if you count the TV too, is focused.

At that moment, maybe for the first time in my life, I realise what Mum is all about. I've always played it down – her mega-fame thing. But when you're caught up in it, when you're swept away by it, when you're blown apart like I was right then – it's like arriving at the bottom of the biggest big dipper ever. And there's only one woman on earth who can do this . . . and she's my mum.

Suddenly the song's over. The last notes fade heartbreakingly away.

When the applause breaks it feels as if it is going to blow the stadium apart.

It's the same for Mum, song after song. You can feel the audience aching with love for her. And she's giving them everything she's got.

She leaves a breathless silence as the final chord of her last song fades into nothingness. I'm left tingling all over with the emotion.

Then Mum coolly blows a kiss, turns on her heel and leaves the stage.

But the audience isn't having it. They start chanting:

'Kandhi! . . . Kandhi! . . . Kandhi! . . . Kandhi! . . . Kandhi!
. . . Kandhi! . . . Kandhi . . . Kandhi . . .'

They want more. They're begging for more. Feet are
thundering on the ground. The chanting continues, growing
faster and louder. I can see the organisers in a huddle. Some
guy's come out on stage trying to lull the crowd. But it makes
no difference. There's nothing else for it. They have to give
in. They have to bring Mum back on.

As she walks to centre-stage the respectful silence that
falls over the crowd is like a religious moment.

She gives them what they've been pleading for. She sings
'Home is Where Your Heart is' once again. If anything more
emotionally than the time before.

As the last notes hang on the air I can see *tears* in the eyes
of the people nearest to me.

And then I realise that this is what Mum lives for. This is
love like love has never been. She has the love of millions.
So much love you could fill a supertanker with it. She doesn't
need to be loved by any one individual. She doesn't need
Oliver's love. She doesn't need my love. A single person's
love is just one tiny drip in the whole ocean of love that's
engulfing her. So small it's meaningless.

As this thought follows all the emotion that's come before,
I feel drained. I feel small. I feel like nothing. I realise that
I'm nobody. Nobody that matters to Mum at any rate. I
recognise, in a great wave of misery, that Mum doesn't need
me. I'm simply a nuisance to her.

Gi-Gi is pulling at my sleeve.

'Is it over?' she mouths against the blast furnace of applause.

219

I nod.

'Hmm,' says Gi-Gi in my ear. 'No doubt it will all go to her head.'

I didn't think I could face the stampede afterwards. There was bound to be a big party with Mr Dee and Mr Schwarz and everyone from the record company getting totally smashed and I'd feel so out of it.

'You OK?' asked Gi-Gi.

'Are you tired, Gi-Gi?'

Gi-Gi squeezed my hand. 'How's about you and me, we go home and celebrate. These people, they make so much noise.'

So that's what we did. Gi-Gi and Thumper and Karl and I celebrated curled up on Gi-Gi's big comfy couch. We had poppy-seed marble cake and sweet Russian tea. And, in spite of the diet he was meant to be on, Thumper had his very own slice of poppy-seed marble cake.

Sunday 16th March
Flat 209, Hillview Mansions, Maida Vale

I stayed over at Gi-Gi's. I guessed no one would really need me around on Sunday. Like, they'd all be recovering from the night before.

I was tired out, anyway. We hadn't got home till way past midnight and then I found it hard to sleep my mind was racing so much.

I spent all Sunday making this huge 'Congratulations' card on Gi-Gi's kitchen table. She'd managed to find glue and Christmas sparkly stuff and even some sequins, so it was quite a work of art.

When I got back to the Trocadero late that afternoon I crept up to Mum's suite. Mum wasn't around. I guessed she was still in bed resting. The suite was full to bursting. There were loads of flowers and cards and boxes and stuff piled up outside Mum's bedroom door. I was just about to prop the card up on top of the pile when Mum's bedroom door opened. But it wasn't Mum who came out. It was Oliver.

'What are you doing here?' I gasped.

I mean, it was a pretty stupid question. Not that he was in his boxers or anything. But he wasn't exactly overdressed. He had on Mum's bathrobe over his trousers.

'I could ask you the same thing. Come to borrow some shoes, maybe? Or were you checking as to who turned up for her lunch date?'

Maybe it was meant to be funny but it came out in a nasty sarky way. They'd obviously been talking about me behind my back.

'I just wanted to say congratulations to Mum.' I held out the card as proof.

Oliver took it in both hands. 'Oh, a card! How nice. Oh, and you made it yourself?'

He was really talking down to me. Suddenly the card looked like the dumbest most childish thing ever. You could even see where the sequins had been stuck on – the glue was going brown around the edges.

'It's not important.'

'Oh, but it is.'

'No. It's not.' I tried to snatch the card back. The paper wasn't that thick and it tore in two right across the front.

'Now look what you've done,' I stormed.

'What's going on?' Mum's voice came from the bedroom behind Oliver.

'It's Hollywood. She's got something for you.'

'No I haven't.'

'It's got torn but I think we could stick it back tog—' started Oliver.

'Why don't you both stop treating me like some kid? And why don't you leave my mother alone? She doesn't care one bit about you. She only wants to be seen with you 'cos you're famous.'

With that I stormed out of the suite.

Later that night Mum called down and said that I had to apologise to Oliver. I said I'd think about it. She said, 'You do that.'

Monday 17th March, 10.00 a.m.
Suite 6002, The Royal Trocadero

I have not apologised to Oliver. In fact, I can now add that to the list of things I have not done.

a) Not apologising to Oliver
b) Not getting the Blahniks back

c) Not doing either of the two essays Rupert set me before he was suspended.

At the very thought of the essays I go into the deepest gloom. What's the point in doing them if Rupert isn't going to mark them? I might as well leave them till I get a new tutor.

And then I have another thought. Why do I need a new tutor? Now 'the nasty threat thing' is all done with, I could go back to school. With that thought I get out of bed, shower and dress and head up to see Mum.

Mum's having a diary session with Vix. At least, Vix is reading from a list of journalists who want to do interviews with Mum and Mum is staring absent-mindedly out of the window saying, 'Yes . . . no . . . maybe . . . I'll think about it . . . tell them to call back . . .'

'Mu-um?'

'Yes, Hollywood? Can't you see I'm busy?' Mum's tone is ominous. She obviously hasn't forgiven me over the Oliver episode.

'You don't want me around – you don't need me here – why can't I go back to school?' I say all in one breath.

'School?' says Mum, turning on me as if I'd suggested running away with the gypsies or going down the mines.

'Yes. I mean, why not?'

'School? What on earth can you mean, Hollywood – I don't need you here?'

'Well you don't . . . do you?'

For an instant a brief flicker of indecision passes across Mum's face.

223

Vix clears her throat and snaps her file shut. 'Maybe we should do this later . . .'

'No, don't go, Vix. I won't be a minute . . .'

Mum turns back to me and opens her arms. 'Come here, Hollywood.'

Obediently, I go to her and snuggle up.

'Now listen to me, babes. We may not always see eye to eye. I may get angry with you at times. But I'm always your mum and you'll always be my baby. Right?' Mum has this choked sound in her voice that shows she's really sincere.

'Re-ally?' I can feel tears starting in my eyes.

'Really. Now you put those silly ideas of yours about going back to school right out of your head. You hear me?'

'Yes, Mum.'

'Come on, have a good blow. Vix! Tissues.'

Vix passes the box of tissues with a frown. I blow my nose.

'Better?'

'Thanks, Mum.'

I go back downstairs feeling loads better. See? Mum cares about me after all.

Tuesday 18th March, 9.00 a.m.
Suite 6002, The Royal Trocadero

'Home is Where Your Heart is' has gone straight to number one. It was confirmed by Mr Schwarz, who rang Vix this morning. In fact, virtually every channel I switch to on

224

the TV this morning seems to be talking about Mum. They're playing the new 'Home is Where Your Heart is' video on MTV, complete with Mum in her new 'homemaker' outfits. I switch to breakfast TV. Hang on, it's Mum they're interviewing.

Mum's had a total change of image. The black has gone, she's all in soft baby colours and, for the first time I've seen in my life, she's actually wearing a skirt that covers her knees. The two commentators are doing the laughy-jokey-off-the-cuff bit and being all smarmy-flattery to Mum and she's lapping it up.

'So tell us a bit about your new hit, Kandhi.'

'Well, I suppose you all know how "Home is Where Your Heart is" comes from this un-be-lievable musical by this really talented guy . . .'

Thanks, Mum. She's doing a plug for Jasper. Isn't that nice of her?

'So are we going to be seeing this musical on stage?'

'I can't really say anything. It's all in the air. Everything is moving so fast,' says Mum. 'Of course my life has totally changed recently.'

'Yes, we hear you have your daughter living with you now?' the interviewer is saying.

'Oh yes, little Hollywood Bliss. You know, all those years of not being able to be with my very own child. That's one of the hardest things to take about being a star.' Mum has that sincere choked sound in her voice, like yesterday . . . 'Believe me, I've suffered,' she adds, looking away from the camera and biting her lip.

The lady interviewer makes some comforting murmuring noises and Mum, with difficulty, regains her composure.

'Hollywood's just so cute, you know. And she's so-oo talented.'

I'm all ears. I creep nearer the TV. What is Mum going to say next?

'I guess a performing career is a natural for her, with you for a mother,' says the male interviewer.

(OH, NO. You don't know me, Mr Interviewer. Oh, SO NOT.)

But Mum continues, warming to the subject: 'Yes, it looks like it. Of course, I'd hate to dictate to her. But singing and dancing just come naturally to Hollywood. I'm trying really hard to keep her focused on her studies though.'

'The big question.' The interviewer leans forward. 'Is Hollywood going to follow in your footsteps?'

'Oh yes, I'd say so for sure. She's really committed.'

I practically fall off the chair. Me committed!

The interview is cut short by a commercial break.

What is Mum up to? What is going on? I'm puzzling over this when there is a smart rap on the interconnecting door with suite 6003.

'This is your cue, Miss Hollywood Bliss . . .' It's Jasper.

'Hi. What are you doing here?'

'I'm your music tutor, remember?'

'But you must be far too important to teach music now.'

Yet it seems that in spite of the fact that 'Home is Where Your Heart is' is at number one, Jasper is still going to continue with my music lessons.

Jasper starts playing the piano. 'Number one . . . strum
. . . Thanks to . . . Hollywood . . . strum . . . Bliss . . . strum
. . . Winterman . . . strum-tee-tum,' he goes.

'Yeah well, and Mum too. Hey, you know what! She was
on TV this morning and she said there might be a chance of
the musical going on stage for real!'

'Fingers and toes crossed. Harold Schwarz thinks he's got
backers.'

'He does?'

'Sev-e-ral!'

'If he thinks so. He's got backers. Mr Schwarz knows
everyone.'

'I sure hope so. But I'm not giving up my day job.'

'Good. Because I missed you when you were working
with Mum.'

'Hey! I'm flattered. And I missed you too, Holly. But, hey,
sob, enough of all this emotion. We have gotta get down
to work.'

Wednesday 19th March
Suite 6003, The Royal Trocadero

My school work has been put on hold while Vix tries to find
me a fill-in tutor. I'm trying to think of ways to sabotage her
search so that they have to forgive Rupert and let him come
back and teach me.

Meanwhile, Jasper has started me on two new songs and
Stella's back too. It seems it was only a sprain after all.

227

10.45 am., mid-music lesson

There have been rumours from the penthouse floor and I know that emails have been flying back and forth between New York and London.

Jasper is so tense, his hands shake so he can barely drink his coffee. He's on tenterhooks waiting for news from Mr Schwarz.

So later that day when Mum herself rings down and asks him to come up and see her, we both totally freak.

Jasper looks at me with a raised eyebrow. 'Uh-oh, I sense news.'

I swallow. 'Surely it's too early to hear anything?'

But as he goes out the door, I shout, 'Good luck' after him.

'Thanks. I'll need it.'

Jasper was gone for ages. I'd even taken to picking out on the piano some of the backing line from one of the songs he was teaching me by the time he came back.

He flung open the door with a really sad look on his face. My heart sank.

Then he flung open his arms and said, 'Guess what!'

'What?'

'They're pulling that new musical *Blondes* off the West End. It's bombed.'

'So?'

'They want to stage *Metropolis* in its place, as soon as. Schwarz has got the backing. It's all go. I think I've died and gone to heaven. Look, I'm gonna have to sit down.'

'But that's brilliant!'

'I can't believe it. Look, sorry. Look, I'm gonna cry.' He took out his hanky and started blowing his nose.

'Cry? But you must be so happy!'

'Hollywood, babes – I am crying because I'm so happy.'

I was nearly crying too. 'Oh wow, Mum must be over the moon.'

'Yeah, she is. Oh, yeah.'

'But is she going to have time? I mean, what about the Heatwave Tour . . .?'

'What about it? What do you mean?' asked Jasper, having a really big nose blow.

'Well, if *Metropolis* is staged for real, Mum will play the lead, won't she?'

Jasper shook his head.'Oh no. Not on. She's too old. The way we sold it to Schwarz was for it to have a child cast – apart from the five character parts, that is. Kind of like *Bugsy Malone* but with adult voices too – to give it more oomph.'

'Oh. I see. So Mum wouldn't be in it at all?'

'Your mum's got a lot of mileage to make up. She may be back up at number one in the UK but that's not going to keep her happy, is it? She's going to have to follow it up. You know Kandhi – today she conquers Britain, tomorrow the world.'

Later that day: the bar, The Royal Trocadero
There wasn't much point in trying to continue with my singing class that day. Jasper was just out of it. Instead, he took me down to the hotel bar and bought me a 'Pussyfoot Cocktail' and then he bought drinks for everyone in the bar.

After that he started calling people up and Vix and Daffyd and June and Sid and Abdul and even Sit joined us. So it turned into a kind of party.

And just when we were getting really rowdy Mum came down and she gave Jasper a way big kiss and he picked her up and sat her on the piano.

'So OK, folks. What shall I sing?' said Mum.

So that afternoon, a group of six Japanese businessmen, two ladies from Bognor who'd dropped by for a cup of tea after shopping and the barman of the Royal Trocadero had their own private Kandhi concert.

After the 'concert' Mum took me and Jasper to the Royal Trocadero restaurant, which is plush. She said I could order what I liked from the menu and she'd turn a blind eye.

When I went off to bed she gave me a big kiss and a hug as if she really meant it.

'You mean a lot to me, Hollywood,' she said with a funny look.

'Thanks Mum, sure. You mean a lot to me too.'

Later still, Suite 6002

I couldn't sleep that night. Mum's being so nice to me. I wonder what she's up to? I lie there fantasising that Mum's really like this all the time. That we've even got a proper house to live in. And that Thumper and Gi-Gi and Karl have come to live with us.

Thumper and I have the top floor all to ourselves and we've put that false grass stuff down instead of carpet and we've got proper plants in boxes like flowerbeds and maybe even an indoor pond with real frogs in it and goldfish and . . .

I guess I must've fallen asleep then.

Thursday 20th March, 11.00 a.m.
The Penthouse Suite

I'm just about to go up for my dance lesson when there's a ringing on my door buzzer.

Sounds as if someone is leaning on it. It's probably the chambermaid trying to get in to fix my room.

'OK. OK. Coming.'

I fling the door open.

It is not the chambermaid. It's Shug.

'So what do you want?' I demand. I know I sound rude. I mean to.

'Can you stop your mother like fooling around with my dad?'

(Hang on a minute. Isn't it him who's fooling around with her?)

'What do you mean, fooling around?' I demand.

'She should leave him alone.'

'He should leave her alone.'

'She like picks him up when she needs an accessory to hang on her arm. And then she drops him.'

'Drops him?'

'Yeah. They were flying to Vegas this morning and she didn't show.'

'To Vegas? She didn't tell me. What for?'

'What do you think people fly to Vegas for?'

'Gambling?'

'Oh, pl-ease.'

'What, then?'

Shug glances over his shoulder. I follow his gaze down the corridor. A chambermaid wheeling a trolley has come within earshot.

'You better come in,' I say, standing aside.

Shug comes into the suite and stands in the middle of the room looking uncomfortable.

'V-e-g-a-s,' says Shug patiently, spelling it out letter by letter as if I was a moron or something, 'Vegas is where you can get a special licence, without any fuss, to get hitched.'

'Married!'

'Except they're not. 'Cos this little wedding ceremony is lacking one essential. The bride.'

'Oh my God, why didn't Mum tell me?'

'Probably 'cos she was planning to blow him out all along.'

'She wouldn't do that.'

'Wouldn't she?'

Then I have this horrible sinking feeling. Oliver stood Mum up, didn't he? And knowing her she'd have to get her own back. Only she'd have to go one better. In order to prove who was the bigger star.

But I say to Shug, 'Oh, come on, you mean to say that poor little Oliver Bream isn't able to look after himself?'

'If she goes on like this, he'll have to go see a shrink.'

It's news to me that someone as cold and distant as Oliver can actually have feelings. I'm about to say something cutting but I pause for a moment. Shug seems genuinely upset.

Instead I find myself saying, 'You mean, you think your dad is genuinely keen on my mum?'

Shrug turns, sticks his hands in his pockets and swivels round on his heel.

'Amazing as it is. Yeah, I reckon.'

'But they're always fighting.'

'You don't fight with someone you don't care about. Do you?'

'But do you think my mum cares about your dad?'

'I dunno. She's your mum. You should be able to tell.'

'I can't. Mum has loads of boyfriends. You can only tell if she really likes them if she marries them.'

'That's what I mean. I don't want my dad getting messed up in all the shit.'

'Well, I don't want my mum getting married to your dad, thank you very much.'

'So we're agreed on one thing. We don't want them to be together.'

'No way. They're totally wrong for each other.'

'OK,' says Shug.

'Right then.'

'Umm.'

He leaves after that. I shut the door on him and lean against it, my mind reeling. What's Mum up to now?

Then I shoot up to the penthouse suite to check if Mum's still there.

Immediately after – the Penthouse Suite

Phew, she was.

I found her in bed. Her face was all pale against the pillows. She didn't have any make-up on. I'm always shocked to see Mum without make-up. She doesn't look like herself at all. When I got closer, I could see her face was all blotchy. She must have been crying.

I went and sat on the edge of the bed and said gently, 'Mum, what's all this about you going to Las Vegas with Oliver?'

Mum sniffed and then blew her nose. 'How did you know about it?'

'Shug told me. He dropped by this morning. He said you stood up Oliver. You two were going to Vegas to get married. Why didn't you tell me?'

'I didn't tell you because I wasn't sure. And then I decided he wasn't really right for me anyway.'

'It's marriage you're talking about, Mum. Not some new outfit.'

'No need to start moralising, Hollywood. I feel bad enough about it as it is.'

'That'll be a first.'

'No, you don't understand. I thought going out with Oliver would change me somehow. You know, be good for my image.'

'Mu-um!'

'No, don't stop me, Hollywood. So when he proposed, I thought, great. You know. New image – me the home-maker and all that. New family. It's just what I need. But

234

then, I realised I couldn't do that to Oliver. He's just too nice a person.'

'You mean, you didn't marry him because you really like him?'

'Yes . . .' said Mum and she started crying again.

What a pair, I thought. Jeez, those two were mixed up.

Later

I spend the day pampering Mum. Believe me, this is a tall order when you consider she has everything she could possibly want. But I fill her suite with her favourite flowers – gardenias. I get Thierry to track down a crate of fresh raspberries which are her favourite food and I put on her favourite DVD.

I've got to swear you to absolute secrecy here – promise you won't tell a soul? Because it's *The Sound of Music*. Sad but true. It was the first musical Mum ever saw and it was then she decided to become a star.

Friday 21st March
The Penthouse Suite

I wake up as usual thinking about RUPERT and wondering what he's doing right now. But I don't have peace to really ponder over this as Vix has called down to say that there will be no classes today because Mum's got some people due in at ten who want to meet me.

'Meet me? Why?'

Vix is vague. 'Oh, I don't know, she didn't say.'

I go up wondering if Mum's still in the state she was in yesterday. But not a bit of it. True to form she's totally recovered.

I find her talking earnestly with two people who are introduced as Fiona from 'Inspiration' PR Agency and Jeremy who is a casting director.

Fiona is wearing a neat little black linen skirt suit and has perfect streaked blonde hair and shiny tanned legs. Jeremy is lounging on Mum's couch as if he owns it.

'Oh, hi,' says Fiona, coming over all gushy-gushy. 'So you're Hollywood? I've been so dying to meet you.'

I sit down on the seat Mum pats beside her and cast a searching What-is-this-all about? look in her direction.

'Oh, yes,' says Jeremy to Mum. 'Oh, yes indeed.'

The room feels heavy with some meaningful conversation that has taken place in my absence.

Fiona continues to Mum, 'I can just see the story. Now this would totally change your image. Gone the old sex-kitten, she-devil Kandhi – that's so yesterday. In with the new caring Kandhi. It's that mother/daughter thing. It's one of the great Universals.'

'Fiona's right,' chips in Jeremy. 'Absolutely perfect.'

'What's perfect?' I ask.

'You are, babes.'

'Perfect for what?'

'Perfect for playing me at your age in this biopic we're planning.'

'Me? Playing you?' I'm starting to get panic-vibes here.

'Hollywood, babes, you're the obvious choice. I mean, you are my daughter.'

'But I don't look anything like you.'

'There are ways and means,' butts in Jeremy. 'Make-up, camera angles, digital enhancing –'

'But, Mum. I can't sing like you. I can't dance like you. No way!'

Fiona interrupts. 'Look, Hollywood. Or would you rather I called you Holly?'

I shrug. 'I don't mind.'

'We only want you to audition. OK?'

'What's the point in auditioning if I don't want to play the part?'

I notice an eye-flick between Fiona and Jeremy.

'It's just for the story. It's a mother and daughter thing.'

Jeremy agrees over my head. 'It's got legs, Kandhi. It's like Liza and Judy all over again.'

'Listen, Holly, this is going to be really big. We're calling it *Supernova*. It's all about your mum's life.'

'I don't see why it has to involve me,' I say, staring down at my hands.

Fiona leans forward and looks me straight in the eyes. 'The film company know what they're doing. They're not going to simply give you the part. There are loads of stage school kids who'll come to the castings. If someone's better than you, then that's it.'

This is reassuring. Stage school kids are bound to be better than me.

Mum adds, 'Listen, babes. Won't you do the audition, for me? It would mean a lot.'

'It would?'

Mum nods. 'We don't have a chance to do much for each other. Do we?'

'I guess not.'

I think guiltily about all the things I haven't done. Like not apologising to Oliver . . . And worse. The things I have done. Like auctioning the Blahniks and talking to the press and going to the Globe . . .

Suddenly I have this vision, as if I'm looking at myself from the outside. Seeing me from Mum's point of view – I am SO NOT a daughter she can be totally proud of. No, I'm sitting here like some sulky teenager. When what she'd really love is a daughter who's really successful. I mean, even Becky is up for Young Musician of the Year. While I'm totally nothing.

'I'll think about it.'

'You do that,' says Mum, giving me a big showy hug.

'You can trust us.' Jeremy is leaning back and smiling indulgently at me.

'Thanks, Holly,' says Fiona earnestly.

Saturday 22nd March, 8.00 a.m.
Suite 6002, The Royal Trocadero

First thing in the morning, I get a text from Becky:

Guess what?

young musician violin trials

I came

```
a) first?
b) third?
c) nowhere?
Bx
```

No exclamation marks. This doesn't look like good news. I text her back.

```
?????
```

Almost immediately I get a reply.

```
b)
```

Oh God, I feel so gutted for her. Poor Becky. How's she going to live with this? I try and think of ways to make her feel better about it.

Send her flowers? Too like a funeral, could make it worse. A big showy card? That's like she was sick or something . . .

I'VE GOT IT. A surprise visit! She came to see me, didn't she? And it's Saturday too, so no classes. Brilliant. I bet if I bribe Abdul with that second kilo of jelly beans he'll take me in the limo. I better clear it with Mum first, though.

Mum must really want to be in my good books. She hardly makes any objection.

'It'll be nice for you to see your friends again,' she says sleepily. 'And the drive will give you time to think . . .'

'Sure, Mum. Thanks.'

I'd made up a hasty comfort pack from everything I could raid from my suite. I'd filled the little basket from the bathroom with loads of free stuff and some of those chocolates the Royal Trocadero leave on your pillow each night which I'd been hoarding. I'd decorated the basket with flowers from my vase and added a mango from the fruit bowl.

All the way I tried to get Abdul to drive faster. The journey seemed to take for ever and I kept thinking of Becky sobbing into her pillow or playing really sad stuff on her violin. But at last we were sweeping through the gates with the big SotR crest on top.

I made Abdul drive round to the back of the building where the kitchen supplies are delivered and the limo drew to a halt without anyone seeming to notice us.

Leaving Abdul peacefully reading his newspaper, I slid past the kitchens. There was a distant clatter and a smell of cooking from the far end, but the only sign of life was the school cat, which came and rubbed itself against my legs and purred in welcome.

I crept up the back stairs to the dormitory floor. No one around here either. Very gently I opened the door of the room I'd shared with Becky. She wasn't in bed sobbing her heart out. The room was empty. The two beds stood neatly made-up. Someone else's pyjamas were folded on what had been my pillow. There were someone else's family photos on the bedside table, someone else's posters on the wall and a tangle of their clothes on the chair. All signs of my presence had been totally eradicated. As if I'd never been there.

'*You're going to have new friends now*.' An echo of Mum's voice ran through my head.

I went and stared out of the window. I could hear familiar sounds of girls' voices coming from the other dorms. This is what it must be like to be dead, I thought gloomily, and to come back as a ghost and find everything going on without you, totally heartlessly.

That's when the door was flung open behind me.

'Holly!' screamed Becky. 'I don't believe it!'

Once we'd sorted out how I'd come, how long I was staying, etc., I composed my face into a suitably sympathetic expression and presented her with the basket.

'Cool,' she said. 'Thanks.'

'Third's not bad, you know,' I said comfortingly.

'Not bad? It's brilliant!' she said. 'The others I was up against were older than me, I didn't think I stood a chance.'

This was a novel way of looking at things. Quite the opposite of Mum's 'not first, you're nowhere' philosophy.

'And I can always try again next year. So it's good experience.'

'Umm.'

'I'll just have to practise harder, that's all.'

'Becky, if you practise harder you'll wear your violin out.'

12.30 p.m., SotR dining hall

They say your memory only retains the good things. So true. Mine had totally wiped SotR's lumpy gravy.

A load of us, Me, Becky, Portia, Marie, Candida and Lim-Ju (plus Abdul who is sitting some way off, trying to

241

ignore the fact that he is the only male in this all-female environment) are having a noisy lunch of beefburgers and mash (and gravy).

The hot topic of the day is whether I should or should not audition for Mum's biopic. Or rather they are discussing it. I'm finding it difficult to get a word in edgeways. In fact, I'm sitting like some vegetable while the discussion rages round me.

'Of course she should do it. She owes it to her mum,' says Lim-Ju.

'No way!' says Portia. 'If Holly doesn't want to do it, it's her affair.'

'Gosh, imagine. Holly, you could be really famous!' says Candida.

'I don't want to be famous,' I chip in. 'I'm suffering enough from second-hand fame as it is.'

'She's right. She'd totally lose her anonymity,' points out Marie. 'Once she's been seen on screen, she'll never be left in peace.'

'They should pay you loads to do the part,' says Portia. 'Will they?'

'I bet you haven't even thought about money,' says Marie.

'Surely she can't expect to be paid for acting the part of her own mother,' says Lim-Ju.

'Stop, everyone!' I interrupt. 'I think I should be the one to make the decision, don't you? Now will someone pass me the ketchup, please.'

It was Becky who had the last word. As I was leaving she leaned in through the car window, saying, 'If you're not going to get the part anyway, what's the big deal? Why not do the audition and get it over with?'

I wake up with a strange foreboding feeling. Then I remember Mum's biopic. *Supernova!* The very word has brought on a mega-attack of performaphobia.

Imagine, if by some absolute fluke of fate, I get the part. Like every other girl auditioning developed rampant tonsillitis, for instance. Or the set collapsed with everyone on it but me . . .

I decide to go downstairs and have a soak in the jacuzzi to calm myself down.

8.30 a.m., The Royal Trocadero jacuzzi (the prime bubbly bit)

I have the jacuzzi all to myself so I'm lying with my eyes closed concentrating hard on slow breathing to stop my heart pumping from panic.

The hot water is bubbling all around me with a comforting 'globble-globble-globble' sound. I am just getting back my composure when: SPLASH!

Some totally inconsiderate person has jumped in.

I open my eyes to protest and come face to face with SHUG.

'Hi! Fancy meeting you here,' he says.

I close my eyes again with dignity.

'You still hanging around?'

'Uh-huh. Bit moody today, are we?'

'I was just enjoying a little peace, that's all.'

'OK. I'll keep to my side.' He squeezes himself up as small as possible against the far wall of the jacuzzi and sits staring at me.

I can feel myself going hot and bothered under his gaze.

'How's your dad?' I ask, trying to deflect his attention from my least impressive measurement.

'He's still in the States. Unlike you and your mum we're not attached at the hip.'

'Is he OK?'

'After his lucky escape, you mean?'

I ignore this. 'So what are you doing with yourself all on your own?'

'I'm here to record a new song, as it happens.'

'Oh, is your brilliant recording career taking off? Or is your dad paying for this one?'

This gets to him. I have the satisfaction of seeing him flinch.

'I don't see you doing so brilliantly.'

'Oh no? I've just had an offer of a part in a film, actually. The lead.'

'The lead! What's the film? *Godzilla*'s *Child*?'

'Ha ha, very funny.'

He is silent for a moment, swishing water round with his toes. Then he asks, 'So when d'you start filming?'

'I haven't decided if I'll accept it yet.'

'Oh, wow! Too many other offers to consider?'

'Not exactly.'

'What, then?'

'For your information, I don't necessarily want a brilliant career in show business. I might do something more worthwhile.'

'Oh, spare me the sermon . . . Like what?'

'As a matter of fact, I was thinking of becoming a vet.'

Shug laughs so much he practically chokes. Then he goes under the surface and comes up again spouting water out of his mouth.

'That's rich. I really like that one. Florence Nightingale to all our furry friends!'

I think at this point that I've had enough of being insulted and start to climb out.

'You know what I think?' says Shug.

'What?'

'I don't think you've got the guts for show business.'

'Oh yeah?'

'No. I think you're chickening out because you're too damn scared.'

'It's only acting, not sky-diving.'

'You haven't got the courage to stand up in front of people and perform.'

'Rubbish.'

'Prove it then.'

'I just might do that,' I snap, wrapping a towel round me. I make for the changing rooms.

I stand under the shower thinking about what he said. The truth stings. He's right. I'm scared. I'm scared stiff of being a failure.

Once I'd dried off I went back upstairs to ring Mum.

I stared at the phone for a long time before I picked up the receiver.

'Mum?'

'Yes?'

'I've made up my mind.'

'Ye-es?'

'I'll do it. I'll do the audition.'

'Hollywood, babes. I knew you wouldn't let your mama down.'

Monday 24th March
Suite 6003

Vix has just told me that a date has been set for the *Supernova* castings. It's next Monday. The very thought makes my stomach kind of turn over with a thump and brings on a mega-attack of performaphobia.

How does Mum go out in front of all those millions of people and sing?

But there's no going back now. I've said I'll do it, so I'll have to go through with it. It'll only take a few minutes before they realise I'm rubbish. I can just shoot in, do my bit and be off. But every minute being rubbish is hard to take.

I send Becky a text:

How do I get through this audition without
a) Drying up?

b) Tripping up?
c) Lousing up?

I get a text back almost immediately:

a) practise
b) practise
c) practise

She's right. I have to work harder. I mean, I kind of thought either I had to be a mega success like Mum, or I was rubbish. Now I've come to terms with the fact that I am somewhere in between. And that if I work hard enough I can improve.

SO.

Monday 24th March through to Monday 31st March

a) I have been practising my scales
b) I have been doing my breathing exercises
c) I have even been studying my music theory
d) I have gone over and over the songs till I can sing them in my sleep.

As for dance:

e) I have stretched every sinew of my body
(Now my SO NOT fallen arches are totally like

247

Roman Arches staying there of their own accord)

f) I have practised and practised and practised each dance routine

g) I have even mapped out the moves on a piece of maths exercise paper so that I can't forget them

The good thing is I only have to perfect one piece for the audition.

Monday 31st March!!!!!!!!

I'm in the limo with Mum, Abdul and Sid heading irretrievably closer and closer to the scene of my total and complete humiliation. Naturally, I am feeling sick with apprehension.

I pass the time by trying to rate on a kind of Richter scale of misery how bad I feel. As bad as being taken to the dentist? No, much much worse. As bad as being driven to the guillotine in one of those tumbrel-thingies? The guillotine was meant to be instant, my suffering is going to last agonising minutes ... As bad as ... Oh my God, I think we've arrived!!!

Mum is peering out of the window complaining, 'This can't be it. It all looks so run-down.'

But it is. There's a guy behind a security grille who's asking for I.D. When Abdul points out Mum in the car, the guy lets the barrier up and salutes.

'Lot 32,' he says. 'Fifth building down.'

'Hmm,' says Mum. 'I should think so too.'

We drive round to Lot 32. It looks like a factory. There's a queue of girls of about my age waiting in line to go in. Most seem to have come with their mums.

'Just drop us at the front,' says Mum to Abdul. 'Holly can come in with me.'

'Mu-um? Aren't I meant to queue like the others?'

'Don't be ridiculous, Hollywood, you can't be expected to stand outside. It's starting to rain.'

'But they are.'

'Yes, Hollywood. They are.'

'But that's not fair.'

'Maybe Holly's got a point,' agrees Sid.

'Life's not fair,' snaps Mum. 'If life was fair, we'd all be stars.'

'Well, I am not going to get special treatment,' I say. 'Let me out now.'

I won the argument in the end. I even got them to drive to the far side of the building so no one would see me get out of the limo. Mum went in at the front entrance. Apparently she was on the selection committee.

By the time Sid and I joined the queue, it was raining quite hard. Sid looked pretty fed up about it. But I decided to ignore him, fair was fair.

There was a small skinny girl in front of me with red hair and freckles and a big wide grin. She was with her mum, who was one of those big cosy kind of mums carrying a bulging plastic bag that looked as if it was about to burst.

'Hi,' said the girl. 'Didn't I see you at the *Geraldi* casting last week?'

I shook my head. 'No, that wasn't me.'

'My name's Gina. What's yours?'

'Holly.'

'Hi, Holly. Funny, I'm sure I've seen you somewhere. Maybe you were at *The Nutcracker*?'

I shook my head again. 'No, not me.'

'You at stage school?'

'No. I just came along to like try. Are you?'

'I'm at the Arts Educational. Is that your dad with you?'

'Erm, no.' (And then I realised I could hardly say he was my bodyguard.) 'He's my step-dad.'

'Nice of him to come with you. Couldn't your mum come?'

'Errm, no. She's busy right now.'

'She at work?'

'Kind of.'

'There are loads of people. This is going to take hours. Haven't you brought your lunch?'

'I didn't think.'

'You can have some of ours. Can't she, Mum?'

Her mum looked at us sympathetically. 'Oh my. Haven't they got anything at all?'

I shook my head.

'Oh, you poor dears. Of course you can.'

The queue was dribbling in, in ones and twos. As we entered there was a girl at a desk who took our names and addresses and handed each of us a number. I gave Gi-Gi's address. Well, I could hardly say I was staying at the Royal Trocadero. Then we had to have our photo taken holding our number, like prisoners do when they're admitted into jail. I was number sixty, so you can see how many people there were.

Once inside, the mums and all the others who were accompanying people were sent to sit at the back of the set. We were taken to a side room and shown where we could hang up our coats and change into our dance shoes. There was a bathroom alongside and I lingered there because I'd really started to feel sick again. In fact while I was at the basins combing my hair, I thought I might actually be sick.

Gina was beside me tying up her hair in a ponytail band. She looked at my reflection curiously in the mirror.

'This is your first time, isn't it.'

'How do you know?'

'You look kind of green.'

'I feel it. On the way here, I was trying to think of all the things that would be worse than coming here.'

'So? What was the worst?'

I shrugged.

'Go on. Imagine! Having your legs sawn off,' she said, rolling her eyes. 'Being slowly boiled in oil! Sizzle!!!!'

I giggled.

'See, it could be a lot worse!'

Groups of girls were being taken on to the set ten at a time. I was relieved to find that Gina was in my group. We waited for what felt like ages. I managed to calm down some, so that my heart stopped doing wobbly-jittery things. But then it did a double somersault. A woman was reading our names from a list.

'58 Francesca Simmonds . . . 59 Gina Locardi . . . 60 Holly Winterman . . .' This was it.

We had to form a line and then we were marched down the corridor. I supposed I might have felt worse if I'd known there was an electric chair up ahead. Marginally.

As we paused in the doorway, I whispered to Gina, 'I've just thought of it.'

'What?'

'The very worst thing that could happen to me.'

'What is it?'

'Getting the part. I don't think I could do it.'

'Then you won't,' said Gina. 'So you can relax.' And she gave me one of her big wide grins. 'Break a leg.'

'You too.'

The set was just a big empty space with loads of scaffolding and electric wires snaking everywhere. An area of the floor had been marked out with strips of bright yellow tape, to show people where to stand. And there was a bank of lights and cameras between us and the rest of the space, so you couldn't really see who was watching. I thought I could make out Fiona's legs in the distance and what could be Mum beside her, her hair just catching the light.

A girl with a clipboard seemed to be in charge. And there was a guy with a headset who kept asking for silence.

We were sent to sit on a row of chairs and then, one by one, each girl was called up in front of the cameras. My goosebumps calmed down somewhat as I watched the girl ahead of us. She wasn't bad. But she wasn't a patch on what followed.

The minute Gina got in front of the cameras she kind of radiated. I can't think of any other word for it. You just had to watch her. She was doing this song from *Grease*. It was a song written for a boy, but she didn't care. As she acted, you'd have thought she really was a boy. She was brilliant.

But there was no applause. Just a voice from the darkness saying, 'Thank you. We'll let you know.'

After that there was a horrible pause. I can't remember NOTHING happening for so long in my life. I could hear my heart thumping in my chest. And then the voice came: 'Next. Number sixty: Holly Winterman . . .'

I walked across the set and handed my music to the lady at the piano like the others had done. I could actually feel my legs shaking.

I was told to go and stand on the yellow cross in the centre facing the cameras. I stared out into this great black scary void and wondered if Mum was nervous for me. I couldn't see anything out there because the lights were full in my eyes. Then the pianist looked over, gave me a nod and played the opening bars of 'Home is Where Your Heart is'.

As I came in I could hear my voice in my head and it sounded horribly thin and tinny but I struggled on and I guess all the coaching Jasper had given me paid off because I found I was singing. And my feet seemed to fall into Stella's step routine without me having to tell them what to do. I mean I kind of went through the song like a robot. So I got to the end somehow.

The voice came to release me at last. 'Thank you. We'll let you know. Next.'

I sat through the other auditions in a daze. Most of them were good, far better than me. But none of them was a patch on Gina.

When we got back to the changing rooms we found Gina's mum was there. She gave Gina a hug.

'Well done,' she said to me.

'But I was terrible.'

'Not once you got started. You were fine,' she said. 'Now, sit down with us and eat something. You look white as a sheet.'

She opened her carrier bag and passed a pack of sandwiches round. They were peanut butter and cucumber in thick white bread. I'd totally stopped feeling sick by then and was ravenous. They were yummy.

Abdul appeared as I ate my third sandwich. He was holding my coat. 'You better put this on, it's still pouring with rain,' he said.

'Where's Mum?' I asked as I got in the car.

'I dropped her off earlier. She didn't want to hang around.'

So I'd have to wait till later for her verdict on my performance.

The limo swept off through the rain. Some way down the road I caught sight of Gina and her mother, making for the underground. They were getting soaking wet but they didn't seem to care. They were laughing and chatting together. I was just about to tap on the glass and tell Abdul to stop and give them a lift when I thought better of it.

I felt ashamed somehow. Me being in the limo and them outside in the rain. And I was kind of envious too. Not just because she was so brilliant at singing. But because of the way she was fooling around with her mum. They looked so . . .

So like a mother and daughter ought to look.

8.30 p.m., the Penthouse Suite, The Royal Trocadero

Mum's called me up to see her.

She's lying in the bath when I arrive.

'It's OK, you can come in. God, that was exhausting.'

'Was I really bad?'

'Course you weren't, babes. With a bit of help from some sound fellas you'd've been fine.'

'The others didn't need any help. Did you see the girl before me?'

'Babes, there were so many . . .'

'No, but you must remember her. A redhead. She did a song from *Grease*.'

'Hmmm, ginger hair. I never could stand redheads. They look so undercooked somehow.'

'Mum, I'm talking about how she acted. She was brilliant. She should get the part. You did vote for her, didn't you?'

'Hollywood, I am only one little person on the selection committee. Besides, it's all confidential. I can't disclose how I voted. If she's as good as you say, I guess she'll get on the shortlist.'

'Shortlist?'

'Umm. You can't cast a movie in one day, you know, babes.'

'Mum. There's no way I could get on that shortlist. Is there?'

Mum looked at me wide-eyed. 'How should I know? It depends how the others voted.'

This was reassuring. I wouldn't put it past Mum to vote for me. But the others couldn't be blind and deaf.

'Well, I just hope they hadn't all fallen asleep when Gina came on, because she's really nice. And so's her mum. They shared their lunch with me.'

'And just think. If you hadn't been so stubborn and queued like that, you could have been through and done in no time, and had lunch with me and Mr Schwarz at the Ivy.'

'You went off for lunch?'

'Holly, there were eighty-something girls to see. There is only so much a person can take.'

'Mum, I don't believe you even saw me. Or Gina.'

'What I saw or didn't see is beside the point. Now could you just leave me, please, to get some peace?'

Mum had on her ominous 'I want to be alone' face. So I left.

That beats everything, I thought. She didn't even see my

audition. So there's no way I could get on the shortlist. That's for sure.

Tuesday 1st April, 9.00 a.m.
Suite 6002, The Royal Trocadero

Vix has rung down to say that she's had an email to say I'm on the shortlist.

'Oh ha-ha, very funny. April Fool to you too.'

'No, but really. I'm not fooling.'

'Then they must be.'

'No, listen, Holly. No one is joking, OK?'

I head straight up to see Mum to find out the truth.

Mum comes bursting out of her bedroom saying, 'Hollywood, babes. I've just heard. I'm so proud of you!'

I'm on the shortlist.

She's hugging me as I protest: 'But that's impossible!' I remind Mum how good the others were.

'Have you no faith in Jasper as a teacher?'

'How short is this shortlist?'

'How short is it, Vix?'

'Umm, around ten, I think.'

So that's nine other people who are way better than me.

'Do you happen to know if a girl called Gina is on it?' I ask Vix.

'Yep,' says Vix, peering at the screen. 'There's a Gina. Gina Locardi.'

'That's her. She was brilliant! I mean, Mum, Gina actually looks like you – you'd only have to change her hair. She's petite and skinny and she's got this knock-out smile. You'd better make sure she gets it.'

'You really don't want the part, do you, Holly?' says Mum with a pout.

'You know I don't.'

'I hoped things might've changed. You'd think you'd have some of your parent's ambition, that's all.'

'I just hate performing in front of people.'

'But you did it for the audition.'

'That was different. That wasn't a proper performance. And since I didn't want to get the part anyway, it didn't matter. There is no way I am going to do another audition.'

Mum is silent for a moment. Then she folds her arms and walks over to the window and stares out.

'Of course, the next audition is going to be way harder,' she says.

'Exactly,' I grunt.

'There'll be spoken dialogue too. You're going to need a voice coach.'

'No, Mum, listen. I'm not doing –'

'Now what was that piece you were doing with Rupert . . .?'

'Rupert . . .?'

'Umm, that "Shrew" thing. I think in the circumstances I might have to reconsider my decision to suspend him. It could be really hard to find someone to coach you at this short notice . . .'

Rupert. She's going to consider getting RUPERT back? I am going to have to reconsider the audition.

'I remember he said there was one piece you did so well . . .'

'It was Shakespeare. From *The Taming of the Shrew*.'

'Whatever. Would Shakespeare be all right, do you think, Vix?'

'I should think Shakespeare would be perfect,' says Vix.

'He's probably not free,' I say.

'Vix has already rung him. He'll be back this afternoon,' says Mum with an angelic smile. She gives me a another big hug and leaves.

2.30 p.m., Suite 6003, The Royal Trocadero (otherwise known as heaven)

RUPERT is back. He's even wearing his navy blue polo-neck (sigh). I find him with his head down marking the stuff I did while he was away. He's given me an A+ for the page I did of the dance steps. (He thought I was a plotting a graph.)

The rest of the morning is spent going through my speech from *The Taming of the Shrew*.

'My God, your mother's got ambitions for you,' says Rupert as we take a break. 'You should have heard her on the phone.'

'Mum rang you?'

'Yep, she was very persuasive. I was about to leave for Tanzania.'

'Tanzania?'

'Umm, I've got this teaching post for a year. Setting up a

259

school in this really remote area. I managed to put off going for a week, though.'

'So you're leaving?'

'Not for a week.'

'But won't it be very dangerous there?'

Rupert looks at me curiously and then laughs. 'Hey, Holly, you sound almost like a girlfriend.'

I feel myself blush scarlet at that.

'No way!' I say. 'Yukkk!'

'OK,' says Rupert, handing me my copy of the play. 'Let's get back to work. Now where were we?'

We go over the speech where Kate really has to spit out the words at Petruchio. The one he said I did so well that time way back. But my heart's not in it. I keep on thinking of Rupert going away for a whole year and getting this big lump in my throat.

Rupert stops me mid-sentence. 'Will you please concentrate, Holly? Don't you remember how you did the speech before?'

I shake my head.

'What's up?'

'I don't even want the stupid part anyway.'

'You don't?'

'No, it's all Mum's idea. She won't be content until she's turned me into a clone of herself.'

'It's only natural, I suppose, to want you to follow in her footsteps. You are her daughter, after all.'

'But I'm nothing like her. And I'm no way as good as the others.'

'Then you won't get the part.'

'You're right. There's this girl Gina. She even looks like Mum. I don't stand a chance against her.'

Rupert shakes his head at that and says with a simply adorable smile: 'You're a funny girl, Holly.'

'Am I?'

Wednesday 2nd April
Suite 6003

I have spent most of the night wondering if 'You're a funny girl' counts as a compliment or not. I have decided to give it the benefit of the doubt and make the most of the one last week I have with Rupert.

I get up early and spend an hour in the bathtub learning Kate's speech off by heart. Eventually my copy of the play is so soggy I have to put it on the towel rail to dry.

By nine thirty I reckon I've got it off pat. Which is handy because I find I can't peel the pages apart to check.

At ten Rupert arrives for an extra run-through. We've hardly started when the phone rings. Rupert answers it.

It's Vix.

'She says your mum wants you to go shopping with her,' he says.

(You'd think, in the circumstances, Mum would want me to concentrate on my run-through, wouldn't you?)

'Shopping!'

'That's what she said.'

Thanks, Mum. She even has to louse up one of my last precious days with Rupert. I head upstairs to ask what on earth she's on about.

Mum is dressed-down. She is so dressed down she hardly looks like Mum at all. She's wearing a pair of old blue jeans and a grey crew neck. And her make-up is artfully done to look as if she isn't wearing any.

'Hollywood, babes, come and give Mama a kiss. I just thought you could help me buy some nice ordinary clothes to suit my new image. You and me, we never do anything together these days.'

'But aren't I meant to be . . .?'

'No, this morning, we are going to have a girly morning together.'

'But Rupert's here for a run-through –'

'You've spent enough time on that speech of yours. I want you to help me buy, you know, stuff that ordinary people buy.'

'But Mum, this speech is really imp—'

'You don't want to get stale, do you?'

'No, but –'

'So where are we going to shop?'

I give up. 'I dunno. Where would you like?'

'Where do ordinary people buy things?'

'Anywhere. You know, like high street shops, I guess.'

Mum rings down on her mobile. 'Abdul, do you think you could find us a high street?' She turns back to me. 'It's OK. He's on to it. He wants to know the names of some shops.'

'How about Gap? Or maybe Kookai?'

Mum frowns. I don't think Gap or Kookai have ever featured in her shopping listings. 'Whatever, I'm sure Abdul can track these places down.'

A high street (not quite sure where)

As we leave the hotel a hidden army of photographers leap out from behind the Trocadero's row of sculpted bay trees.

'Don't take any notice,' says Mum, giving them her Winning Press Smile. 'They're only doing their job. I have to put up with it, being as I am at number one.'

We climb into the limo and find it difficult to close the doors as several photographers seem intent on getting in with us. As we set off there is a little cavalcade of them following on motorbikes.

'Mum, I don't know how you can live with all this.'

Mum's W.P.S. has set in for the day. She's doing little accompanying mirror faces through the car windows. It's really difficult to speak when you're busy pouting, so I have to wait till we're out of camera range before she replies.

'You get used to it. In fact, after a while, it seems kind of odd when they're not there.'

'Well, I wouldn't stand for it.'

'Hollywood, babes, when you're famous you have to do these things for your fans. Basically, you owe it to them.'

I thought it would be wiser not to comment on that. 'Pass the bucket' was about the only thing that came to mind.

There follows a girly mum and daughter morning which is as normal as it gets when you have a frantic trail of photographers on your heels. We get out of the limo and Abdul kind of kerb-crawls alongside as we stroll down this high street trying to window-shop.

Once inside Gap, Mum is recognised and the assistants are fighting to serve us. The guy who actually gets the job is so overcome he's shaking. He brings us virtually every item in the store.

I settle for a selection of cropped trousers to try on. Mum's in the next changing room trying on T-shirts. By eleven I've tried on at least twelve pairs of trousers and am feeling frayed. I suggest stopping for a coffee.

'Yeah, sure, good idea. I'll ask the assistant.'

'Mum, they don't serve coffee in Gap.'

'Oh, really? They always do in Versace.'

I take her over the street to Starbucks. It's a small Starbucks, so maybe we can get some peace. The photographers are left outside and have to content themselves with snapping us through the window.

By midday, Mum and I are back in the limo having successfully bought some totally normal T-shirts, some really ordinary cut-off trousers, a couple of casual sweaters and two identical pairs of trainers.

Hang on a minute. What's going on? I'm confused now. I was meant to be getting to look like Mum. Now she's getting to look like me.

The second casting had to take place in the evening to fit in with Mum's schedule. I didn't see why she even had to be there, seeing as she sneaked off halfway through the last one.

Mum's so laid back about this one we actually arrive fifteen minutes late. Abdul drops me off like before and takes Mum round to the far side of the studio. I rush in, in a fluster at being late, and find the others are all assembled in the changing room. At first I don't see Gina and then I spot her familiar red hair at the far side of the room. She's bending over to button her character shoes.

I bounce up behind her and say, 'Hi there!'

Gina turns. For a split second I think I've got the wrong person. This is not the bubbly Gina I know. Her face hardly registers recognition.

'Oh, hi, Holly,' she says flatly.

'You OK?'

'Yes, fine. Why?' she continues in the same cold tone.

I can feel myself going hot and bothered trying to work out what I've done or said. 'You must be nervous . . .' I try. 'I mean, you shouldn't be. You were brilliant last week.'

Gina shrugs.

'No, really, I mean it. You'll get the part, I know you will . . .'

'Thanks. But I reckon that's already decided. Don't you?'

'What do you mean?'

Gina exchanges glances with the girl beside her. They're both staring at me, saying nothing. I feel really terrible.

'Look. Please tell me. What have I done? What have I said?'

The other girl glances down. On the bench there's a newspaper open at a double-page spread showing Mum and me on yesterday's shopping expedition.

Above a picture of us having our lattes at Starbucks the headline says:

'HOLLYWOOD TO PLAY MUM?'

'Oh my God!' I exclaim, picking it up. 'What's all this about?'

'What do you think, Holly*wood*?' says the other girl.

Gina stares hard at me. 'Well?'

'You don't think they've already decided . . .? No. That wouldn't be fair.'

(An echo of Mum's voice comes back to me at that moment: 'Life isn't fair, Hollywood. If it was, we'd all be stars.')

I can feel tears pricking in my eyes.

Gina notices. She says resentfully, 'You could have told us who you were.'

'I didn't see the point. It would've been like showing off. But I still don't think they'd give me the part. I'm no way good enough.'

'That's show business, Holly. You'll get it because you're Kandhi's daughter. It doesn't matter how good you are. It doesn't matter if you're total rubbish.'

'So why are they doing all these auditions?' I point out.

'Haven't you noticed? They've been filming everything. They'll probably make it into a reality TV show. Will Holly get the part or won't she? We'll all be on the edge of our seats . . .'

'I bet she's known all along . . .' a third girl butts in.

'Believe me, please. I didn't.'

'You must've. Look at her in those pictures,' adds a blonde girl, pointing at the newspaper.

'No . . . Honestly. I thought all the fuss was because of Mum being at number one . . .'

'Sure . . .' says the blonde in a nasty way.

Gina frowns at her. 'It's not your fault, Holly. But you can't blame us for feeling this way . . .'

A voice cuts across Gina's.

The woman who had been in charge the time before had appeared in the doorway with a clipboard in her hand.

'Ready, girls? I'm going to take you through now. Can you get in line in the order I call out your names. Quiet, please! Thank you.'

'Jessica Blandford. Juliet Crome. Sally Eames. Gina Locardi. Holly Winterman . . .'

We were led up as before to wait on the row of chairs.

While the first few girls did their singing, dancing and spoken pieces, my mind was racing. Were they right? Was the audition fixed? Had Mum known all along?

So many things came back to me now. All those little looks and hints. Those glances between those publicists. I reckon even Vix was in on it.

They had got to Gina by now. She was as brilliant as before. Even in her spoken part, which was a piece taken

267

from *Alice in Wonderland*, in which she went on about the curiousness of it all.

'Curiouser and curiouser . . .' That's how it ended.

'Holly Winterman! On camera two, please?'

'Holly Winterman. Are you there?'

Through the confusion I realised my name had been called a second time. I got up from my seat.

All of a sudden, I wasn't nervous. Not one bit. I walked out in front and handed my music to the pianist as if sleep-walking. Then as I went to stand on the yellow cross, my mind magically cleared.

It was so simple. No one could make me do what I didn't want to do.

The pianist came in with the opening bars and I just stood there NOT singing, doing nothing. The piano faltered over a few bars and then came to a halt.

The pianist looked up and nodded to me.

'From the top, dear . . . Shall we try again?'

She started from the beginning once more. I still didn't come in.

In fact, I stood there and made a complete dick of myself.

And I didn't care one bit. Because I was angry. I was furious. I was making a stand for every single one of those girls who had been walked over simply because they weren't famous enough.

The notes of the piano faded away. The pianist got to her feet and said into the darkness, 'I'm sorry, what do I do now?'

A voice came from the back.

'Is there a problem, Holly?'

I held up a hand to shield my eyes from the lights. At that moment I didn't care that I was out in front of a load of really important people. I just wanted to get back at Mum for putting me in this positiion.

'Yes. There is a problem. I'm sorry, I'm not going to audition. Every single one of the other girls is ten times better than me. So there's no point.'

'Hollywood!' Mum's voice came from out of the darkness. 'It's not up to you to judge. You've got to audition. You can't let me down like this.'

'You can't make me. It's not fair on the others. I'm sorry. Can I leave now?'

I could hear Mum saying to the others, 'She's just nervous, that's all. It's stage fright.'

'I have never been less nervous in my life. It's no good, Mum. I'm going now.'

As I left the set everyone seemed to be talking at once. Except for the girls who were behind me, who were stunned into silence. One of them squeezed my arm as I went by.

That really gave me a lump in my throat. I found I was shaking when I got back to the changing room. The people who had been on before me were sitting in a little huddle. They must've heard what was going on.

I went silently to my pile of clothes and started to change my shoes. I'd hardly got my dance shoes off before Mum stormed into the changing room. Her eyes were blazing.

'Hollywood. You go back in there, do you hear me? They've agreed to give you another chance . . .'

'But I don't want another chance, Mum.'

'Oh yes, you do.'

'No. I don't.'

That's when Gina got up from her seat and came over and stood beside me.

'It's not her fault, Mrs Winterman,' said Gina. 'Holly doesn't want to audition because of us. Because of what we said.'

'So? What did you say?' snapped Mum.

Mum's not very big but she looked ten times bigger than Gina at that point. But Gina stood her ground.

'We said that we didn't think the audition was fair. None of us stand a chance of getting the part. We think Hollywood's already been chosen, because she's your daughter.'

Mum stood there seething. You could see from her face that she couldn't come up with an answer to this. She turned on her heel and said, 'I'm going to get them to stop the audition. Right now.'

I watched helplessly while Mum went back inside. They couldn't drag me back on to the set. But nonetheless, I wasn't going to hang around. Who knew what Mum would do next. The limo was standing outside waiting. There was no time to lose. I flung on my coat and dashed outside.

Abdul took one look at my face and turned on the ignition.

'Can you take me back to the hotel? And go back for Mum later?'

All the way back Abdul was making comforting noises

about how the audition was no big deal. But I was still shaking from the tension. My brain had gone into a flat spin, trying to judge whether what I had done was right or wrong. I tried to remember exactly what I had said out there.

I mean, I know what I did was right. Or at least 95% right because what I'd done was both fair and honest.

But it was that niggly little 5% that I couldn't rid my mind of.

It was that niggly little 5% that said I should have stood by Mum. I'd made her look a total failure as a mother. A daughter who stood up to her in front of everyone and practically called her a cheat. How could I have done that?

It was that tiny little 5% that made me go cold inside. How could I face Mum ever again? She was going to be so mad at me. This was going to be like the seafood-platter-and-the-Blahniks-and-wanting-to-be-a-vet-and-talking-to-the-press-and-going-to-the-Globe-without-permission all rolled-into-one.

Later: the steps of The Royal Trocadero

As I got out of the limo outside the Trocadero I was practically blinded by camera flashes.

'No, look, guys. It's only me . . .' I protested.

'Hollywood, over here!'

'Holly, give us a smile.'

'Hey! Can I come to your première?'

'How does it feel to be playing your mum?'

Shielding my eyes from the glare, I stumbled up the hotel steps, pushing my way through the circular doors into

271

reception. I paused for a moment in the hushed haven of the lobby as the terrible truth sank in. It wasn't Mum they were after, it was me.

I shot into the elevator and slammed my hand down on the button, my mind racing. So is this how it starts? From a tiny beginning . . . the ball of fame starts rolling and rolling . . . and getting bigger and bigger . . . and gathering speed . . . carrying you with it, until there's nothing in the world you can do to stop it?

As soon as I reached my floor I ran down the corridor and unlocked my door with a shaking hand.

I slammed the door behind me and gazed around the now familiar surroundings of my suite. The bed turned back ready for the night. The lights on low. My few possessions tidied with military precision. What was I doing here? Was this what life was going to be like from now on? A prisoner to fame with the press clamouring at the door? Mum was going to be in her seventh heaven with all this publicity. And she'd want more. Dragging me ever deeper in with her. How could she do this to me? A shudder ran down my back. I had to escape while there was still time.

Without really thinking what I was doing, I went to the closet and took out my backpack. I crammed in my teddy and my pyjamas and my toothbrush. I tried to fit in the shoebox with My Personal Private Collection of Very Precious Objects. But it was too big, so I took out the little pink chocolate heart that Rupert had given me and packed that instead. Then I grabbed my mobile and raked through my purse.

I hadn't any money.

But in the little pocket at the back of my purse I found the Gold Card Mum had given me for 'emergencies'. Yep, this certainly was an emergency.

I stared at the Gold Card. It was one of the best cards you could have. Since it was on Mum's card, the money you could take out was virtually limitless. I could go anywhere on this.

I considered the options:

a) Gi-Gi's (nope. That was the first place Mum would look for me)
b) School (that was the second place she'd look)
c) Dad's . . .

Could this card pay for a ticket to New York? 'Course it could, that's what it did all the time.

I had to be quick before Mum got back. She could arrive at any moment. I opened the door of my suite and peered out.

'Good evening, Miss Winterman,' said a voice.

Just my luck, one of the security guards must've popped up to do a routine check. Curses. What did I do now?

With sudden inspiration I slipped my towelling robe over my clothes and hung a towel over my backpack. Then I sauntered out into the corridor.

'Just going for a swim,' I said.

'Have a nice one, Miss Winterman.'

'Thank you. I will.'

Don't arouse suspicion. Keep a clear head. Nice and

slowly into the elevator . . . Right! I pressed the button for the lower ground. My heart was doing double somersaults as we passed the ground. 'Please, please don't stop,' I prayed.

It didn't. We arrived at the lower ground and I headed out past the kitchens to the secret back exit by the swimming pool controls. Nobody around. Not a soul had seen me.

There were the emergency doors marked 'Press Bar to Open'. I pressed. They opened. I was out in the back alley. I shoved my robe and towel into a trash bin and started running as fast as I could.

Once in the street I realised it was late. Very late. I glanced at my watch. It was eleven o'clock. I wondered how late the tube trains ran. And whether planes flew that late. Sure they flew that late, they had headlights, didn't they?

Within minutes I was across the street and racing down the steps into the station. Once inside the tube station, I found the place almost deserted. Just a few stragglers hanging around and a drunk guy who was singing.

I went to the machine where I'd seen Rupert buy tickets. There was a slot for credit cards and it accepted Mum's card from my shaking hand. It delivered a single ticket to Heathrow Airport!

I waited in an agony of impatience for a train to come along, thinking irrationally that Mum might at any minute appear on the platform like a ball of fury to drag me back.

At last a train rumbled in and I slid gratefully into a seat. The rest of the journey to Heathrow was easy. The airport was at the end of the line. I didn't even have to change trains.

11.30 p.m., Terminal Four, Heathrow Airport

Airports are no problem. I know them inside out. I know that for long-haul flights you have to go to Terminal Four. I even know exactly which desk you go to for last-minute tickets. So that's where I went.

'A first class single to New York, please.'

The woman at the desk leaned over the top and asked in a surprised way, 'Hi there. You travelling alone?'

'My dad's meeting me the other end.' This wasn't technically a lie, since I was going to call Dad the minute I was safely on the plane.

'I see. Right. Your passport, please.'

'Passport?' My heart sank. I hadn't thought. Vix looks after all the passports while Mum and I get kind of wafted through.

'Do I really have to have a passport? I'm like half-American.'

The woman looked at me pityingly.

'Yes. You really do have to have a passport.'

'I could have it sent on after.'

'How old are you?'

'Sixteen,' I lied. I did lie this time. Reverend Mother, please forgive me. I could feel myself blushing scarlet.

'Do your parents know you're here?'

'Yes, sure they do.' After one lie the others are easy. They just kind of tag along.

The woman picked up the phone on her desk and said something I couldn't hear.

This was it. At any moment some creepy lurking member

275

of airport security was going to take me off and interrogate me. So I shoved my backpack over my shoulder and said, 'Going to get my passport. Goodbye.'

And fled down the concourse.

I went back down into the tube station. The late, late tube was waiting there. I climbed in, trying desperately to think things through. There was no way I could get my passport without Vix knowing. She kept them in the hotel safe.

The train set off and I sat staring blankly at the window. It was dark outside so I couldn't see out. All I could see was my own reflection staring miserably back at me. All I could think of was how I'd messed up. What on earth was I going to do now? I knew if I stayed on this train I would get relentlessly closer and closer to the Royal Trocadero. I couldn't go back there. I couldn't face Mum.

So on to Plan b): School. That's where I'd go. I'd get Becky to hide me in her room and I could cut off all my hair and pretend to be a new girl. Not a brilliant idea. But the best I could come up with.

I knew the train for school left from a station called Paddington. So I switched trains and made my way there.

1.00 a.m., Paddington station

Paddington station was horribly empty. I could see from the departures board that there weren't going to be any trains leaving until 6.00 a.m. the next morning.

The station was cold and gloomy, lit by a dim icy light.

I suddenly found I was dead tired. I slumped down on a railing that was only big enough to perch on. There wasn't even a bench to curl up on.

And suddenly Jasper's words came back to me:

'. . . it's night and it's creepy and there's this girl all alone centre-stage and she's homeless – she's got nowhere to go. There's a single eerie spotlight on her. She starts singing . . .'

And then I thought of Mum singing that song at the Heatwave and how brilliant she was. And I couldn't help feeling a bit proud of her. I could picture her now, a tiny figure in the centre of that vast arena. Every eye on her, every breath held . . . and then her voice, so pure, so strong, so beautiful all alone out there before the backing thundered in.

I huddled myself down further into my coat and leaned against the railing and I guess I must've drifted off . . .

The next thing I know, someone is shaking me. It's Mum. This must be a dream. But the shaking continues. This is no dream. It *is* Mum!

'Mum! What are you doing here?'

Mum turns round and signals violently to someone to keep back. In the distance, I can see a load of policemen with tracker dogs.

'Give us a minute alone, OK?' she calls out.

Mum's crying. She's scrabbling for a tissue. I find a crumpled one in my pocket and hand it to her.

'Hollywood. Oh, Hollywood . . .'

'Mum, will you stop saying my name and tell me what you're doing here?'

'I was so worried about you. I thought I'd lost my baby.'

'I'm not a baby, Mum,' I protest as I struggle to get properly awake.

'No, but you are and always will be my baby. Oh, how could you go off like that?'

'Mum, there were all these photographers and it was me they were after. How could you do this to me?'

'Oh, Holly . . . have I been such a terrible mother to you?'

'You could just listen to what I say now and again . . .'

'I am listening now, Holly . . .'

'But you didn't listen when I said I didn't want that part . . .'

'Oh, that doesn't matter any more . . .'

'It doesn't?'

'No. It's not important.'

'Not important? But I thought you'd be so mad at me.'

'I was proud of you, baby. You stood up there and you said it from the heart.'

'I did?'

'For once I could see a little bit of me in you.'

'Now look, Mum . . .'

'No, it's OK, Holly. I'm not going to force you into doing anything you don't want. That's all going to change. When I found you weren't there I just felt so . . .' Mum pauses for a beat. 'So alone.'

'You, alone, Mum! But you're always surrounded by people.'

'People I pay. People who are fans. People who want Kandhi the singer. I don't have a single person who would pass the time of day with me if I wasn't who I am. Holly, if you don't care about me, nobody does.'

'Oh, Mum. Of course that's not true.' I put my arms around her all the same and give her a hug.

But then something odd strikes me.

'Mu-um? How did you find me? How did you know I was here?'

I follow Mum's eyes. She's looking at the bulge in my pocket where I keep my mobile.

My mobile. The mobile she gave me.

'Mu-um! You put a chip in it. You've been tracking me, haven't you!'

'Hollywood, I –'

'Tell the truth, Mum . . .'

'Well, only because . . . because Holly . . .' Mum blows her nose and wipes her eyes and looks me straight in the face. 'Because I need you, Holly. I need you with me. You are the one thing that makes my life feel real.'

I stare back at her and am kind of engulfed in a great big wave of feeling . . .

(Hang on, this is where the music would fade in if this was the movies)

. . . because in spite of everything, she's my mum and I've got to forgive her. Because whatever your mum's done, your mum's your mum, and you only get one, so you've really got to love her whatever . . .

That is until she does the next totally random thing . . .

To order from Bookpost PO Box 29 Douglas Isle of Man IM99 1BQ www.bookpost.co.uk
email: bookshop@enterprise.net fax: 01624 837033 tel: 01624 836000

BLOOMSBURY

www.bloomsbury.com